All Change Please

Danielle West

In modern day London, the lives of three close friends are instantly set off course when their mutual friend, Laura, is suddenly killed. The three friends – Ophelia, Elise and Kat – find that their current lives are far worse than they could ever fathom. In the light of Laura's tragic death, do any or all of the women decide to grab life by the horns and do something about how their own existences have exactly lived up to expectations? In a peculiar sort of way, Laura's death not only shakes the three to their foundations, but it also wakes them out of their own personal slumbers.

One of them is suffering through a dead end job with no appreciation or any advancement coming anytime soon. All this after she had moved from the United States to the UK in search of a happy, meaningful life and career. She was wrong and now she feels trapped in a city she has slowly learned to loathe and isn't sure if she's going to try and move out of London or stick it out. Her love life is pitiful as well, which doesn't help matters.

Another of the three eventually finds herself questioning her marriage, though she deeply loves her husband. However, like many a marriage, her in-laws don't respect her and she finds herself constantly walking on eggshells. It doesn't help that her husband is a struggling writer who coops himself up in their house all day. Does the love of her husband help her endure her own troubles?

The third woman is a struggling artist who can't seem to ever catch a break. Her relationship with her parents isn't what one would describe as peachy, either, because of how vastly different she is from them. Constantly at odds with herself and society, she desperately searches for answers to her questions that she's struggled to find her entire life.

All Change Please takes you on the journey these women find themselves on together over the period of a few months towards the end of the year. They lean on each other for support when grieving Laura's death and they feed off each other in trying to make the best of their own situations.

All Change Please is a story of life's great failures and the lessons learned, and it's told with a superb dark comedic undertone. Enjoy the tale of Ophelia, Elise and Kat as they try to overcome their lousy states of existence via turmoil, death, stumbling drunkenness, anger, sarcasm, love, expression, frustration, and the determination of breaking the shackles of monotony.

16 September

The bunnies stared up cautiously; keen to see if they'd make it to work with Ophelia. Their ruse was spoiled when she dropped her lunch all over the front hall. She sighed and ran back upstairs to the flat to find a pair of shoes that didn't have fuzzy ears attached plus some kitchen roll to mop up the carrot and coriander soup she looked forward to having.

Later, as she passed the shops on the high street she tried to avoid looking at the usual throng of pollution-stained pigeons vie for position over a puddle of sick leftover from a heavy Saturday night or a football victory celebrated late into Sunday; the unfortunate confirmation that it was indeed Monday in London.

The air was cool and wet with a perfect mist to start the day. Spiders' webs stood out on the hedge rows with fine crystallised embroidery being carefully weaved to trap unsuspecting flies hurrying through. She took her place among the suited zombies trudging to the Tube station. A smirk slowly spread across her face as she imagined she was racing them to the finish. The trophy would have to be a gold-plated skull crammed full of brains- hopefully her line manager's- which she could eat or fling at passersby.

Or to cure the drones of their misanthropy she thought of creating and marketing a breakfast cereal loaded with anti-depressants- a very concentrated dose of antide-pressants. The cereal would have to have marshmallows, miniature ones. Ophelia's biggest disappointment upon moving to the UK was the absence of breakfast cereals with marshmallows. The only breakfast cereals on offer that would even remotely interest an American palate raised on Lucky Charms and Count Chocula were Shred-dies, which brought Ophelia to tears when she first tried them five years ago. She desperately rang a friend begging for boxes of neon coloured flakes crammed with marshmallows, cartoon characters and implausible back stories in the ads involving kids solving crimes in abandoned mines or caves with bowls, pitchers of milk and overly enthusiastic cartoon mascots that appeared to be on copious amounts of ephedrine.

She joined the ranks at the platform jostling for a position near the carriage doors. Ophelia's thoughts wandered as she searched her bag in vain for her iPod. She couldn't tell if it was her job that was getting to her, or if she was in need of a holiday. She never pictured herself dressed in a dull grey suit watching black mice scurry along the platform while she hoped for a spot on the carriage to grab a bit of the rail. The trained groaned to a stop, opening the doors to reveal a pack of hostile groggy faces amongst papers, mobiles and cosmetic mirrors.

On the train sandwiched between a stout, ruddy -aced man in a grey suit no younger than 50 reading the Times and a thin, younger man in a dark suit and a loud tie reading the Sun, Ophelia assessed her travelling companions. The Sun reader was definitely in sales. It was the stiff, product-ridden hairstyle that gave him away. It was as if he had doused his hair in a mixture of PVA glue and water and walked through a wind tunnel on his way to breakfast. He wasn't reading the Sun so much as checking the sports scores and ogling the page 3 model's fun bags. The older man looked as if he was in finance. His suit was subdued, though obviously a very expensive blend of cashmere and wool. The Times financial section had been taken out and put in his briefcase as if he were worried his poker face would give away precious trade secrets to his fellow commuters. The poor sod looked so drained; his eyes sunken and tired, vessels on his nose confessing to countless lost weekends on the drink. He must have stood on the same train five days a week for the past 30 years.

'Could anyone imagine they would end up like him?' She wondered. 'This can't possibly be all there is to life. This can't be my life. I worked so hard and hoped for so much more.' The air in the carriage felt thin to Ophelia as she reread the predictable ending of her book to avoid eye contact and tried to shake her panicked thoughts.

She was tempted to flee the carriage at the next stop and skive off work. She yearned to amble up to the first half empty café and order a jam doughnut and coffee for an unhurried hour just eyeing passers-by, taking mental notes on how they should have dressed before leaving the house that morning or what hairstyle would be most flattering. Or she'd simply picture them in kinky knickers, leather ones with the bum exposed for a fat and harried barrister or a rubber nappy for some stuffy secretary. Then she could create bizarre and dramatic back stories to their lives and what brought them to pass her at that moment in time. Afterwards she imagined strolling to the nearest bookstore, picking titles at random sat in a corner scanning a few pages or chapters. The West End theatres were virtually empty on a Monday morning, giving an entire theatre to cheer, heckle or scream at the screen with no annoying teenagers or nattering twats on their mobiles. She could probably even sneak into a second film as well before going to browse the shops in relative solitude or wander the National Gallery.

Just as she was getting to Van Gogh, the announcement chimed, "The next station is Oxford Circus".

Ophelia's plans quickly evaporated as she reluctantly gathered her bags and stepped onto the platform into the stream of people. 'So close,' she kidded herself as she was swept up the escalator like cattle in a slaughterhouse. If only it were like school where your wrist was slapped for truancy or worse, they called your folks. With the way things had been lately, it would have taken ages to find another staggeringly boring job that she would grow to loathe despite the fact it paid her bills. Ophelia felt trapped and somehow cheated. It seems cruel and misleading to ask kids what they wanted to be when they grow up; most kids were going to end up in the rat race trapped in a dull job wishing they had done something else.

-

"Okay, when you say that it burns all over, where do you mean exactly?" Kat sipped her tea trying hard not to sound impatient. Quickly glancing over her shoulder, she furtively opened her web browser and checked her inbox. "Is this the first time you've used this particular product?" Ignoring Dorothy's two emails from Friday, she went straight to Ophelia's. "Well, is this the first time you've experienced this sort of reaction?"

>Kat, PLEASE say you are around for lunch today!! Need to whinge REALLY bad.
>Those shoes don't fit me either, would Elise wear them?
>-O xoxo!

"I don't mean to pry Mrs. Molloy, but have you engaged in any rough sex or foreplay in the past 24 hours?"

>Hey Ophelia,
>Lunch sounds fine as long as you aren't whinging about shingles, post coital >drip or rectal itching. See you at one, Oxford Circus?? Should I ask Elise along >as well? Then she can try the shoes on.
>Kat

"No, I'm not getting fresh with you or poking fun." Kat smirked at her own pun. "I'm merely asking as sometimes rough sex can cause minor abrasions and the spermicidal creams or foams can cause irritation or a burning sensation on open or sensitive skin. Uh huh, okay, well I would suggest taking a warm or lukewarm bath and soak in

12

it for a good twenty minutes. And don't use any bath oils or bubbles, as those could cause irritation as well. Then thoroughly dry the area with a towel and throw on a pair of cotton knickers. Don't use nylon, lace, nothing fancy or synthetic. The cotton will allow the area to breathe. If you're still experiencing irritation tomorrow morning, I suggest you ring your GP. Okay? Is there anything else I can help with? Thanks for calling."

Kat groaned as she slipped the headset off and said to herself with a smile "Well, I can't exactly wish them a good day, now can I?" she looked around and announced, "I'm going to the kitchen. Does anyone want anything?"

Kat managed to get a job within two months of moving to the UK at one of the call centres that are contracted by the NHS for health enquiries. The phone line had initially been set up by Labour as a PR stunt to guarantee seats for an election, in a misguided attempt to help surgeries hit targets by allowing people to call with questions and concerns. Instead it cost more money than initially thought to run but faced outraged by Daily Mail and some lupus or eczema charity when they attempted to close it down. It was being run in a small space in the Department of Human and Health Sciences at the University of Westminster where half the staff were NHS nursing students on work experience and the rest were staff trained by the NHS specifically for the call centre. At first, she was enthusiastic though nearly five years on and no real hope to move up or grow and Kat was beginning to feel disillusioned.

-

The mornings at Ophelia's office were monotonous and routine. She declined any meetings before 10.30 unless it was with her line manager to ensure she had a cup of proper coffee and herbal tea. She scanned her inbox for leaving do invites which was code for: "I have been sacked, you could be next. Let's get pissed and you can ask to take my stapler." After those emails were seen to, she had to go through the emails of those above her in the office pecking order and usually answer inane questions or simply refer to old emails where she would copy and paste responses she gave them or other managers already. She even developed a filing system to find answers quickly. After those she took an hour to go through personal emails, check eBay bids and then the BBC news to feel as if she were doing something grown-up and business related.

After toiling for four years at university in Boston and then a year in London, Ophelia found herself at a global corporation that promised her challenges and excitement in a fast paced environment. Instead, after her orientation on the first day they told her to stick to the template and held an annual personal growth seminar for a weekend once a year at a resort in Spain or Gran Canaria where days were spent playing charades or building the ideal teammate using a balloon, construction paper and yarn while evenings were spent getting drunk and intimate with colleagues that normally wouldn't even speak in the communal kitchen while making a cuppa. For the rest of the year the company would send quarterly newsletters either thanking you for contributing to the quarterly profits on behalf of the shareholders or telling you if the company's profits dip then they would quite easily send one of their precious assets packing to placate said shareholders.

Ophelia dreamed of meeting one of the shareholders one day. They seemed awfully fickle for people that had so much say in her future. If they weren't happy with the company's earnings, someone lost their job. These shareholders probably had big houses with several cars, the odd yacht and didn't seem to mind someone earning £22k a year lose their job, flat, etc if the company's profits didn't meet expectations. Every year in December redundancies made their way around various departments to even out any potential concerns in terms of profit so the shareholders would enjoy a pleasant Q4 while a few unsuspecting victims would spend Christmas and New Year

14

on the dole. Ophelia created a spreadsheet of her life and realised that 30% of her time was spent at work. The only thing she spent more time on was sleeping which dominated 33% of the pie. After creating the chart she posted it on her wall and noticed that 8% of her time was also spent commuting which meant that 38% of her time was spent on something she enjoyed less than a bikini wax. It just didn't seem fair to her, although nothing seemed fair after leaving university and joining all the other grown-ups queuing up to do exactly what was expected of them before retiring or having a nervous breakdown.

Ophelia was an online marketing analyst, hence the 3D pie chart. The reports across the departments would vary which provided a small amount of variety in a job that was otherwise fairly monotonous. She spent days creating reports from the response cards sent in with coupons or competitions on the type of cat food lonely spinsters purported to buy or how many men under the age of 30 were losing their hair and considered using aerosol head paint to cover it up. These reports were initially interesting but after a year she grew bored and then became frustrated. Her manager was always tasking her at the last minute with detailed case studies and reports which on more than a few occasions he took full credit for. It all felt a bit dissatisfying and pointless in the grand scheme of things and was far from what she had envisioned when she started university majoring in liberal arts and photography. Ophelia had secretly harboured hopes of having some of her work "discovered" at one of the coffee houses that allowed her to "exhibit" or hang her photos while she invited her mates there for copious amounts of coffee, weak American beer and onion rings or Buffalo wings. After two years of watching digital cameras grow in popularity, sophistication and affordability she started to notice that everyone harboured the same hopes and dreams and that her photographs weren't any more remarkable (or to be fair, any less!) than anyone else's in the class. Most of the friends that graduated were shooting pictures of Bar Mitzvahs or developing film at CVS.

Ophelia changed her major at university when she assisted her friend Marisol photographing a family portrait of what had to be the vilest family in New England at a Wal-Mart. It was a group of obese rednecks from Seabrook, New Hampshire. The family greeted Marisol, who is Colombian, with cold hard stares before slowly and loudly trying to explain that they were there to have pictures taken. Ophelia snuck a glance at Marisol who discreetly waved it off as a regular occurrence. Whenever Marisol asked them to sit a certain place or move they rolled their eyes and mumbled to each other or asked her to repeat what she said in English. Aside from several infants sporting confederate flag bibs with eyes set too close together or too far apart, the adults demanded they be allowed to smoke (not a chance), spilled cheese curls everywhere and left orange handprints on the chairs in the waiting area (which Ophelia got to clean as the assistant) while the school aged kids picked up equipment and poked each other with said items.

Marisol actually grew up in Switzerland, was then sent to a boarding school in the States and her accent was almost undetectable. Aside from English and Spanish she also spoke Italian, French and Mandarin. The family portrait lasted an agonising ten minutes before they finally said to Marisol that they would feel more comfortable having Ophelia shoot the portrait. Marisol smirked, shrugged and held the camera towards Ophelia. They looked at Ophelia expectantly as surely as the white worker she understood what they meant. She folded her arms over her chest and as calmly as she could, said, "Creo que todos tenemos que salir ahora." The puzzled family looked from her to Marisol who explained that Ophelia asked them to leave.

The following Monday Ophelia changed her major to Business studies. The photography helped with the marketing and advertising courses since she understood how composition or lighting or colour affected a mood or conveyed emotion. After finishing her degree, she still didn't feel quite ready to join the rat race and managed to get into

16

a post graduate programme at Birbeck and head to London for adventure, fun and direction.

-

"The leather is a soft kidskin available in three colours; black, white or tan. And it can be embossed in silver or gold with a classic Times New Roman font or script. Ooh, we also have the Footprints board game on special this week. This game rocks! It traces all of Jesus' steps throughout his life. As you can imagine, the board is enormous but folds up so you can take it with you on travels or retreats. Also, and I think this is so neat; there is a small windup donkey and magic jug of water! It has this little transparent plastic jug- shaped thing with a tiny red bulb inside so he can change water into wine. It takes triple "A" batteries, though only one and it's not included. I'm sure you have loads stuck in your sofa cushion. At least that's where I find my batteries and loose change. It's only twelve quid this week. Aw go on, the kids will love it! ...Two, Mrs. Dobson? Fab! Okay now, what shall we put on your King James Bible? Ooh I love black leather, it's so chic. I'm sure your husband will be thrilled. I know I would be if I got one for my birthday. These should reach you in about five working days. Have a lovely day and remember: Jesus loves you very much!"

Elise entered the last few details on the keyboard and switched her phone to the break setting.

"How do you do it, Elise?"

"Do what?"

Startled, Elise turned and stared blankly at Norbert. She made note of his sweater pattern. Today it was ducks. There was a whole army of little yellow ducks marching across the green woolly background of his lanky torso. Norbert had what Elise considered to be the largest naff sweater collection in all of Great Britain, if not the world.

"Up-selling. That woman rang to order a plain canvass Bible and ended up getting the deluxe leather bound edition; embossed no less, a Last Supper tea set and two of those board games. I'm amazed. You're up for review next week and your figures won't go unnoticed."

Elise smirked as she rose to her feet. "Cheers Norbert."

'He must still live with his mum', she thought as she made her way to the candy machine. What grown man wears duck sweaters to work except one whose mother still dresses him? Elise had been working at the Jesus Loves You Ltd. Call Centre for almost three months. A staunch atheist, she found the job provided her with endless amusement on top of commission. Elise didn't need to work. Her parents bought her a property as a gift when she finished university. She picked a modest Victorian house in Hackney to her parents' horror but insisted, saying the house had lots of historic value and she could rent the rooms until she found a respectable job or husband. Her mother immediately agreed upon mention of a husband and Elise moved in. She mainly worked to meet people or inspire her artwork and let a few of the bedrooms to local artists for additional income. The resident numbers varied, as many of the occupants would just show up on the futon one morning and stay for days, months or years and then disappear just as mysteriously. The term artist should be used loosely as some of the residents were indeed artists, photographers, musicians, or designers who were very serious about making a career out of a passion or talent. Although there were also a lot of homeless junkies, runaways or people that showed up to a party, passed out, woke up and stayed for weeks after.

After devouring her second chocolate bar, she picked up the phone. As she waited for someone to answer, Elise got the cello tape from her drawer and began to randomly stick the plastic barnyard animal figures on her monitor to a long strip of cello tape. A few colleagues watched for the distraction.

"Yes, I wish to speak with Katherine North please."

She took the label off her empty water bottle and wrapped the cello tape animal garland around it.

"This is her mother-in-law. Please tell her it's urgent. I had the reform club over for a wild sex orgy last night and now I am pissing razors!"

A few of Elise's colleagues brazenly looked over their cubicle divides as Elise shot them an exaggerated grin and waved excitedly at them.

"Nutty cow? Don't be daft, that was funny. I bet all of your co-workers got a chuckle."

Elise secured the tornado-themed water bottle on her monitor with a sticky wodge of blu-tack.

-

Kat rolled her eyes to herself feeling everyone's grins on her. "Well what's up?"

"Just wondering what you're doing for lunch today." Elise queried.

"Ooh, I'm so popular today. Ophelia emailed me this morning and needs to moan. No, not like that! You are such a dirty slag, Elise. Oh, she said those shoes I gave her didn't fit, want them?"

"Are those the heeled ones with the rings or the platforms?"

"The platforms. How are things in the Holy Land? Are you free?"

"Sure."

"See you at one outside Shelley's in Oxford Circus."

-

The dark clouds loomed heavy in the sky threatening to burst at any moment. All the cheap cafes were packed so Elise dragged Ophelia and Kat to her favourite haunt. "You two will like it, I promise! It's nothing like the scary Krishna café. This one has no preachy smelly bald guys and the food looks and tastes like real meat!"

Kat grinned at Ophelia "You mean like hot dogs?"

Elise furrowed her brow, "Don't be disgusting, Kat! Everyone knows that hot dogs are made from circus animals."

"Don't you mean lips and arseholes?" Ophelia chided.

Elise shook her head and flagged down the waiter. Kat looked over at Ophelia as she sighed and slid her mac off.

"Cheer up chicken. It can't be that bad. The week's only just begun."

"I should've skipped work today. I nearly did but remembered this report that Mr. Jerkface will want to take credit for."

Elise finished ordering and looked over, "Do you mean Toupee Guy?"

Ophelia nodded.

Elise slammed her hand on the table. "That is bang out of order. You've got to do something, Feelie. What about telling another manager or his boss? Maybe sabotage the reports?"

"I really can't be arsed today. Plus that would leave me screwed when I get sacked and need a reference. How's your joke job going?"

Elise stiffened in mock offence "It's not a joke. Look, I even dress smart for it." She stood up to show off her oversized charity shop men's black jacket and trousers with a worn and baggy t-shirt.

Kat motioned for Elise to turn round as if she were a catwalk model. "I hate to break this to you Elise, but I don't think the Jesus and Mary Chain is a Christian band."

"Elise is right. She's been there for what, three months now? That's a record. And that suit! It just screams 'I mean business'."

Kat couldn't help laughing. "That suit screams, 'spare some change.' What do you have up your sleeve, Elise? I still remember Nike Town."

Elise mock pouted, tossed her nose in the air and sat down. "Nothing. The job offers me hours of amusement and I'm helping spread the good news about Jesus rising from the dead to eat brains from leper skulls. I'm a fucking hero, really. And Nike Town was totally different. I was there fighting global capitalism and helping to dress chavs. I was basically taking them down from the inside like a double agent."

"I hate to remind you 007, but your cover was blown after three weeks. That's pretty suck-tastic for a secret agent." Ophelia sniffed her tea suspiciously before adding sugar.

"Double agent." Kat corrected.

"Okay, I admit I should've staggered my activities maybe on a month rather instead of weekly." Elise blew on her tea with a smile. "I bet they're still finding letters in their trainers to this day. I was quite chuffed with that, very clever if I do say so myself!"

Elise had decided to give the Nike factory workers a voice and did so by writing frantic notes on scraps of paper like "Help! I am tortured, malnourished and overworked so you can buy these ugly overpriced trainers!!" and "Nike gives me 10p a day to get my twelve-year-old fingers caught in the rivet machine, please free me from this slavery!" then stuck them in the trainers right before they were purchased. Her sales pitches were sardonic but were ignored by customers. Her favourite closers were 'Just think of how quickly you can run to the sofa in these!' and 'You'll be the most active looking sedentary person with this tracksuit!"

Elise shook her head. "Nah, the jumper incident got me sacked." Elise went to work as usual on a Saturday and at the busiest point of the shift, removed her jumper to reveal a t-shirt with the boldly printed slogan 'Nike. Helping Indonesians afford penny candy since 1972.' She managed to shift a few pairs of trainers and a few customers even asked if the shirt was available in the store before a manager took her aside and had security show her out.

"I'm still banned from the Oxford Circus branch!"

Kat smiled at Ophelia. "See? Things could be worse. You could be crazy like Elise."

"When I moved here I honestly thought I'd be living an exciting life with a high paying job at a swish agency. And here I am doing detective whether women prefer wings on their panty liners in an office full of petty wankers."

"Poor you. No offence, Elise. Everyone has delusions like that. I thought I'd be home with a baby or doing something I actually enjoyed. At least you're not on the phone to the physically and mentally challenged all day. You don't realise how stupid people really are until you've sat on a phone with them all day asking how to affix plasters or worse how to fucking unwrap them!"

Elise squealed with glee as the food arrived. Kat twirled her noodles with her fork then paused and grabbed her bag. "Elise, before I forget, here's Dorothy's latest tips for living. I'm starting to feel like some mad bag lady carrying these things around."

Kat's mother-in-law was endlessly clipping articles in the Times or magazines and giving them to Kat. The clippings ranged from the innocently helpful concert dates or articles on vitamins to the almost passive aggressive clippings on diet tips, cleaning and how a woman's biological clock only ticks for so long. As these "helpful" clippings piled up mocking her in the recycling bin they became a source of arguments or resentment towards her husband Ian. When she mentioned this over beers one evening Elise volunteered to incorporate the clippings into a sculpture she was working on and Kat was happy to oblige.

Elise solemnly tucked the papers into her Jesus Loves You Ltd. carrier bag. "Ta, Kat. The piece is really coming along. It may even make it into the show at Zee's gallery."

Kat smiled relieved to be rid of the pages. "Elise, I'll buy the finished piece off you. Can you put a sold notice on it at the exhibition if you show it?"

Ophelia eyed Kat suspiciously over her imitation chicken roast. "You aren't going to give it as a mothering Sunday gift or something, are you?"

"Don't be silly, it's going in the flat." Kat quipped. "So, how was your weekend, my sad little sausage?"

"On Friday I went out with the banker that Elise's mother's been trying to pimp out. Elise, you owe me for five hours of my life which I will never get back."

Elise's mother was determined to bring her only daughter into the old money fold and her method was by playing matchmaker with some of London's most prominent bachelors. On the evening this Mystery Date was available, Elise had to attend a friend's opening. Plus, she disapproved of the company he worked for, something about funding labs that test on animals or arms dealing. Ophelia was free, up for a gratis meal at a four star Michelin restaurant and hadn't been lucky in the man department so volunteered before the unsuspecting suitor spent the evening having red paint thrown at him by Elise and her mates at the anti-vivisection league.

Elise made origami cranes with the extra napkins. "Was he that bad Feelie? Worse than that arrogant city trader chap with the wonky eye?"

"Walleyed! I thought he was drunk when I arrived!! Elise this guy was so frigging boring! All he could talk about was money. The FTSE did this, my stocks did that, what does your investment portfolio look like? Oh, it went on like that over the cocktails, and then it was about the various clubs he belongs to over appetisers, his sports car with limited edition colour during the main course which I think it was peacock green in case your mum interrogates you. Like I give a shit. It wasn't even worth dinner at Claridges! I could have had saveloy, chips and Stella while I watched a DVD or even watch grass grow and had a better night out."

"Was it just dinner or did this go on even longer? Did you at least get a shag out of the deal?" Kat asked.

"After telling me all about his sports car? Ha! Still you owe me five hours of my life I'll never get back. If only it was just dinner, I would've had time to do something else! I couldn't just say I was going to the bathroom and leave or tell him he was boring the fuck out of me, could I?"

"Why not? I would." Elise remarked. "I should've brought him with me to the opening. It would have been funny." Elise grinned as she set all the cranes down on her empty plate. "Funny for me."

"I didn't want to be rude so I stuck it out for the night. He took me to a couple of swish clubs to talk to some of his swish friends while I got drunk and pretended to be interested. He may have asked me back to his flat if I hadn't thrown up all over his shoes!"

Kat's eyes and mouth dropped wide open. "No."

She nodded, slightly embarrassed and a little smug. "They looked expensive. Well before I puked all over them. How was the opening, Elise?" She asked eager to shift the focus.

"Ace. There were a few people from the Guardian there and her dad showed up. Isn't that sweet? I couldn't drag my folks to an opening. They went to my first show and were horrified by the food, location and cheap wine. As if I'd ask them to cough up the dosh for some expensive Chablis that would just get pissed or sicked up all over an alley or doorstep later. Nigel was there with a few of his mates so I chatted with him and snogged him quickly before I left. Maybe I'll call him this week and accost him this weekend."

Elise had her eye on Nigel for the past month after seeing his band play at Koko. Ophelia looked over as Kat furtively shook a fag out of the pack.

"How about you, Kat?"

Kat pushed her empty plate away and tapped the filter end on the table. "It was pretty quiet on Friday and Saturday we went to the theatre with his cousin who I hate! He's such a letch. Sunday I dragged Ian to Spitalfields to avoid brunch with the in-laws. Mission accomplished. Nice quiet weekend for the old married couple."

-

"You're back a bit late, Ophelia. Have a nice lunch?" Clara grinned as she looked up from her PC.

"Yes, Clara. Thank you so much for caring."

26

Ophelia used her most patronising and professional smile. Clara Ritchie (or Clara Bitchy as she was known by Elise) was the office busybody. Her lisp only served to reinforce her serpentine attributes. Every office with more than twenty members of staff seemed to have an official busybody or two. They were often observant colleagues who were often making tea for the management team and happy to offer unsolicited comments on them from time to time. Ophelia suspected every company had them on hand for when times get tough; then the office busybody could produce a nice stack of notes on who should go first and why. Whenever redundancies made their way round the office, the busybody always eluded the sack. Coincidence?

Clara sat opposite Ophelia so she had a lot of time to devise an entire back story and conspiracy theory about her. Their line manager John, also known as Toupee Guy, had been with the company for nearly a decade. It appeared that his job was quite possibly his whole life. He was often situated by the water cooler gossiping with the ladies and keen to the point of obsession about attending company events until he became the chair of the monthly drinks night. He stayed late every night and was usually in before anyone every morning.

Ophelia learned this the hard way coming from a mate's (err, that she slept with one night after too much to drink) flat one Monday morning at 7am. Instead of taking the Tube all the way home and then back through Monday morning rush hour, she walked since this mate lived in Holborn. She grabbed a breakfast bap at the local take-away and headed to work. It was a beautiful summer morning and she looked forward to going into an empty office to go through emails, surf the web, do a bit of shopping, or work on some research in the vast quiet of the empty building. To her horror she saw Toupee Guy hunched over his desk, typing away. It was 7:30 and he smirked as she continued her walk of shame to her desk to find her spare clothes for just such occasions in her pedestal drawer.

Ophelia half-listened to her voicemail while she checked through her emails. To her surprise, there was one from Dave. He was the first person she met at Birbeck and her first friend in London. He was next to her on their first class and about twenty minutes into a dry lecture on business economics Dave began to furiously scribble. Ophelia peeked over his shoulder and couldn't help but laugh out loud at his elaborate doodle of T-Rex dinosaurs taking on an army of bears. Dave looked over and sheepishly grinned. At the end of the class he gave her the drawing which she framed, and still had hanging in her flat. Dave went on to design creative for telly which were mainly station idents or children's programmes though he started making shorts that were gaining a global following online. He lived out in Richmond and despite working in London they rarely saw each other. Ophelia hadn't seen Dave since her 26th birthday nearly two years ago so she was hoping he emailed to meet up.

>Hey O
>Don't know if you heard yet, but Laura died on Sunday night. The funeral's
> Wednesday. I'll text the details once I've got them. Mark's obviously shaken
> up, but still taking calls at home.
>Love
>Dave

She reread the email five times.

>Dave, are you sure there isn't some mistake?? Rumour, maybe?? Was she poorly?
>O xoxox

She forwarded the email to Elise and Kat asking if they heard anything about Laura. Laura was the second friend Ophelia made after coming to London and it was through her she met Kat. Ophelia knew Mark as well but was nervous about calling him especially since he knew her more as a friend of his wife. Numbness spread

28

through her slowly as she logged out of her email account. She was stunned at how quickly the day shifted. The news seemed unreal. She switched her voicemail to instant pick up, slipped her earphones on and buried herself in her report for the afternoon.

The walk to the station took ages in the dark night. At only half five, the sky was black. The streets were slick with a light rain reflecting the sodium lights and neon signs. Ophelia hadn't spoken to a soul all afternoon. She didn't feel sad or sorry or angry. She didn't seem to feel anything at all. It was like the comic strips where something confusing or surprising occurs and the character just had an exclamation mark over their heads without a speech bubble. Oblivious to her fellow commuters and their cornucopia of odours and peculiarities, Ophelia stared into space not thinking or feeling.

-

Elise logged off her PC and slid her earpiece off. The second shift trickled through the door. She waved to no one in particular as she bounded out the door. As she wandered down Poland Street she noticed a homeless woman in a doorway asking passers-by for change. Elise stopped and fiddled around in her bag.

"Shit, I'm out of change. Listen, have you eaten yet?"

She shook her head. The woman couldn't have been much older than Elise. Her clothes were worn enough to show she'd been on the streets for a good few months. Her hands were really grimy around the nails though her face and hands weren't that dirty.

"Okay then, you can be my dinner companion tonight if it suits you. I'm just going to Pollo on Old Compton Street. Interested?"

"Thanks." The woman got to her feet and brushed herself off, grabbing her bags. "I'm starved, actually."

"I'm Elise." She smiled and offered to take a bag.

"I'm Sara. "

"Nice to meet you." The two walked through Soho quickly as they were both hungry and eager not to be caught in the rain. Elise opened the door to the café and waved her dinner date in.

"Order whatever you like, the food here is amazing! It looks like a total dive but it's my favourite for Italian. The portions are huge. "

"Thank you." She looked at Elise briefly then self-consciously back down at the menu.

Elise shook her head "It's nothing, really. It beats dining alone. So no worries. "

-

Kat walked briskly from the take-away hoping she wouldn't need to reheat the food when she got in as she was ravenously hungry and didn't feel like messing about in the kitchen. The clouds were parting to reveal a dark blue sky and a sliver of the moon. This was Kat's favourite Chinese take-away as they not only included free prawn crackers but also fortune cookies. Upon first moving to London, Kat was confused that there were no fortune cookies offered at the end of her meal in Chinatown.

30

Kat wore a general expression of horror around London when she first moved over. Most people got culture shock when moving to a new country, though Kat was already pretty neurotic. She also craved routine and familiarity so the little things like no fortune cookies or calling pants "trousers" really bothered her. After about a year, she began to accept if not enjoy some distinctively English things like prawn crackers or always being able to find Guinness on tap or the fantastic holiday packages offered to full time employees.

Kat broke into a jog a block away from her flat fuelled by hunger and the scent of spring rolls wafting from the bag. Taking the steps two at a time, she burst through the door and paused. There was the distinct aroma of pizza wafting from the living room. Kat followed it, puzzled. Ian sat on the sofa devouring a large pizza with extra cheese.

"I thought it was my turn to get take-away this week?" she asked.

Ian dropped the slice he was ravaging. "No, last week you brought home sushi so I figured I'd grab a pizza on the way home from my meeting."

"Meeting?"

Ian nodded as he muted the stereo speakers. "I told you about it on Friday. I went and showed my script to Tony in EC1. He wasn't too impressed, but he didn't say no, either. So I'm staying hopeful until he says 'It's crap and we ain't touching it.' Oh, Ophelia rang, said to call her back as soon as you got in."

Ian was a struggling playwright. He had done great in school but for some reason he had trouble selling his plays in the real world and didn't think a conventional job would allow him the creative freedom to focus on his work. Ian generally wrote existential

31

pieces, though he was big on symbolism and surrealism so a lot of the characters that would normally be people would be pieces of furniture, food or animals. It was an odd combo, though Kat had faith that soon he would be in the West End or at the very least teaching. Every time she tried to start a conversation about a job she saw in the papers or about money being tight, Ian would quietly get up and leave the room. On a few occasions when Kat was persistent he would leave the house and drive to his parents nearby.

"Screw that, I'm so hungry. I'll ring her after dinner."

Kat grabbed a slice of pizza and ate it as she walked into the kitchen and grabbed two plates and chopsticks.

-

"Some days it feels like I'll be here forever, but it does have its good points."

Elise looked up from her cassata raising an eyebrow. "Really?"

"Yeah, there's a freedom in not having to answer to anyone. I never have to be any-where by a certain time or live up to anyone's expectations." Sara sipped her coffee thoughtfully. "There are loads of crap things about it, too. I'm sure you can imagine. The worst is that people act like you're invisible; they just look right past you. I'd ra-ther have them tell me no, or apologise and say no or even to say piss off and get a job. When they pretend not to see you, well after a while on some days I start to feel invisible. Like a ghost."

Elise looked at Sara sympathetically and nodded. "What would you do if you could do anything right now?"

Sara shook her head. "I don't even know anymore. It's been seven months but it feels like I've been on the streets seven years. I wouldn't even know how to be normal anymore."

"I don't know how to be normal either if it makes you feel any better."

"When I first got out here I kept saying that any day I'd get a job and maybe a council flat. Days turned to weeks. It seemed less likely. I just don't know anymore. I don't even know if I care." Sara's eyes gazed wistfully into space, and then she shook her head and smiled self-consciously. "Sorry, didn't mean to go on like that. Pity party for one please! Thanks again for dinner, I really appreciate it. I gotta get back to my space before someone nicks it."

"Sure. Thanks for the company." Elise waved as Sara gathered her bags and left. Her smile faded as she sighed and paid the bill. There was a light rain falling, though not heavy enough for an umbrella. A Londoner could easily spot a tourist in this weather since they had their umbrellas out for it. Elise walked up Charing Cross Road then stopped short, inspired by the sheer genius of an idea. She popped into the bookstore and went up the stairs to the first floor where they carried their stationery and gift items. Her eyes scanned the shelves until she came upon a few rubber ducks. They even had miniature ones. Perfect! Elise smiled as she paid for the ducks.

-

Ophelia crashed through the door and peeled off her mac, jacket, blouse and trousers on her way to the kitchen. Leaning over the sink in support hose, knickers and cami-sole she ate some tuna out of the tin and tried to gather her thoughts. Ten Jaffa cakes and two glasses of wine later she felt ready to ring Mark. After four rings, the machine picked up and her thoughts started to race. What should she say? Should she ask what happened?

She was grounded by the high-pitched tone of the machine. "Uh, Mark? Mark, it's Ophelia. Hi, I was just…-"

"Hello?" She could barely hear Mark over the screeching distortion of the answering machine. "Hey, hang on; I have to shut the machine off. Ophelia? Hey." His voice was gravelly and distant like that of someone jolted out of a dream and still disoriented from being awakened so suddenly.

Ophelia's heart sank. "Hi, um, are you okay? Well as okay as you could be all things considered. Fuck, I'm sorry. That sounded awful!"

"No worries. You know, then."

"Yeah. Dave emailed me this afternoon. What happened? Did you want to talk? I'm here to listen if you need, or not if you don't want to talk. Can I do anything?"

Mark sighed and paused. "I was out at the rugby and she was out with her mum. Her mum had a row with her dad or something and they were out when…" I could hear a sharp intake of breath and a pause as the tears started. "She was struck by a car in a zebra crossing. The fucking bastard sped off. Someone called 999 and…" Mark was now sobbing openly.

"I'm so sorry. Do you want me to get a cab over?"

"No, no. I need to be alone now."

"Did you want me to come to the funeral with you?"

"Listen can you ring tomorrow? I'll get her mum to text the details." Mark hung up and Ophelia sank to the floor feeling like a complete doughnut. She never had anyone close die. She hadn't spoken to family in years and couldn't recall if her grandparents were even around when she was a girl. She realised how lucky she'd been. Up until then her friends managed to elude the grim reaper. When family members of friends passed away they were usually uncles or grandparents or aunts. Ophelia was completely unfamiliar with the protocol in dealing with deaths. She wanted to help or offer some comfort but she couldn't raise the dead or reverse time so realistically she probably couldn't offer much in the way of help. She turned the kettle on and rang Kat.

-

Kat and her husband Ian moved to Essex five years ago. Ian had been living in the US for ten years and since neither was familiar with London Ian suggested they moved close to his family. His mother was only too happy to help find and decorate a maisonette flat for them complete with an extra bedroom containing a bassinet. At first it was helpful having some local knowledge and advice though five years on and Kat really loathed the colour scheme selected for the flat that Ian insisted remain to avoid hurting his mother's feelings. She hated the ubiquitous orange perma-tans afflicting men and women alike, and the compulsory Sunday brunch at the in-laws. They had a back garden patch where Kat started planting roses and some herbs soon after they moved in. Though after a few dour comments from Dorothy and starting her new job, Kat lost time and interest and abandoned the project altogether. There was also the matter of the little old widow in a council flat across the street that owned 13 cats all of which loved to soil their now overgrown garden.

Kat finished the last drag of her cigarette and went back inside. Ian looked over from his game of Tekken and sighed.

"When are you going to quit?"

"This is my last pack, I swear!"

"You said that two months ago. Kat that shit's so bad for you and you stink. I don't know how anyone who spends that much money on perfumes, soaps and creams can justify smoking. You just smell like fags. It's a waste."

Kat rolled her eyes as she stormed into the kitchen and grabbed the half-eaten bag of prawn crackers. The wrinkling of the plastic bag prompted a chorus of high-pitched squealing from the guinea pigs. One of Elise's weekend activities was hanging out with her chums at the anti-vivisection league and rescuing animals from labs. Elise usually kept as many as she could for pets. Though for some reason last year, she felt the little critters would be ideal Christmas gifts and told everyone that received one they should feel honoured she trusted them enough to care for these traumatised creatures. Kat managed to end up with two (the second for Ian, perhaps?). Although initially timid and quiet, they quickly became Pavlovian nightmares. Guinea pigs are apparently easy to train and seem to respond to conditioning. Whenever a plastic bag was rustled, it was followed by a frantic squealing since they associated the noise with their food bag being opened. Kat marched back into the kitchen and grabbed a few pieces of lettuce. They eagerly rose to their feet expectantly when the phone rang. Kat stopped and grabbed it.

"Kat, did you get my messages?"

"Ophelia, hey. I was actually about to call you. Ian said you rang."

36

"Did you see my email?"

"Mmm? No, it was really busy after lunch and I haven't had time. Why? Is something wrong?"

"Laura died yesterday. She was hit by a car. The wake's a week Wednesday."

"Oh... Have you talked to Elise?"

"I've emailed. I figured I'd call you first as Elise usually gets in late. Are those the guinea pigs I can hear?"

"They're relentless. Hang on."

"Listen, I'm gonna go. I'll talk to you later."

Kat fed the guinea pigs and went back out on the balcony and lit another cigarette. Normally, Kat would discreetly step out for a smoke or try to wait the craving out. She struck the match and wondered if she heard Ophelia correctly. As she slowly exhaled, tears welled in her eyes.

'Laura had only just married Mark last summer and, oh Christ! Mark! Set to spend his whole life with someone who was suddenly gone. How do you pick yourself up and move on from life's big plans? What do you do with such finality as death? There were no Plan B's to resort to, or negotiations to be made; they're dead. Anything you forgot to tell them before their last breath will be forever left unsaid'.

Kat was now sobbing as her hand shakily drew out a second fag from her pack. She snuffled the mucus seeping out her nose and tried to look through the tears to light her second cigarette off her first. As she did this she was startled to find Ian watching her on the other side of the glass door. He slowly slid the door open waiting to see if Kat wanted to be approached.

"Hey, what's wrong?" His eyes surveyed Kat sympathetically as he held out his arms.

"Laura died yesterday." As Kat finished the sentence, she began to sob louder as if her saying it aloud confirmed it. Ian hugged Kat tightly, trying to ignore the smoke. She dropped the butt off the balcony and sank into his embrace as their breath rose up in the cold night air.

-

Elise frantically burst in the house and ran up to her room. She found her favourite blue sweater and attached the rubber ducks to it with safety pins. A grin spread across her face as she wondered how long she would be able to mirror Norbert's sweaters until he cottoned on. She didn't want to make him insane or paranoid but loved the idea of making artistic interpretations of his naff sweater collection. It would make a great photo series, she thought. It would be even better if she could get photos of Norbert. She found her Polaroid and mercifully it still had film in it. She would have to accost one of her flatmates in the morning and get a picture of her in the sweaters. Elise began to snigger as the phone rang and she was startled out of the reverie of her Turner Prize acceptance speech. "I'd have put far too much effort into it to ever win a Turner Prize." Elise smugly muttered to herself as she answered the phone.

"Hello?"

"Elise, where the fuck have you been? Don't you check your messages?"

38

"No, I usually wait for them to accumulate for a few days so I feel popular. Kidding! What's up?"

"Laura died. Car accident. The wake is Wednesday."

"Bloody hell, you're joking."

"I left you six messages Elise, and I emailed you."

"Sorry. I was out for dinner and they get real bent out of shape if we're online at work so I usually check it at home. Can you email me the details of the wake and I'll get time off."

"Sure. You okay?"

"Yeah. Just shocked, you know? Look, can I let you go? I'm gonna check my messages and email. I'll try and ring you tomorrow, we can meet for lunch?"

"Okay, I'll talk to you tomorrow. Cheers."

Elise slowly finished pinning the rubber ducks to her sweater. She was quite stunned as she attached the last miniature duck to the blinding turquoise of her sweater. Her motivation wound down and she decided against going through messages or her email. She kicked her trainers off and curled up on her futon in the clutter of blankets and dirty clothes. She sighed as her mind drifted, blocking out any feelings of sadness with sleep.

Ophelia was up early the following morning and couldn't recall a single dream. She almost always remembered her dreams. It was more a curse than a blessing since the dreams were a disturbing amalgamation of Fellini, David Lynch, Salvador Dali and the Magic Roundabout. Her radio alarm may be partly to blame since it was set to the news station for travel updates and weather (overcast and rainy, what a surprise!) forecasts for the day. The problem was that the alarm went off at 6:11-the weather report is done at 12 past and 42 past every hour- and she pressed snooze continually until 6:42. This allowed the grisly and sensationalistic headlines of London and the greater UK to creep into her dreams, creating a subplot or bizarre twist to the already disturbing apparitions.

This basically meant she would dream she was in the financial district about to get onto a bus that was driven by Margaret Thatcher who was eating the passengers as they board, when thirty OAPs dressed in Man United kit grab her and frogmarch her into an alley to recruit her to spearhead a campaign against Genetically Modified cheese spread. As if there was any other kind. Or Batman and Ophelia were being chased by a giant and then stop at Selfridges for their annual sale, then stopped by the filth and told if they don't hand over their mobile phones the Japanese stock market will crash.

Ophelia woke relieved, albeit suspicious that there were no vampire accountants demanding sexual favours in exchange for her tax return or plasticine gargoyles pushing her off the Centre Point building to recall in the shower or over a cup of tea. Sleep had been a black hole the night before without the nasty hangover. Maybe this is how people feel after alien abductions or how most normal people wake up every morning, she wondered. She looked at the clock and tried to recall why she had gotten up so early without the alarm. Laura! Her memory clicked and calmly in an almost detached fashion she recalled wanting to get in early to speak to John and get a card for Mark and Laura's family.

This was one of those scenarios that served as a reminder that life was a constant and unbiased force that carried on like a powerful locomotive running to its own universal timetable. No matter what angle she looked at, the facts remained the same. There was nothing anyone could do or say to change things. No one had any control over death or when it would make an appearance. Laura hadn't planned to get killed by some knob driving carelessly, it just happened. Ophelia shivered as she sipped her tea and dressed for work. She was disappointed to reach the Tube station early and find it even more crowded than usual. 'Keen little wankers', she sneered.

She didn't bother to analyse fellow commuters; she was distracted wondering how she would go. If Ophelia died that morning she knew her obituary would be a few pathetic sentences about a dull conformist life. She was so busy ticking all the boxes; school, go to uni, get a job, get a flat, etc. She hadn't really stopped to think of how it would look in retrospect. Was this what she wanted or was this what she was supposed to want? It wasn't torture but on the same hand she couldn't say her life was rewarding or fulfilling. She certainly never set out to be one of the faceless many with their nose to the grindstone. It hadn't crossed her mind that she could still die young and suddenly despite following the rules. Life didn't owe her a thing and it certainly didn't owe her a long and predictable run. She wondered if Laura felt the same way. Were there things Laura had been meaning to get to? There must have been. Or did she go with regrets? At 27 she must have racked up a few. Was her life even headed where she had hoped before it was cut short? Ophelia felt her eyes start to swell and she grabbed a free paper to distract herself.

She scanned the pages while thoughts streamed through her head like elusive schools of fish. When she tried to grasp an idea or particular thought mid-stream, her

41

thoughts dispersed and left her struggling to recall any until she relaxed and the entire process would start over. Her eyes pored over meaningless articles on the world's ugliest dog or some outraged family that had been wronged by the council or the NHS or a cereal company. Then there were pages devoted to celebrities. Ophelia was always a bit suspicious of what was so fascinating about these people with their ultra white teeth and their escapades. Few of them seemed to actually do anything worth celebrating. Some could act or sing if pushed, but mainly it seemed like they had great stylists and agents. Was this what she was supposed to aspire to? Ophelia tried to picture their epitaphs and couldn't see aside from some poor wardrobe choices how theirs would be any more meaningful than hers. If anything she may have even beaten a good few C-listers in terms of substance. Would a different career given her life more meaning? Or perhaps if she was more selfish with her time and actually spent it with her friends instead of nursing hangovers from work drinks or lame dates that never amounted to anything meaningful.

Ophelia finally pinched a thread of her thoughts and realised what was niggling her most was that her life recently seemed rather devoid of purpose. As she realised this it felt as if the past fifteen years had been in vain. All her efforts and hard work to achieve and accomplish what; to show to or gain approval or praise from someone? Everyone else had their head down moving along the same game of snakes and ladders which was what greeted her as the doors opened at Oxford Circus and she seemed to notice the tiles as if for the first time.

Street cleaners were cleaning the gutters as pigeons busily scavenged for spilled chips from the night before. The main roads were just waking up to the light smoke coloured skies. A few early risers briskly walked to the cash points or cafes for coffee or bacon sarnies. Ophelia ducked into the bookstore to look through the cards. There were so many in the condolences section much to her relief. She couldn't think of what would be appropriate to write and it wasn't like any of the cards would lessen the grief or wake the dead. She wanted to find something that wasn't overly sentimental or religious. She wasn't sure if Laura even had a religion and the religious cards seemed the least comforting. It was like saying 'God loves you so much he has decided to take someone close to you away and leave you here in the material world with a broken heart. Hey, at least you have spiritual comfort.' After fifteen minutes of rereading several cards she settled on a blank one with a photograph of a tree in winter. She would have to simply sign it with condolences or that her thoughts were with them, or just send with a bouquet of flowers and sign her name. She headed to work and laid the card face down on her desk, vowing to deal with it after the morning tea ritual.

-

Kat stretched and wiped the thick crust of sleep from her eyes. She could already tell they were very puffy. She closed them again and lightly ran her finger over them, cringing at the thought of how red and blotchy they must be. The cotton duvet felt soft and comforting against her skin. It wasn't too warm, or stuffy, or chilly. She felt perfectly content and mused that this was one of her favourite feelings. She exhaled and tried to savour the moment, knowing it would be fleeting and quickly forgotten.

'It's the nice mornings in bed, the way grass smells after it's just been cut, the way hot soup feels in your belly on a brisk day, the perfect post-coital snuggle, spontaneity.' Kat smiled as she sighed. It was these things she wished she could hold onto and keep forever. It was these things that she would miss when she died. It wouldn't be the holidays she broke the bank planning, or the shoes she spent over £200.00 on (and told Ian they were £50.00 in the sales) or all the late hours she put in at the office.

"Shit, work!" Kat bolted upright in a panic and glanced over at the clock face that dispassionately read 10:15. "Fuck! Ian!" she moaned throwing the duvet off and stumbling upright.

"What is it, love?" Ian bounded up the stairs.

"I'm so fucking late! Why didn't you wake me? They're going to fucking kill me!"

"Calm down, Kat. I called your manager and told him you wouldn't be in until Thursday or Friday. You look a right mess. How's about a cup of tea?"

Kat's shoulders sank with relief as she smiled. "Thanks. Tea would be great."
Kat tried in vain to find that comfy spot she was in only moments ago and after several failed attempts, got out of bed. She shuffled downstairs to see that Ian had cleaned the entire flat and was in the kitchen getting her tea.

"Am I in the Twilight Zone? Are you my husband?" Kat looked around in wonder as she took her teacup to the table.

Ian smiled shyly, "I couldn't sleep last night so I tidied the flat and was up early this morning. You were in such a state I figured I'd clean up a bit so you could just relax today. You were just tossing and turning all night. How do you feel this morning?"

"Puffy."

Ian smiled tenderly. "My puffy wife, why don't we have a nice quiet morning, maybe take a walk or something?"

"Thanks."

-

Elise rolled out of bed and threw the duck clone sweater on over yesterday's t-shirt and a pair of trousers peaking out from under the bed. She was late and doubted anyone would be able to smell her over the phone. She bounded downstairs into the kitchen and found James buttering a piece of toast. He assessed her briefly before returning his attention to the toast.

"What the hell are you wearing?"

Elise smiled weakly as she studied the ducks suspended from her sweater.

"This? Just an experiment in paranoia with 'Johnny-God-Boy' at the office."

James grinned to himself as he poured the tea. "Elise, you are going to land that poor man in therapy. Don't tease the Christians, sweetie, they might get mad and send those men in suits to our door armed with bibles." His grin spread menacingly across his face as he set his plate down.

"You need a therapist, James." Elise sighed. "Pass me a banana, please."

James was Elise's first housemate. He moved in about six months after she did, four years ago. James wrote short stories for a gay fetish magazine and was a freelance copywriter for industrial safety product websites and brochures. He normally spent the first half of the week penning pornographic short stories to accompany the particular theme for that issue like gay space invaders on the pull, or the living dead hungry for bottoms, or the police officer arresting the naughty crook. The latter half of the week was spent examining various safety goggles or cooling gloves and trying to write

45

enthusiastic copy for them. And the time in between was spent trying to complete his first full length novel despite drawing a blank every time he sat down to work on it.

Jo (who would sometimes add an "e" to the name depending how the week was going) was a drag performer in the West End as well as a regular cabaret act at the Bethnal Green Working Mens Club and did bit part acting mainly for commercials or as an extra. His favourite persona was Rosemary Clooney. It wasn't so much he was a fan, but that he looked an awful lot like her. Or perhaps Rosemary Clooney looked a lot like a drag queen.

A youth worker named Mahesh rented one of the other bedrooms. He was a great cook and was the only one in the house with any DIY skills so everyone was keen to keep him around as long as possible. He moved in a week after Delilah had moved out over the summer to pursue work as a designer in New York City's fashion industry. Elise envied her terribly and wanted to go with Delilah. She even booked a return flight but thought better of staying more than a weekend since Delilah had a bit of a problem with cocaine, making her moody and at times unpredictable. If Elise was going to leave London, she wanted to be sure she'd never have to return, especially as a failure.

Elise usually rented out three of the four bedrooms to cover the mortgage and maintenance expenses, which was supposed to leave her free to enjoy life as a lady of leisure. Her mother often got indignant when Elise made excuses to avoid yet another lunch at Harvey Nichols or The Ivy to discuss her future or hear about how well everyone else's daughter and now even grandchildren are doing.

"Earth to Elise, you okay?"

"Huh? Yeah. A friend died Sunday. Still shocked."

James adjusted his napkin awkwardly, studying the crumbs on his plate. "Oh. I'm so sorry. Who?"

"Laura Thompson. You've met her. Tall, long brown hair, she did some headshots of Joe last year for his portfolio."

"Were you close?"

"I don't know," sighed Elise as she tied her hair up with the rubber band that was rolled around the newspaper. "Are you ever not close enough with someone to shrug off their death?"

James grimaced. "True enough." Elise quietly trudged to the front door, slowly un-peeling the banana. The sun tried in vain to break through the grey wall of cloud as they misted down on the pavement and cars, covering everything in a light net of rain.

-

Ophelia finished going through her inbox of business spam and called John over.

"Yes?"

She looked for Clara Bitchy who seemed to be in a meeting or away from her desk which was a relief since she didn't want her to see or hear. "John, a friend of mine passed away on Sunday and I need time off tomorrow and Thursday to attend the wake and funeral."

John nodded solemnly. "Of course." She was a bit taken aback after expecting some grumbling or forms to fill out or something. "Are you all right? If you need to, you can take today as well."

Ophelia was in complete shock. She half expected him to turn into a pigeon, shit on her desk and fly away. She certainly did not expect this reaction from Mr. 'Jobs Worth' at all. She weakly replied. "Thanks. I have the McKinley report to do but maybe I'll go after that. Thank you."

Maybe John was human after all Ophelia thought and immediately felt silly for worrying about getting any opposition from him. She poured a cup of milky coffee and opened the first card. It was as if she stored up years of grief into a plastic carrier bag and the handles just snapped. She had spent the last ten years focused on surviving, succeeding and escaping her childhood. Ophelia thought she managed to bury her vulnerable self or at least suppress it when instead she managed to build an intricate structure of past hurts and future worries that upended from the weight of Laura's mortality. She was overwhelmed with sadness and regret as the tears fell slowly in heavy drops by her keyboard. She tried to manage her breathing and remain inconspicuous. She pursed her lips and reached for her coffee with shaky hands and reminded herself that she was at work though the reminder did little to abate the tears. She sat as still as possible hiding behind the monitor until she felt a hand lightly on her shoulder and turned around, startled to find John.

"I'm awfully sorry." She muttered. "This is not the place to do this, I know. I really thought I'd be okay. I'm so sorry."

"Take the rest of the day off and get some rest."

"But the McKinley report? It has to be done." She feebly protested.

48

"Don't worry. Go home."

It was 10:45 and she was leaving at John's behest. She sent the unfinished report and switched of the pc. She walked to Oxford Circus in a daze bumping into distracted tourists, the odd outburst of tears stopping her at every block or so.

A faint jazzy tune echoed through the ticket hall. It sounded like a tinny old horn being broadcast on an old short wave radio. Ophelia paused to hear the tune as she fed her ticket through the Barrier. The echo grew louder and the sound harder as she descended the escalator. She was surprised to find someone dressed in a furry black cat suit wailing happily on a trumpet. She smiled at this despite herself at the eccentric busker or potential psychopath as she rooted about in her purse for some coins. The tune was familiar but just out of reach. She tried desperately to place the cat's melody. She had no change so placed a fiver in the cat's empty coffee cup.

As Ophelia walked over to the platform she looked at the clock and thought, 'why go home and wallow in depression?' She turned around and headed back towards the jazz cat and the escalator. Her hums evolved slowly to a song as she found the lyrics softly at first and then louder as she realised no one would hear her over the din of the horn bouncing off the tiles. It was a swing rendition of "Dream a Little Dream". The music seemed to propel her up the steps and into the streets with enough life to get her to Old Compton St.

She sat outside the café filling out a few quiet sentiments to Mark and Laura's family. She spied a motley group walk past kitted out in worn t-shirts, denim vests, plaid trousers, blue or green hair and sighed, recalling when she dressed like that and yearned to tell them so. She knew they wouldn't care nor would they believe they can't stay that way forever. Someday they would either choose to or have to grow up to allow another generation to experiment with shocking identities, radical politics and remind them of everything left behind and taken for granted in a frantic search for direction. Go on and laugh at the sell-outs, conformists, capitalist pigs, but they'll be among them one day to pay rent or buy groceries; up at six, shuffling to the station with the suited zombies to a job that couldn't be further from what they'd set out to do when they dressed like that. 'Enjoy it while you can,' she thought. 'The cycle is ruthless and inevitable.'

The sun muscled its way through the cloud cover by half eleven as she sipped a latte and listened to ubiquitous melody of neighbouring and passing conversations. Ophelia always considered London to be cosmopolitan but as she heard the voices around her, speaking Urdu, Italian, Polish, Farsi, Cantonese, Punjabi, Japanese, Portuguese, French, and English laughing and debating, arguing and confiding, screaming and whispering; she realised how vibrant the streets themselves were to the ears. Like birdsong in the early hours of dawn it was something that went on all the time but only heard for the first time when relaxed. Ophelia listened to the rich rhythmic pulse of the seemingly often heartless city. For the first time since she wore an adolescent's sneer she wasn't furiously rushing off to a meeting or tethered to a mobile deep in shallow conversation or cocooned in earphones. She simply sat quietly taking in this cultural orchestra under a sunny sky with nowhere to be and gracefully accepted the nicest gift London had ever granted her. She could stay all day to watch the secrets and dramas of the city unfold before her.

She watched the women assess one another with sharp eyes and snap judgements. These exchanges were subtle to most but a constant source of anxiety of any female over 12. Just as men steal a sneaky glance in the locker room or at urinals, women check the perceived competition. After a late night session over gin and tonics Ophelia found that women all seem to compare or measure different things. Ophelia compulsively checked shoes, boots, trainers and such whereas Kat compared figures which drove Ian mad when she hissed as a woman passed by, "is she bigger than me or thinner? Does my arse look like that? Was I ever that thin?" It went on and on. Elise checked for unusual apparel or evidence of cosmetic surgery. She was in search of perfection or symmetry only to prove it didn't exist. For a brief period, she carried around a camera to record her findings until she had a small run-in with a very sensitive and outspoken woman from Essex on a hen night. There was a strange comfort seeing others engaged in the same assessments serving as subconscious assurances that a level of uncertainty exists beneath even the most opaque veneer of confidence.

-

Elise turned looked around to see if Norbert was in yet. She caught sight of a brown and green argyle jumper hunched over a logbook and headed towards it.

"Um, Norbert?"

Norbert turned to face an army of little rubber ducks pinned against the giant woolly backdrop. He regarded this vision thoughtfully before his glance drew up to meet Elise's. "Yes?"

"A friend of mine passed away on Sunday and the funeral's tomorrow. I'll need the day off."

"If it's not the death of an immediate family member, you'd have to take it as holiday and you took all your days already."

Elise stared blankly at him "You're fucking joking."

Norbert winced. "I'm sorry, but I'm afraid I'm not. I can ask my manager if you can take it as unpaid leave or make it up by covering an evening shift."

Elise's nostrils flared as she shook her head in disbelief. "I don't think I'm hearing you right. A dear friend has died and I'm asking for some time off to bury her and mourn my loss."

Norbert held his hand up to cut in. "I understand what you're saying, Elise, but the policy is for deaths of immediate family. As a Christian organisation we must follow the rules like sheep follow their shepherd."

"Can't you just say that it's family?" Elise cut in impatiently.

Norbert gasped in horror. "Elise! I just said this is a Christian organisation and Christians don't tell porkies. I must say I'm shocked and a bit disappointed that you'd even suggest such a thing."

She inhaled deeply and retreated to her desk. She regarded her PC and then Norbert before remembering she wasn't there out of necessity.

"Fuck this."

She grabbed her bag and marched over to Norbert's desk and in a fierce whisper that gradually blossomed into an outraged boom she spat, "I'm not one of your sheep and I don't give a toss if this company is Christian, or Jewish, or Hindu, or Muslim or bloody Jedi! If someone dies their loved ones need to mourn. This is what makes us human. The last thing I should be worried about is getting time off. My relation to her is immaterial. If this is how Christianity works I want no part of it and I'll be damned if

I'll be contributing to its profit margins. Send my final paycheque to my home address. I won't waste another second here."

Elise stormed out of the office and onto the streets. Adrenaline coursed through her as she moved upstream against the current of commuters. 'Bunch of cunts,' she cursed to herself. Anxiety flooded through her chest as she headed for the bus stop. She paced irritably as she waited for the bus. She sneered at ads on passing taxis and the buses that weren't hers. After ten minutes the bus arrived and she was flushed with anger. She fought her way on and squeezed into a corner.

The jumper was glued to her back by a thin sheen of sweat. The windows fogged with heat and humidity from the crowd within. She glared at the writhing mass while they elbowed, jostled and bickered for space. Her rage simmered while she struggled to hold back tears of frustration. She reassured herself that her house wasn't too far and tried to control the tremors in her hands.

Frustration, grief and anger brimmed over into the corners of her eyes. Her frustration boiled within as she recalled her last conversation with Laura just two weeks before. They had met up to attend a screening of a Thai film at the BFI. Laura boasted that she'd already started her Christmas shopping. It struck Elise then how those gifts will probably never make it to their intended recipients. Laura had no way of knowing her life would end so suddenly. She told Elise about how she was thinking of changing jobs. She loved working in the charity sector but she hated the commute. They discussed possible holidays and all sorts of other vague plans for the future that would now never happen. Laura's life had really only just began; all the schooling behind her, found a partner and managed to buy mid-terrace in need of repair. She was looking forward to eventually having children, probably even grandchildren perhaps, or travelling to South America.

Her life was now frozen in amber at age 27. Her 27 years a question cut short. She'd never go grey or worry about menopause. Elise would be swept up in the relentless waves of time pushing forward through decay while Laura was mired in the sand at the tipping point of youth. The pressure overwhelmed her and dissolved into a muted sob. Her chest heaved as hot tears fell from her eyes onto her shoes. The passengers stepped back half a metre en masse. Elise felt utterly alone in the packed bus. The drops swelled to a steady stream.

Her sobs grew louder as she gripped the pole, fighting the shaky gravity of the jerking bus and bumpy roads. It bumbled through Angel past shops being opened for the day and cafe crowds thinning out. The city felt out of reach and was unable to sympathise with her feelings of loss.

The bus finally reached her stop. Elise struggled to gather her bag along with the emotional refuse that seemed to trickle down into the invisible boundaries her fellow travellers allotted her. Public transport was no place for emotions. If there was a delay or signal failure, a sigh or roll of the eyes would suffice. Or when drunk, laughter, slurring or anger was tolerated by fellow passengers. Raw, sober emotions, however, were completely unacceptable. It was an unspoken rule of London public transport that emotions were to be suppressed. Grief had no place there.

After frantically jiggling the keys into the stubborn lock she fell through the door and found James in the kitchen sitting down to a plate of Jammy Dodgers and a cup of tea. Elise stared at her flatmate in surprise assuming the house was empty. James straightened in his seat and indignantly declared,

"One must have their elevenses." He paused to examine his watch "And what brings you back in such a state? Did they send you home to find God, sweetie?"

Elise erupted into tears and wailed, "I left!" and she ran over to hug James.

"Please don't cry, especially on my shirt, dear. It'll be okay. I'm sure they need you a hell of a lot more than you need them, honey."

James tentatively petted Elise's head as he fumbled for a supportive phrase.

"It's not that," she wept. "It's everything!" She exhaled only to crumple onto James' back and sob. "The job wasn't much, just the straw that broke the camel's back." Elise sniffled as she wiped her face on her sleeve.

She tried to regulate her breathing before looking around. "Is anyone else home?" She could feel her sinuses swelling as her nose oozed steadily onto the back of James's vest. She hastily wiped it and began to rub his back in an effort to seem like an inconspicuous gesture.

"I don't think so. Just me and the biscuits, I'm afraid."

Elise nodded as she straightened her posture. "Good."

James nodded as he opened a Jammy Dodger to lick the jam off the biscuit. "I'm here until 1, then off to a meeting with the publishers. Want me to get anything while I'm out? Tea, tissues, diazepam, Prozac, rum or maybe some jam doughnuts?"

Elise cracked a weak smile, "No. Cheers though. Might have a bath or a nap. It's been a messy day and it's not even lunch time."

As she turned to go upstairs, the phone cut through the quiet of the house. She stiffened uncomfortably and shot a pleading glance at James. He rolled his eyes dramatically. "Yes, of course, my lady."

"Hello? She isn't in at the moment. Had an interview with the devil, apparently he's hiring. Shall I let her know you rang? Mmm, okay Norby. I'll tell her."

18 SEPTEMBER

The morning of the funeral was grey and cold, with miserable drizzle. The weather was similar on most mornings that September without the funeral though Ophelia noticed it was actually appropriate for the occasion. The taxi drew up to the old church. Mark looked as if he hadn't slept in days. Ophelia couldn't find the appropriate words to express how she felt despite a bulk of her journey spent searching for a comforting or reassuring word or gesture. She wanted desperately to make him feel better but ultimately felt powerless. Mark was so enveloped in his own grief he wouldn't process much that was said anyway. She gave him a hug and whispered "sorry."

Laura's mother, Colleen, finished speaking to the minister and gave Mark a firm hug. He slowly collapsed, sobbing loudly on her shoulder. Ophelia looked away to give their grief some privacy, feeling displaced like an emotional spectator.

She couldn't believe Laura was dead. She remembered all the lost summers and holidays spent with Laura, once invincible super-humans pumping any and every substance under the sun into themselves, staying up all night on ecstasy and amphetamine mixers dancing and dodging death. They survived that and for what; to feel the intangible restraints of duty, responsibility and adulthood tighten? How did they get there from their dreams? What did they sleep through? As she gazed at the tombstones she wondered where did she seriously expect to be at 28? She didn't care if she ever moved ahead in that job and had no intention of living forever in that flat. What did she even want out of life?

She thought of the first time she met Laura. Ophelia missed freshers week thanks to a screw up booking the flights and still felt dizzy with jet lag after landing the day before classes started. She barely managed to stay awake and had a terrible time understanding the professors' accents. By the time the last class ended she felt ready to

57

cry before noticing she felt a tap on her shoulder. She turned to see a friendly smile surrounded by a long kinky mane of brown hair.

"You all right?"

Ophelia immediately felt at ease after several days of poker faced travellers on the tubes and buses followed by a day watching alliances that formed at the freshers week she missed. Laura's smile was a welcome and much needed reprieve. They went for mezze at a small Lebanese place nearby and shared histories; slowly and carefully at first then manically and carelessly after three bottles of house red. She was born and raised in London but her parents were from Limerick in Ireland. Laura laughed for ages when Ophelia asked if everyone had Lucky Charms for breakfast and used Irish Spring soap. She was a bit embarrassed when Laura confessed she had never heard of either. Laura had walked Ophelia back to her rented room and they made tea and continued to talk late into the night. As Ophelia lost herself deep in a forest of reveries, the murmur of condolences drew her back to the church yard.

Behind her came the soft rustle of withered leaves being crunched underfoot and turned to see Mark. He was slightly more composed, slumped next to Colleen, smoking a cigarette and settling into a bench. She gingerly sat down beside him and squeezed his hand softly. He nodded almost imperceptibly. A melancholy parade of friends and relatives slowly milled past, offering comforting words before heading into the church where they filled empty spaces with a soothing buzz of memories and even the occasional outburst of laughter or tears. She stayed by Mark as he sat on the bench smoking one cigarette after the other while Colleen busied herself with arriving mourners. Perhaps that was how she was able to get through the day, Ophelia thought. Mark was in no shape to talk as tears gently ebbed and flowed to the tides of thoughts and memories.

Kat arrived with Ian. She looked around anxiously for some familiar faces. Her eyes were red and swollen from crying. Ophelia motioned to her and slowly rose. Kat briskly walked over to meet Ophelia, her lips pursed in a mournful frown to keep the weeping in. Her hands trembled as she drew a cigarette from her bag. Ophelia quickly met the tip of it with Mark's lighter. She leaned back as she inhaled, trying desperately to catch her breath.

"I am so sorry! I really thought I could handle this, but it just makes it hurt more…" Kat trailed off. Ian slowly walked over and gently rubbed her back.

Ophelia nodded sympathetically and embraced her. Elise arrived shortly thereafter with her parents and quietly headed over to Colleen. Her mother took Colleen's hands in her own before embracing her and Elise. The usual frenetic energy that radiated from Elise was noticeably subdued. Her hair was tied back and she was wearing an expensive looking black suit making her seem older and sophisticated. Her features looked tired and drawn with the faintest beginnings of lines around her eyes. She kissed her parents and Colleen before she headed towards Mark. She held him tight and cooed, "She wouldn't want us to mourn her life; she would want us to celebrate it." He choked back a sob and nodded. Elise's embrace stayed firm until the wave tears passed.

People quietly crept in to the pews. Their expressions were sombre but also of shock. There was hardly any time to prepare for the loss. The casket dominated the altar; surrounded by lilies, azaleas, roses and baby's breath. Ophelia found it hard to believe the intimidating mahogany casket held her friend. She recalled how Laura had a strange aversion to musicals and after a debate with Ian spent an entire day spontaneously launching into song about renewing her bus pass or buying groceries. She remembered how Laura could sew almost anything. She used to make her own clothes at Birbeck and always inspired enquiries of where she got the dress or top whenever they went to a gig. All of these attributes and memories seeped out of the box and flitted through her mind. Ophelia wondered what, if anything, would be re-membered of her if she were to go suddenly. She doubted the ability to drink most folks under the table would feature or all the marvellous flowcharts and pivot tables she made.

Elise was sat in the back pew with her back straight against the bench staring straight ahead at the casket. She dabbed at her eyes and sniffled as she looked over at her two friends.

"I still can't believe how sudden this all came about. It's not like we knew she was going to die. There was so much I should have said to her the last time I saw her. All the questions I wished I asked. You think you have time to recall and ask but then they're dead."

Kat tapped her foot compulsively and Ian tried to soothe her by patting the other. The funeral was the first time in fourteen years since she set foot in a church. She grew up attending Catholic School in the States and hated sitting through Mass. Her mother dragged her literally kicking and screaming every Sunday, pulling her hair into tight, painful plaits staring reproachfully at Kat before shoving her into the passenger seat of the family car. Her patent leather shoes always seemed too small or too big and the priests often spoke with thick Italian accents or Irish brogue making them impossi-ble to understand which would draw the inevitable pinch from her mother every time she fell asleep. She wasn't sure if her mother was being sadistic, trying to indoctrinate her or was just simply being Catholic. She noticed the seams under her arms were hot stains of sweat that travelled with alarming speed towards the front of her blouse. Her hairline felt slick with a cool sweat and she couldn't stop flipping through the psalm book distractedly, desperate to keep her shaky hands busy.

She thought of Laura and how if she were there would have swapped the psalm books with Razzles or added hand scrawled lyrics to contemporary songs. Laura loved mischief. Kat laughed easily which made her the perfect partner. Whenever Laura pulled off a stunt Kat would reward her with rich laughter and a willing accomplice. It would start with a little giggle over something like pigeons squabbling over a bun or an unintended typo in an ad. She would cast a conspiring glance towards Kat and the laughter would build into crescendo of banshee howls that lasted ages until they forgot what had started it off and then start again once recalled. Whether they were swapping trolleys of sleepy midnight shoppers at the 24-hour Tesco or belting out the body form jingle at an east London karaoke night, Kat had some of her best late nights and lost weekends with Laura.

Kat met Laura a year after moving to London. She had married Ian just three months before in a rushed civil ceremony attended by Kat's best friend, Beth, her husband and Ian's old Boston flatmate Jim. Dorothy called every day for a month crying and accused Ian of unspeakable cruelty. Having been estranged from her own family for nearly six years Kat couldn't understand why Dorothy was so hurt by them wanting a quick and intimate ceremony. She even offered to have a big reception party but it was too late; Dorothy had already formed an opinion and impression of her new American daughter-in-law. They decided to move to London to further Ian's career and so he could make up for the wedding by being closer to his family. Within a week of arriving Kat had found temp work answering phones at a breast cancer charity to earn money and get out of Ian's parents' house more. There were two other women who shared the desk with her, helped her get used to accents and teased her playfully about her own. Laura commented on the flower arrangements that appeared on the desk every Tuesday. Some were overly creative, looking like Carmen Mirada castoffs or ikebana as interpreted by circus clowns, and one almost certainly looked like a phallic "piss off" from a disgruntled florist on their way out.

On one Tuesday the vase was full of lilies. Laura walked in that morning and stopped short.

"Fucking hell, is business that bad?" Kat looked at her quizzically. "The lilies. You send them as a default flower at funerals and we're working to cure cancer."

Kat paused before bursting into a raucous laughter. They began having lunch together and Laura's mum had a friend who helped find them a place to Dorothy's liking so that they could finally move into their own place. Kat looked at the lilies behind the casket and smiled as tears stung her eyes.

Ophelia couldn't stop staring at the casket. The whispers and sniffles of the other mourners grew muffled and distant as she tried to reconcile the fact that her friend's corpse was in that polished box along with an unfinished lifetime of dreams, hopes, and experiences not shared. It could just as easily have been her or anyone else in there whose life could have been suspended or cut short the way a computer freezes for no discernable reason and all the data are lost. All of Laura's memories and secrets would be irretrievably lost. This struck Ophelia as particularly depressing. She held everything in for years from secrets to grudges to tears not considering when or where to unload all of their baggage. She just assumed she had time to figure it out later. She now realised that later doesn't necessarily have to come. Ophelia noticed the minister slip out to help calm Mark and coax him in.

"Can't blame him." Ophelia muttered.

"Who?" Elise turned her head to watch the minister comforting Mark, who was collapsed on the bench sobbing into his hands.

"Mark. I wouldn't want to be here if I was him."

"Ah, right. It would probably make it even more final or real."

"What do you think she would've made of all this?"

"Laura? Not sure. It's not like she planned for this, is it?"

"I know but they weren't even married in church."

"I'm just relieved she's being buried! I couldn't have sat and watched the casket on a conveyor belt like they have at supermarket checkouts and send her body into a furnace."

"If anything Laura may have gotten a kick out of that." They shared a grim smile.

-

For the reception Colleen rented the function room at the local pub. Ophelia walked over with Elise. It was just after four in the afternoon and the pub was nearly empty. There were a few kids that were furtively nursing pints of cider trying their best to look 18, a group of geezers crowded around a fruit machine trying to double the amount of their dole cheques, and an OAP at the bar extolling the "good old days" to a bartender that looks as if she heard the speech many times before.

Upstairs, the function room was dimly lit and cigarette smoke slowly curled in with the surge of guests like ghosts.

Ophelia felt a soft tap on her shoulder and was relieved to see Dave. Dave smiled and she sank into his big arms. Dave had grown to be a brotherly figure and it was an enormous comfort to bury her face in his chest and sigh. "I'm so glad you're here, Dave!" she whispered.

"Hey Feelie, it's okay. How are you?"

"Sad."

"About Laura?"

"About everything."

Ophelia looked around and noticed a lot of old familiar faces looming about. Older, more tired faces than she remembered. Some were crying, smoking or just chatting. Some had accumulated a few lines and grey hairs, others had grown gaunt and tired, some were filled in and others just looked bloated. How many of these faces would still look this way if we were gathered at a wedding or reunion? She wondered how they saw her face and how many were as disappointed with their life as she was with hers at that moment.

Dave's gaze followed Mark briefly then he turned to Ophelia and shook his head. "I don't know how he's managing. I'd be a fucking wreck."

Ophelia raised her eyebrows. "He is a fucking wreck. Weren't you at the funeral? I find it hard to take in so heaven knows what it must be like for him. I know it sounds daft, but death never occurs to me."

Dave drew a fag from his pack. "No, I know what you're saying. It never really crosses my mind, either. I don't think about any of that shit, really. So when this happened I was shocked."

Mark slowly made his way over holding a pint in one hand and a fag in the other. He sipped his pint slowly and stared into space. "I feel like the living dead. I'm doomed to float around on autopilot for the rest of my time here on earth… In London…In hell."

Ophelia nodded. "London is definitely hell!"

Dave lit a second fag and passed it to Mark. "No, mate. London's definitely more of a purgatory."

Mark broke his concentrated stare to accept the smoke and look at Dave. "Huh?"

"No one's final destination is ever London. Unless they're filthy rich…I mean, think of it; everyone living in London is working their arse off to get the hell out and move to a place with nicer climate, lower cost of living, nicer people, less crime, fewer people, clean air, more space. London is purgatory. It's the bus terminal of life! I can't think of anyone I know who's lived in London all their lives and don't dream of leaving. People living in New York City love New York City. Same with Paris. People could spend their whole life living in Oxford or Bath. Everyone's dying to get out of London."

Ophelia looked at Dave with surprise then glanced to gauge Mark's reaction. Mark didn't seem to register. She searched her mind quickly to break the brief silence. "Why don't I get a round, Dave?"

"Ta. I'll have a pint of ale. Cheers."

Within an hour, everyone in the function room was pissed. The mood was lighter with memories and anecdotes of Laura that connected everyone. Tears balanced precariously with laughter and even singing by Laura's uncles. Mark perambulated around the room, trying to stay composed and thank everyone for coming while accepting hugs and sympathies. Elise emerged from a small crowd, grabbing Mark by the hand on her way and headed towards Ophelia and Dave.

"Hey!" She sighed as she wriggled into the booth and gingerly placed her pint on the table. Dave returned with their fifth round of drinks. Kat and Ian followed closely behind him. Ophelia gave Kat's arm a squeeze as her other arm hovered tentatively over the table searching for a place to flick her ashes. Elise passed the ashtray over to her. Kat inhaled the filter of her cigarette deeply before stubbing it out. "I'm going to miss her so much. She was the first friend I had made in the UK. She could mimic Dorothy's voice perfectly. And dog barks though I'm not sure the two were connected. Laura would terrorise poodles on the street, barking at them." Everyone smiled at the thought. "It was Laura that introduced us, Ophelia. It was at that weird theme party she threw with you, Mark. It was um…"

"Rainbow." Mark finished her train of thought and took a cigarette from her pack as the memory volleyed about the booth. .

"I still can't believe that was a kid's programme! With that closet homosexual pink hippo…"

"Frank."

"Yeah, and the fuzzy orange one with the gimp face."

"Zippy."

"They were more like the usual suspects at an S&M bar than kids' T.V. characters."

"Didn't Laura use a gimp mask and glue orange felt to it for Zippy?"

"It was an old towel."

Ian grinned, "She was so creative. She did a lot of the costumes and the set pieces for my first local theatre play. It was only Harlow, but it was bloody brilliant. It even got a mention in the Observer."

Ophelia raised a glass of port and smiled. "Cheers everyone. To a life lived well and loved lots."

Everyone raised their glasses. "To Laura!"

"I usually only ever have this at Christmas." Ophelia remarked to no one in particular.

"Bollocks." Elise slurred, waving Ophelia off with a tired smile. "'S'only two months early. Drink up."

Mark downed a shot and his eyes welled with tears. He smiled wanly and grasped the edge of the table. "I'd best go check on Colleen."

They watched Mark disappear into the crowd, his posture crumbling with each step.

Kat sighed. "Not to sound morbid, but I wonder if Laura died happy."

Elise cocked her head, slightly baffled. "What do mean? Like the minute before she died?"

"No. I mean generally."

Dave nodded. "Yes, yes, I know what you mean. I imagine she was. Happy, that is. She adored Mark. They just finished painting the house, she had that new job and I think they were thinking of having kids."

"But she went so suddenly. Like, do you think she was content with the way she left things?"

Ophelia knitted her brows. "It's not like she had much choice."

Kat dragged on her cigarette. "Can you imagine all the things she may have meant to do and never got around to?" Kat's trembling hands betrayed her measured voice.

Elise finished her pint and looked over at the crowd at the bar. "She was 27, not 77. You can't live your life like you could die at any second. That's not what it's for."

A thick silky blue cloud of smoke crept out of Kat's mouth, her eyes following Elise's. "If I died tomorrow, there'd be so many regrets. Places to see, the people I've screwed over and never apologised to, or the people who screwed me over that I never told to sod off. I still can't even drive in this country and I've been here for five friggin years. I don't want to just be remembered as the operator of a phone-in STD clinic."

"Kat, you actually help people. If you died tomorrow, I'd campaign for your canonisa-tion. We'd call you Saint Kat and you'd be the patron saint of the sexually pathetic." Ophelia touched Kat's hand, desperate to keep the mood light.

Elise abruptly burst with laughter and Kat smiled as she tapped her cigarette in the ashtray and traded her empty pint glass for Ian's.

"Now puffy," Ian chided affectionately, "be careful not to get too squiffy. I don't want to have to carry you up the stairs. I'm getting a lemonade for me and a water for you. Does anyone else want anything?" Elise, Dave and Ophelia both asked for another pint. Dave offered to help Ian bring the drinks back.

"I know what you mean." Ophelia confided as she lit a fag from Kat's pack. "I've put a lot of things off myself. I'm not that far from 30, I work as a drone in a rubbish company where I'm constantly getting stabbed in the back, live alone in a rubbish flat with the world's loudest rodent, I've not been in a proper relationship in two years…I'd feel a bit cheated if I died tomorrow, actually."

Kat nodded. "I know! Me, too." Kat looked over at Elise. "At least you live life on your on terms. You do it all your own way. And people actually own your artwork! At least you know your name will live on in some capacity. You're never afraid to tell people to fuck off."

"Everyone has fears, Kat." Elise countered quickly.

"I'm afraid I'm wasting my creativity and talent." Ophelia said feeling the alcohol hitting her. "I've been at my job like a little worker bee for so long. I'm afraid if I actually was given the opportunity to be creative, I'd fuck it up. I don't even think I can be creative anymore. I can hardly remember what I even set out to be in the first place."

Kat nodded vigorously and now had her arm around Elise. "I know. I actually wanted to be a window dresser. I know it sounds stupid, but I loved the idea of coming up with amazing scenes for big department store windows. Every month or few weeks it would all change again. Stuff that would stop people or at least stay with them on their way to work, draw crowds or just make kids smile. I've been desperate to redecorate but I know Dorothy will be offering 'helpful hints' or worse: make nasty comments about whatever I do."

"Sod what she thinks, Kat. Do it for you." Elise replied. "You can't worry about what Dorothy says. She doesn't live there, you do."

"Did you see how supportive Mark's mother-in-law was?" Kat grew more animated as she lit another fag. "I mean, I can just see Dorothy in that situation. She'd be complaining that Ian died because I didn't feed him enough."

Dave smiled. "I'm sure she can't be that bad, Kat."

Kat's eyes widened. "When she found out I was headed to a wake, she rang up to give me tips on etiquette and apparel. Like I'm some fuckin Neanderthal." Kat inhaled deeply and exhaled a long agitated sigh as Ian returned with the drinks.

Elise shrugged. "Maybe she is that bad."

"She doesn't mean any harm, love!" Ian said as he set the drinks on the table. "It's all part of being a Welsh woman."

Kat raised her brow at Ian as she took a sip.

"Ian may be right. We had an account at my company once and the contact was a Welsh woman who moaned and complained constantly! She was also blunt to the point of being downright rude." Ophelia explained in Ian's defence. "And she also had this really nasal voice. She sounded like a talking sheep! We all called her Dolly behind her back!" Ophelia began to smirk as she continued. "Every time she visited the office or rang up, I had this sound bite I downloaded off the web of a sheep braying and would play it when she'd leave or after hanging up with her."

 Kat cracked a small grin as Dave interjected "Cor, bet she was popular in the Welsh villages!" After that, the whole table was laughing.

-

Kat and Ian drove home in silence. As he drove, he would occasionally pat her knee or reach over and stroke her hair. She looked out the passenger window as the rain pelted down against it, magnifying small bits of the Epping Forest in the oncoming headlights. The sky ahead was a heavy grey canopy held up by the bare, gnarled branches of the trees. Their slick trunks grounded among the sodden mulch of leaves shed weeks before, rooted to the spot watching with dejected resignation as each year everything that they worked so hard to grow fell to the ground and died.

"Ian?" Kate mused as she watched the forest pass by.

"Yes, love?"

"What do you think happens when we die?"

Ian shook his head as he watched the road. "Nothing."

Kat turned abruptly and faced Ian's profile. "What do you mean nothing?"

"Just nothing. It all goes black, end of story. You become worm fodder and return to the earth, I guess."

The hairs rose on Kat's neck, as she grew anxious. Her voice wavered as she brushed a few stray amber wisps behind her ears. "How can you say that?" she spat.

"What? It's just what I think."

"Yeah but how the fuck can you possibly be content with that as an ending?"

"I didn't say I was content with the idea, but it's the most logical. Well, for me it is."

Kat's thoughts raced in a panic. There was no reassurance in Ian's response whatsoever.

"Then why do you even bother? If you're just gonna end up as fertiliser what's the fucking point? Why do anything or even get out of bed for that matter? I mean what's the use of exerting any effort at all?"

She grew frantic at the thought of her lifeless body enveloped in a heavy layer of soil not dreaming or thinking or being.

Ian seemed calm as he watched the road ahead, oblivious to Kat's meltdown less than a metre away. "I reckon we live on in other ways. Like anything you make or create is still here long after you've gone. Your affects are passed on. Your family and friends' memories of you, if you have kids; all that lives on after you die, I guess."

He shrugged as the windscreen wipers squeaked back and forth between the silences. She pictured worms slithering over her in the ground, paralysed and unable to shake them off.

"But what about your soul?" Ian snorted and rolled his eyes. Kat sighed. "Okay, what about your ID or personality or even your dreams? Why do we have any of that at all then if it's going to switch off at the end? All the memories and beliefs you accumulate in a lifetime are gone with as much effort as switching the telly off? What's it all for then?"

"Kat, they aren't frequent flyer miles or loyalty card schemes. Where would these memories go? Or what would you do with it?" The distance between them seemed to increase as he spoke.

Kat's eyes welled up, her face contorting into the horrified grimace of a child who just watched her dog get hit by a lorry. "That's not comforting at all. That's fucking horrible!"

Ian turned his head, surprised and helpless, as his wife turned to face the passenger window in a sulk. "Well, what do you think happens?" he replied, exasperated.

Kat shook her head slowly as the forest passed like a zoetrope. Tears streamed down her face, mirroring the rain on the window silently falling outside. "I don't know what happens to us, but I always hope whatever it is that I would still be with you somehow."

Houses slowly began to mix in with the trees as they silently made their way onto the high road. As the car drew up to the space, Ian noticed a small figure on the hedges. "Hey Kat, look. Do you think that's the little sod that's been soiling the garden?" As she craned her neck a smile slowly spread over her face.

"Holy shit, Ian! Look!" She giggled. The cat was all white with a small patch of black fur beneath its little pink nose. "It looks like H-H-Hitler." She stuttered. They looked at one another and ruptured into a fit of giggles.

"Shhh. Whatever you do, don't mention the war!" Ian managed before joining in Kat's laughter. Kat tilted her head back as she emitted a throaty laugh and Ian's heart trembled, storing this image of his wife into his own collection of memories.

The cat sat erect by the hedge looking indignant, well aware of the affront. "I wonder if it's that old spinster's cat. Oh my god! He even looks angry. I bet the little fucker knows we're laughing at him," Kat sniggered as she opened the car door.

The cat scurried away into the night as they approached. Kat and Ian continued to laugh, pointing at it in the distance. She hugged Ian and leaned into him drunkenly. "I don't know what I'd ever do without you, Ian. You're the only one in the world who understands my demented sense of humour."

"I love you, too." Ian said as he gently kissed her head and squeezed her back.

-

Elise stumbled out of the pub and staggered onto the bus to the nearest tube station. Being well after rush hour, the train was an amalgamation of the over-worked, over-sexed or overwrought. Her thoughts swam dazedly amid several pints of Stella. Elise loved to take the trains on futile journeys. She loved to natter with the passengers on these idle voyages. She especially loved doing this while pissed.

She often caught them unaware with flattering comments or simple questions and would then proceed to chat with them until one got off. In doing this, Elise had amassed a wealth of random and trivial information such as; discovering 22 different ways to make cheesecake, the number of tones used in the Cantonese language (7), the best place in London for fresh roasted coffee beans (Camden Town), how to avoid a tattoo scarring (vitamin e oil), how to say thank you in 11 different languages (so far, this was an ongoing project) and the history of the Faberge egg (that had been an exceptionally long journey). Elise also managed to build a collection of international email addresses this way. She never emailed any of the people, but kept all the scraps of paper, business cards and club flyers with the addresses in an old shoe box covered in a manic collage of stickers, clippings and pictures.

With the funeral still fresh in her thoughts and a few hours until the pubs closed, Elise reasoned this would be a good time to have a London Underground pub-crawl. Every few stops, she stumbled out of a random station and groped her way to the nearest public house. Initially, she leaned against the bars and quietly observed the other patrons, even ear-wigging the odd conversation. As with most pub-crawls, the atmosphere grew more surreal with each stop. With each drink, Elise felt herself gracefully sinking into an abyss of grief and spirits. Rather than leaning at the bar she waded through the crowd briefly passing through anecdotes, rows, jokes, confessions, secrets and lies until it was a hazy collage of faces, muffled voices and cigarette smoke.

With each drink, the tide of inebriation deepened until it had completely submerged her. The surrounding pubs, streets, alleys and train stations transformed into a pacific manifestation of colours and textures, shadow and light. Boundaries and shapes merged and blurred like jellyfish against the neon lights. Black cabs swam by dreamily as the traffic lights slowly danced from red to amber to green. In this aquatic, muffled state Elise felt protected from sharp voices, words and emotions.

Elise felt five years old again at Harrods shopping with her mum. Her mother would spend hours going through racks of clothing and Elise would walk through the clothes, shutting her eyes and obscuring herself among the soft coats, or gowns, letting the fabrics caress her face while taking in the rich smells of silk, mink and leather. She felt at ease, drifting through the various textures and smells, completely alone and carefree, but comforted knowing that her mum wasn't too far away.

Elise managed to trudge to the station after last call. Although she was actually weaving erratically through the streets, she felt fluid and graceful. The hum and jerk of the train soothed her like an ocean current. As the carriage gradually emptied, Elise noticed a harried businessman shuffling through his papers. His finger seemed to wander listlessly down each page. His eyelids were heavy as his chest carefully expanded and gently collapsed. His head would bob slightly with fatigue then reel back to rouse him and he continued fondling his papers. A feeling of isolation languidly spread through Elise as she watched him. Far too drunk to identify what it was that was so lugubrious about this man Elise felt a stir in her heart. She rose unsteadily and began to pace towards him. She felt a desperate need to hug him or place her hand on his; any sort of contact to anchor her, to soothe her. As she drew closer, the train jerked forward and yanked Elise down. The descent felt abyssal as if she plunged infinitely until her face struck the cold, gritty floor.

Dazzled briefly, she opened her eyes and saw two black shoes slowly come into focus. A face floated towards her, the mouth moving but it sounded as if he were underwater. He helped her up gently, keeping his hands on her shoulders for balance. As Elise gathered what was left of her wits, she grasped the rail with her hand and brought into focus a pair of eyes. They seemed kind and concerned, slightly withered from age and many late nights. Studying his eyes, she was overcome with a wave of loneliness and yearning. She grabbed the sleeve of his coat with her free hand and abruptly leaned forward, kissing him passionately on the lips. She let go of the rail and held him close to her, expressing all the stored up anger and grief in this one act of spontaneous emotion. The businessman went limp with shock. As his mind

76

searched for a reflex, the doors whooshed open and Elise wrenched herself free and stumbled out of the carriage. She weaved down the platform towards the way out.

A couple of weeks passed and everyone seemed to be hibernating to Ophelia. She was on autopilot going to work, attending meetings and going home. She felt more lethargic than ever, constantly oversleeping despite falling asleep on the sofa at 9 or 10 most nights. She grew even more apathetic towards work to the point where she would sit and simply stare at the monitor for hours as if hypnotised, or scroll through sales on eBay.

She found herself haunted by Laura and saw her everywhere; her eyes on the face of a woman on the train, or her hairstyle in an advertisement, or her smile on a woman in a café. She would hear laughter in a shop and pause to look for her or would pass by streets and night clubs where they once stood smoking, talking, drinking or getting up to nothing much. She would pass a deli and the smell would instantly bring lunch with Laura to mind. It was a ubiquitous spectre following her throughout London though she wasn't sure if was a great comfort or a burden.

Ophelia thought about how much time she spent with Laura in the year before she died and felt a niggling guilt she neglected their friendship. Whenever she cancelled a weekend or evening out she reasoned that Laura was busy with her own life, marriage, house and job. Living and working in London could do that. Ophelia rarely saw people that weren't near her office or lived close by. It didn't help that the Tube was such a hassle or that traffic was a nightmare. Mostly, she was too tired or busy to bother. Since Mark and Laura lived on the other side of London, she saw them twice a year at most. Mark worked relatively close by but it never occurred to her to have lunch with him since she had always been Laura's friend. She couldn't think of what it was that actually kept her busy to the point of cancelling plans Laura tried to make. And now everywhere she went she thought of that.

In the weeks following Laura's death, Elise threw herself into her artwork. Her sculpture for Kat was nearly finished. She listened to Kat moan for years about her mother-in-law and decided the most appropriate homage would be a large as life sculpture of Joan Crawford. She found loads of photographs of her from the web and West End movie poster shops. Then, she hounded various boutiques until one was willing to part with an old, bald mannequin. Elise had carefully restored the cracks and painted "Joan" white, and added her features in black, silver and grey. She had even added the thick *Mommy Dearest* eyebrows and one of Jo's old wigs for her hair. The final touch was of course the dress. Elise had managed to construct a 1950s Dior house dress out of chicken wire, *papier-mâché* and Dorothy's clippings. All over the dress, gloves and shoes were Dorothy's helpful hints on keeping house, PMT cures, weight-loss tips and of course information on fertility. It was as if Joan had stepped right off the silver screen and was attacked by a mob of deranged ransom note enthusiasts. Elise was hoping to use it as a central piece in her upcoming show built on the theme of old icons and their enduring relevance.

She worked on the pieces non-stop since her post-funeral pub-crawl. She hadn't left the house once and left her room only for loo breaks or snacks. She stopped answering her phone and email. She never really watched telly anyway and eschewed radio, opting for her record collection instead. Elise cut herself off from the world determined to spend a few weeks in blissful ignorance of political, environmental and social affairs to solely concentrate on her work. Holed up in her room, she needn't answer to anyone. Nor did she have to worry or care about anything. She simply worked and slept, thinking only of her upcoming gallery show.

Or at least she tried to. She often found herself in the middle of glazing the news clipping dress and would be overcome by a burst of sheer rage resulting in her grabbing the first dense object that would fit into her hand to hurl across the room, exhaling as it made a pleasing thud or crash. Elise couldn't quite place what would set her off. She would be painting, filing Joan's features, humming with the music when a feeling of gross injustice or frustration would hit. It would be anything from labs she had broken into with the anti-vivisectionists, the nerve of Norbert to refuse her request to Laura's wake, frustration at Laura's sudden departure or her insecurities. Although the anger would surface quite suddenly, it could take all day for the fury to dissipate. Sometimes the fits of anger frightened Elise, or she'd feel slightly embarrassed when a flatmate would feebly knock at her door asking if everything was okay. Other times, she collapsed in a corner and cried.

The mere thought of going outside exhausted her. She felt safer in her fortress, cocooned with her thoughts. Her gallery show wasn't for a few weeks still, so Elise had all the time in the world. Everything else lost its significance after the funeral. Perspectives unravelled and Elise found herself repeating the mantra, 'Does it really matter?' Aside from abrupt outbursts, she managed to remain detached and indifferent to the world around her. She created a vacuum in an effort to avoid any social distractions and finish her gallery pieces. She tried to harden her emotional skin to an impenetrable callous but Laura's death kept seeping in.

Ophelia felt a confident and professional pride as she walked in wearing her best suit. The suit was normally used for job interviews or important external meetings. Though today, she had neither. After being virtually unreachable for three weeks, Kat emailed her and asked if she was free for lunch. She had a big surprise and insisted Ophelia wear her best suit. Ophelia was hoping she found her the perfect job or even the perfect man, but would have gladly settled for a swish cream tea at some posh hotel. Despite giving the impression of a high-earning businesswoman, Ophelia was in fact completely skint.

She met Kat at her office and immediately began to interrogate her. "Okay, what are we doing for lunch? I'm warning you right now that I'm totally broke and can't possibly pull a runner in these shoes."

Kat smiled mischievously. "I know. I'm broke myself. That's why I thought we could use some cheering up."

"What are you getting at?"

Kat lead them towards Bond Street. "I did this in Boston or the local malls when I was broke or bored and it always made me feel better. Basically, we go to a department store in our best clothes, browse around counters, ask questions and get free samples. Most companies give samples as a marketing tool to lure potential customers. Some are shit like a pamphlet or colour chart but some are really nice like a small vial of perfume or tiny tubes of lip colour or a pot of cream. One time, I got a sachet of mud masque from one counter, a miniature jar of scrub from another and a lovely sample of face cream for free. Anyhow, it's nice to try. Sometimes you walk out with enough for a night of pampering. Other times you get sod all. I figured it might cheer us up some to get dolled up and make like we're important."

"I feel like I'm playing dress up with you now."

"Or con artists?"

"Or still teenagers?"

"Nonsense. It was my Nan who showed me how when I was about 10. She worked at a makeup counter in Filenes and always brought me samples when she visited. And it's good for business, I guess. A few times I've found a lip colour or lotion that works and go back to buy it come payday. The secret is to look like you have money. People are so shallow and judgemental that if you look like you've got money, they kiss your arse, give you stuff and bend over backwards for you, and not just at the cosmetic counters. But if you look poor, they shit on you. It sucks, but that's human nature."

"An exercise in self confidence, basically." Ophelia mused as they passed shop windows.

"Yes! But it becomes a self-fulfilling prophecy since you become more confident when you pretend you are. It's a bit fucked up but it works."

"Kat North, life coach."

"Piss off!"

With just over a month before December even started most of the shops were kitted out for the winter holidays. The windows were filled with powdery imitation snow, colourful metallic baubles, trees, dressy mannequins modelling the season must-haves for the inevitable office Christmas do, and boxes wrapped in decorative papers boasting intricate bows. A few of the larger department stores would dedicate a single window to Halloween in a vain attempt to get Britain interested in what has been a mainly American holiday.

The streets pulsed with hordes of tourists and shoppers busily streaming in and out of stores like ants at a picnic. Ophelia felt she had rank over them since she worked in London full-time. And yet the mob continued on regardless encroaching on London-ers' turf, creating long bus queues, elbowing as they bustled past and walking slowly or stopping to study maps. The only other time the West End became this unbearable was summer. That was even worse because the sun would be blazing and tourists would infest bars, shops, tubes and pubs. Just walking to the tube station was similar to negotiating a mosh pit.

"Just look like you have money. Pretend you turned out exactly how you hoped you would when you were eleven or twelve." Kat coached as they reached the entrance.

"Ummm, a nurse with eight kids, a pony and an ice cream stand?" Ophelia laughed. Kat flashed a serious look. "Okay, okay!"

Ophelia only ever ventured into Selfridges during the post-holiday sales and even then she went at the slowest possible time, to avoid crowds. The place was a buzz of activity, especially the cosmetic counters. Perfumes competed for recognition in the stuffy air and heavily made-up women tried to engage passersby with a free makeo-ver. Kat pushed her shoulders back and relaxed her face into a smile that instantly created the impression of confidence. Ophelia was surprised at the transformation made with such subtle changes and tried her best to follow suit.

"So how are you these days, stranger?" Kat asked as she eyed her favourite counters.

"Alright, I guess. Been blue since the funeral. Plus work's been a bit busy. How about you?"

"We got a new manager named Norman. He started last week. Real quiet which I find unsettling. And he's got a Caesar haircut thing going on. That's a little unsettling, too. He hasn't said much either way, but hasn't bothered me so I have no complaints."

Kat opened a sample and dabbed some lotion on her hand. "Ian's still having trouble finding work. I suspect he's not looking to hard though. I really try to be supportive and he does help around the house, but I find it so frustrating some days. I can't understand why he has such a hard time finding work. It would be nice if he could get something even part time, but he's so focused on this theatre thing. I'm tempted to go with him to these interviews and pitches to browbeat the people into giving him work. He's almost always still in bed when I leave for work in the mornings and when I get home there are dishes in the sink, the beds not made and he then moans he's tired."

They managed to blag enough for an evening of home spa treatments. Ophelia's spirit felt a bit lighter as they headed to a nearby cafe. Kat poured ketchup over the glob of mayonnaise and stirred it with some chips. "I know this is gonna sound random but I can't help but think that if I died tomorrow my obituary would look pathetic."

"Unless you caused some horrid disaster like a jumbo jet crashed into you or you drove a jumbo that crashed into the Gherkin."

"I'm being serious. I was looking through the obituaries in Saturday's Guardian and there was a page full of accomplishments summing up this guy's life. If I died tomorrow mine would probably just included my name, date of birth, cause of death and date. Three frigging lines to sum up twenty seven years! That's depressing."

"Ah, I see what you mean. Did they write one up for Laura?"

"I didn't ask."

"No of course. I guess my obituary would be a few lines max with perhaps a few false lines about how nice or generous or happy I seemed."

"No one's going to say you were a total bitch, are they? It's not nice to speak ill of the dead."

"I can't imagine anyone wrote that Hitler was a nice guy who loved rescuing puppies or that Stalin was a quiet but happy chap."

"They didn't need to; those guys have both left a massive albeit horrid mark on history. Screw obituaries, there are books and documentaries on them all the time."

"Kat, you aren't suggesting we try and overthrow the government and then start killing large groups of people, are you?"

"What? I said nothing remotely like that! What about Mother Theresa? She was a nice woman who had a lovely few pages written about her."

"I'm hardly a candidate for a nunnery. The poor things would have a heart attack if I told them how many guys I've slept with. Besides I don't think she was that nice; didn't a bunch of her orphanages get busted for squalor?"

"Even still, I just can't help but worry that if I went tomorrow I've hardly left my mark. I'm in a job to pay bills, have no hobbies or interests outside sitting on the sofa watching Ian beat a high score or watching some mind numbing reality show on people even more dull and vapid than me."

"You aren't dull at all. You just need to find something you're passionate about. It'll come to you."

"So what about you? Would you be happy with your obituary if you popped your clogs tomorrow?"

"Hell no! Especially since I could totally see Clara Bitchy adding some smarmy backhanded compliment about me. I think my hobby will be thinking of childish pranks that will slowly drive her into the Priory and away from me."

"Harsh."

"But fair."

—

Kat leisurely walked back to work, enjoying the dry break. The sky was still grey but the rain had finally stopped. Kat playfully dodged the mucky puddles and digressed to buy a small bag of caramelised nuts from a street vendor. They never tasted nearly as good as they smelled, but it was worth the pound she paid to hold the warm steaming bag to her nose and inhale in between bites. With a bag full of free spoils and the heavenly smell, Kat concluded today had been a good day so far.

As she walked into the office, Norman quietly poked his head to the side of his monitor and softly uttered, "Kat, can I see you at three?"

Kat nodded as she hung her coat, "Sure, Norman. Three should be fine."

Norman's eyes bulged slightly as if acknowledging her response and his head silently floated back behind his PC screen. Of all of Norman's odd gestures and quirks, his reserved disposition is what unsettled Kat the most. He seemed to silently loom over the office like a miasma with his magpie eyes busily looking about and hardly making a sound. Ian joked to Kat that Norman was probably a ninja, brought in by the witness protection after torching the wrong castle or grassing a fellow ninja.

Kat casually entered the meeting room, noting Norman was slightly more twitchy than usual and assumed his wool suit was probably unlined. His eyes darted nervously from Kat to the empty chair to his blank notebook as he busied his hand tapping his pen. He seemed even more birdlike with his twitching and Kat desperately wished she could have opened the window and see him fly out. As she settled into her chair, Kat felt a tension build within the room. "Is everything okay?" She enquired hesitantly.

"I'm afraid it's not actually," Norman frowned briefly and slightly shook his head. "Katherine I want to talk to you about your attitude." As he spoke his voice seemed to gain momentum getting more aggressive with each syllable. "You do realise you were 30 minutes late returning from lunch today?"

Kat was taken aback by this new side of Norman. "I can make up the time if it really bothers you?"

"That's not the point. By being late you have shown a total disregard for my authority."

"I'm sorry Norman, I never thought of it like that."

"You know, I don't believe you really are sorry. I don't think you even care, Katherine. Is this job a joke to you? It feels like you're having a laugh sometimes."

Now Kat's eyes bulged and her mouth fell open in horror. She was not sure how to respond to any of this, nor was she expecting it. Norman was now tightly gripping the pen and his jaw appeared taught, pulling his lips sternly together.

"Well? Don't just sit there, what have you got to say for yourself?" he demanded.

Kat's affected confidence from her trip to Selfridges quickly leaked from her as she felt herself shrink. She blinked in astonishment and shook her head "I'm, I'm afraid I am not quite following you, Norman." She stuttered.

As Norman launched into a further tirade, Kat fought to hold herself together and attempted to rationalise this sudden outburst. She found herself for the first time ever during her employment at any job feeling like a child being scolded at nursery. Kat managed to distance herself from the words being thrown at her and maintained a solemn expression throughout, trying to nod in all the appropriate places. Focusing on this seemed to keep the tears at bay though she wasn't sure how long she could continue before breaking.

"Listen, I am not going to allow you to make a mockery of me or this company. From now on, you pay attention to your timekeeping and your attitude. Do you under-stand?"

Kat nodded meekly. "Is that all, Norman?"

He curtly nodded and gestured towards the door. Kat scrambled to her feet dumfounded. She felt as if she had just been slapped across the face and wasn't sure how to react. She walked briskly out the door and headed straight for the loos.

Confronted by her own surprised expression in the mirror, Kat blinked hard trying to figure out what just transpired. Doubt set in gradually as she scanned her tired face. First came a few waves of uncertainty about her professional abilities and her perceived position in the office pyramid. A flood of ambiguity about herself as a woman quickly followed this. Kat inhaled slowly, planning how to handle the rest of the afternoon. She certainly couldn't speak to anyone right now, nor did she feel comfortable returning to her desk. She didn't want to be in the same room as Norman. She noticed her hands trembling with anxiety and resolved to leave for the day.

Kat strode back into the office trying her best to appear confident and unruffled. She grabbed her coat and bag and looked around for Norman. Kat exhaled with relief as she saw his desk empty and went over to Ouife. "Hey, where's Norman?"

Ouife looked up from her logbook. "He's gone downstairs to some board meeting. Why?"

"I'm starting to get a migraine so I think I'm gonna head home. Can you tell him for me?"

"Of course. Hope you feel better."

—

By the time she reached Ophelia's office, Kat was a mess. The lift doors opened to reveal a very wet and dishevelled Kat. "Are you all right?"

Kat shook her head silently.

"Okay, hang on. I just have to grab my coat."

She bounded up the stairs and locked her PC. "John, I have to run, there's an emergency downstairs. I'll try and return later tonight if I can."

John looked up and nodded while Clara rolled her eyes and clucked her tongue. The rain pelted down in a cold and steady barrage. She fumbled with her umbrella as Kat drew anxiously on a fag.

Ophelia took her to the local around the corner and hoped there were no redundancies brooding over pints. At the start of the fourth quarter, cuts made their way through the building to ensure the year ended as profitably as possible. People already started to get emails returned or a busy signal when trying to reach colleagues on the first floor. They did it by floor for some reason and being on the fourth floor, the cuts would start for Ophelia's team in about three or four weeks. Sometimes when the economy was doing well the cull would start in October and be over in the first week of November. The year hadn't been good thanks to some scandal uncovered by the Daily Mail involving the numbers used in a study for baby formula and it already seemed like some harsh news would be given to some poor sods in December. The pub near the office was always full of recent redundancies or friends of theirs from the end of October up to the week before Christmas.

They grabbed a free booth and Ophelia scanned the room briefly, spotting a few familiar yet forlorn or furious faces. She waved at her former colleagues and got two pints. Kat gave her account of the meeting with Norman and Ophelia stared in horror.

"What are you going to do?"

"I'm not sure if I should complain to HR or confront him or just pretend nothing happened. Right now I feel like I want to hide under the duvet."

"I suppose there's no reason you can't. Why not pull a sickie and give yourself a day to think?"

Kat nodded thoughtfully before sipping her pint. "I guess, but then what? I mean, right now I feel completely incompetent. I have never doubted myself doing this job and in 30 minutes, this dick manages to completely undermine my fucking confidence. I felt like I was 10 years old."

"Don't let him win, Kat. You can do your job well. This guy obviously has issues. Why not file a complaint with HR?"

"I dunno, I suppose, though I'd rather push him down a flight of stairs. Or maybe piss in his tea."

"Is he always like that? Or did he seem to be having a bad day?"

"Ophelia, this totally came out of the fucking blue. Yes, I was late, fair enough. However, I can't think of any reason to speak to anyone you work with like that. The guy is a fucking creep and I'm now stuck working with him."

"You could always walk out like Elise does." Ophelia winked, hoping to coax a small smile out of her.

"Have you heard from Elise?"

"The last I heard or saw of her was at Laura's funeral. How about you?"

"Same. I've not really felt too social after the whole thing. I haven't even started my shopping for Christmas. Laura's death knocked me for six."

"Yeah, me too."

Kat stared thoughtfully into space. "I'm so scared of dying. Especially since I have no idea what happens afterwards."

"I think I'm more worried about regrets."

"Yeah, I've thought about going for my UK driver's license. I've been putting it off for ages because I've been busy, or didn't want to have to go through the whole learning to drive thing again. Then I thought, maybe I was just afraid to fail. And after Laura and the obituary talk, I thought I should just suck it up and go for it."

"Did you want me to insist that they add that in your obituary?"

"What are you like? Let me get the next round."

"I'll add that you were the generous type as well."

"Shut it!"

A couple hours later, Ophelia managed to haul a less anxious and completely trolleyed Kat onto her train home. She was about to head home and then stopped herself. Mark was working around the corner so she figured she'd pop over. Ophelia was sure he could use the company and really needed to get out of the house. She had been in a funk since Laura's death, coming right home after work, eating frozen dinners and finishing off bottles of plonk whilst gazing at the telly until nodding off.

Mark was in his office and after some gentle cajoling over the phone he agreed to meet Ophelia for a curry. A security guard sent texts with no pretense of looking busy at the front desk. The steel grey marble floors bore the ghosts of hundreds of footprints that passed through in a day. The lift doors opened to a reveal a haggard and broken Mark. Ophelia noticed his trousers looked rumpled and worn, his shirt in need of ironing and face unshaven. It hardly surprised her but it did tug a bit at the heartstring to see him so forlorn. She made a conscious effort and suddenly smiled hoping that happiness was contagious. She gave him a big hug. His body yielded almost reluctantly and he felt thinner, almost weaker than only a few weeks ago.

She took him by the hand and led him down Wardour Street. "So, how's work going?" She opened an umbrella and clasped his shoulder to keep him sheltered. Mark grunted and shrugged as the rain softly pelted against the fabric of the brolly. Ophelia braced herself for an evening full of awkward silences. They quietly listened to the rhythm of the rain falling all around, interrupted by the occasional black cab thundering past or the chatter of other couples and groups heading to the bars or coming out of the theatres.

They ordered beers and naan bread to start. Ophelia felt vaguely anxious and worried that maybe this was more encumbering than comforting for Mark. She tried to consider the silence between them as peaceful or reflective. She wanted desperately to say the perfect thing but knew there simply wasn't anything she could say or do that would help or fix anything. She watched people walk past the window in couples and crowds. The streetlamps cast warm hues over the striped scarves and woolly hats.

She thought about how hard it must be for Mark and worried she made it worse dragging him out to dinner. Although now they were there she was at a loss as to how she could politely extricate herself from what was fast becoming one of the worst meals out she could recall. Perhaps his misery needed company. She couldn't help but think that if there was ever a time that someone would need their friends, it would be then. She thought of all the times Laura came around after Ophelia had a broken heart or suffered a disappointment and knew she should stick it out for the evening.

Mark made no attempt at conversation as he sat across Ophelia. He stared at his drink and fiddled with a matchbook. She wondered how the neighbouring diners interpreted this, certain they looked like a couple at the bitter end of a drawn out relationship trying in vain to work it out. Or maybe they appeared to be a seriously mismatched blind date. She grinned wanly at the thought and finished her beer. She sighed and finally attempted to engage with her gloomy date. "So, how are you doing these days?"

Mark looked up, startled. "How do you fucking think I'm doing?" he growled sharply.

She drew back, wounded by his tone. She never saw him like this. No one in the restaurant would have guessed that Mark could be very funny, charming and supportive. He was always the first to have a cracking anecdote at a party and was an excellent teammate for pub quizzes. He was quick witted with a knack for storing figures and trivial information. Ophelia tried to remind herself of this as Mark slowly turned into a moody stranger over the meal. She felt guilty for being cross with Mark since he was obviously still grieving Laura's death, yet he really seemed intent on isolating

94

himself. She couldn't help but feel annoyed he agreed to dinner if he wanted to be alone.

When he and Laura were first married they had everyone round their flat on the last Saturday of each month. The nights were filled with cheap lager, chips or curry and heated discussions about music, politics, religion, or their respective futures. In the restaurant as the minutes passed into hours those topics seemed frivolous or perhaps they were possibly too taboo.

Fortunately, the wait-staff were swift with their mains. If it had been anyone else, she probably would have simply made a polite exit. She worried if she left he might feel abandoned. She wanted to scream at him or shake him or hold him. She wanted a nice night out like those Saturdays years ago but she knew those days were over.

After she finished her curry and fourth beer, Ophelia reached over and grabbed his hand. His hand stiffened briefly, and then reluctantly acquiesced. His eyes didn't flinch from his bowl as he busily ate not even noticing his hand. It was if he had compartmentalised every aspect of himself to cope. His heart sealed off in a steel locker, his mind in a fog, his feelings behind a brick wall and his hand in hers. They sat in silence while he finished eating with his free hand until the cheque came. Ophelia walked him to the bus stop still holding his hand. As the bus came into view she hugged him tight and whispered "I'm always here if you need a friend."

Ophelia waved as Mark's bus headed up Charing Cross Road and hoped Laura knew she tried her best.

Kat slept in on Friday and had Ian call in for her with a migraine, which in a way was true from all she drank with Ophelia the night before. Her sadness and insecurity morphed into anger overnight and she felt justified in taking a day off. She was tempted to go into work and give Norman a piece of her mind, but Ian managed to convince her that a day off was best to get her thoughts organised. She read through the paper in bed with a big mug of coffee and browsed the jobs in the appointments section with half-hearted intentions of applying.

She decided to pop over to Elise's since she usually gave herself at least a month off after she left a job. She stopped at the newsagents on the way to the tube to grab a newspaper, fags and some bubble gum. She felt empowered as she got on the train not caring a bit about bunking off. The apathy was thoroughly liberating when she defiantly missed her stop for work and continued to Elise's house. If anyone appreciated a rebellious sickie it would be Elise.

James answered the door looking surprised, "Did you actually get an invite from Miss 'I Want to Be Alone'?"

Kat looked at James quizzically. "No, I took the day off and figured I'd check in since I haven't heard from her. Is she in?"

"Is she in? Honey, she hasn't left the house for weeks."

"Seriously? Is she okay?"

"I don't know if she was ever okay to begin with."

"Do you think she'd want company?" Kat asked hopefully.

James shrugged and stepped aside. "It could be interesting to find out and so far would be the most exciting thing to happen today."

Kat could hear music emanating through the door as she reached the upstairs hall. James shook his head and rolled his eyes. "Oh god, not the Stone Roses! I can handle Morrissey and the Smiths, but come on girl! It's like the 90's never ended! If you see her waving a glowstick I want you to take it from her and give her a good hard knock to the head with it."

When he opened the door Kat was met by a gust of music. She scanned the candlelit room noting it was a complete tip. In the centre of it was a heap of blankets and a form that must have been Elise.

"Hey, sleeping beauty, you have a visitor." James gently shook the bedraggled pile of quilts and duvets. "Oh sod it. I'll let you rouse her, Kat. Can I get you a drink? Tea? Coffee? Water?"

Kat shook her head, horrified at the state of Elise's room. Elise was never known for her fastidiousness, but this really took the biscuit. The room resembled a razed ghetto. Sodden tissues were scattered about like carnation flowers, long since dead. Crumbly ashen snakes of burned incense mixed with coagulated puddles of candle wax formed abstract sculptures around the book case and window sills. Furious slashes of paint shone like gashes on the walls; a frantic epitaph of the broken paintbrushes strewn about. Crushed cans and broken bottles reflected the soft candlelight and the occasional beams of sunlight sneaking through the closed blinds. A dense and earthy smell of patchouli hung in the air like thick velvet.

Feeling anxious and claustrophobic, Kat pulled the blinds and cracked the window. The mountain of blankets remained nearly still with the light stir of breathing. "At least she's not dead," sighed Kat.

She managed to get a few bin liners as well as a dustpan and brush from James and set about tidying Elise's room. The debris on the floor didn't take too long to sweep up into the appropriate bags and the brushes were all placed on the desk in anticipation of future repair. The wax was mostly scraped off and the ashes swept away. Kat found cleaning relaxing and meditative. As some semblance of order began to take form, the clouds broke more and a cool breeze made its way through the room. Kat piled what looked like dirty clothes into a corner and put Elise's CDs near her stereo. The music was thumping loudly through the speakers. Kat adjusted the volume.

Elise's hands fumbled out of the duvets. "What the fuck? Piss off!"

"I beg your pardon. I just cleaned your room before you completely disappeared in this mess."

"Kat?" Elise poked her face out looking physically and emotionally drained. "What the hell are you doing here?"

Kat smiled mischievously, "I took a sickie because my new manager is a tosser."

Elise slowly inched out of the blankets. "Christ, what time is it?"

"Nearly two. What say we go get a nice fry up?"

"I dunno if I feel like going out today…"

"Why the hell not? The sky has some big blue patches on it today and you look like you could use some fresh air."

"How long have you been here?"

"Only a couple of hours. Is this CD on a loop or something?"

Elise looked over defensively as she groped around the floor. "So? It's a great fucking album. Hey, where are my fucking trousers?"

"You mean the crusty ones? I put them in the corner to be washed. You so need to do some laundry. What have you been up to?"

Elise wiped the sleep from her bloodshot eyes and scratched her head. "I dunno, getting my pieces ready for the gallery show. Why?"

Kat got up from the floor and grabbed a pair of jeans from the bureau and threw them at Elise, who had now managed to completely sit up. Kat walked over to the window and lit a fag.

"Hey what do you think you're doing? Put that shit out!"

"What? I'm smoking out the window. I just cleaned your whole room and this is my thanks? You're so grumpy when you first wake up."

Elise groaned. "Just finish that one and light some incense, it stinks." Kicking off the last layer of sheets, she clumsily wiggled into her jeans. "Why don't I just grab some snacks from downstairs?"

"No. For once the weather isn't completely shit and I have the whole day off. I don't want to waste it vegging out at your house."

"Yeah, well I don't feel like going out."

"Elise, if I didn't know any better, I'd say you were depressed. And going out's the best thing for it."

Elise rolled her eyes as she surveyed the room.

"And besides, it's the least you could do after I tidied your room."

"I didn't ask you to do it, you're just completely neurotic."

"And you're depressed. Come on, we'll get smoothies and fry up. No more arguments. I'm prepared to carry you. I'll even buy you a new CD. Get your trainers, we're going."

Elise shook her head. "You are such a bitch." She smiled and hugged Kat.

As Kat and Elise made their way downstairs Kat tried not to snigger as a blue rendition of Anything Goes was heard in the living room. As they neared the racket, Kat could no longer control herself at the site of Jo dressed as Nancy Reagan and another drag queen dressed as Margaret Thatcher bowed to an applauding and giddy James.

Elise looked on soberly as Kat nudged her and whispered. "Come on, that is pretty funny."

"Hey sugar, how are you?" Jo cooed as he scurried over with his lone false breast bobbing furiously. "I was starting to worry about you." He sang as he swept Elise into his arms, cradling her exaggeratedly.

"Thanks for caring. Please let go, your tit is crushing my nose." She murmured.

"Woops! Sorry about that, love! Having just the one is really throwing me off today."

"It's good to see you out and about." James called over between nibbles of a pasty.

"We were just gonna grab breakfast. Does anyone want anything?" Kat asked wiping the corners of her eyes.

"Besides my other fun bag, I can't think of anything." Jo sighed with his best American accent. "And if anyone offers you girls drugs, I want you to just say no."

"Nancy! You worthless trollop! Stop faffing about and get your arse over here," trilled Thatcher.

"Piss off, you tarty cow." Jo shouted over his shoulder as he adjusted his wig. "Hey, why don't you two come the premiere tonight? We need all the people we can get to fill seats and it'll be fab, I promise!"

"I can tell! Elise, we should go! I can ring Ian. I'm sure he'd love to come."

Elise looked at Kat and then at Jo. "I really don't think I'll be up for it. I'm sorry."

"Oh rubbish! You must! It's opening night. And this Nancy ain't taking no for an answer. Kat, make sure she goes. I'll put you three on the list at the door."

As the girls made their way up the street Elise shielded her eyes as they adjusted to the light outside. "I dunno about tonight. I just don't think I'm in the mood to laugh."

"Right. Well, let's see how you're fixed after a nice bit of brekkie. Reckon it's safe for you to be out in the sun, dearie?"

"Not funny. Now let's just go before I change me mind."

Being well after lunchtime the café was virtually empty. Disco music crackled like hot grease out of two tinny little speakers of a radio with a rusty coat hanger antenna. The nicotine-stained walls were lined with framed autographed photos of both famous and obscure celebrities who had eaten there or popped in to ask for directions. Kat grabbed a window seat hoping the intermittent sun lifted Elise's spirits.

"So how are you really? And don't you dare give me some lame one word answer or tell me you're fine because the state of your room says otherwise."

Elise poured a little water into her black coffee and sipped it. "I've been down, I guess. I feel like all the expectations I had of life and the world were way off. I'm angry that all the faith I had in humanity was a waste. I miss Laura. I'm freaked by the thought of my own mortality and that my whole existence could be snuffed out like that. It just puts things into perspective and right now everything seems utterly pointless and false and stupid. I'm not sure what I'm trying to accomplish anymore."

Kat sipped her smoothie unsure of what to say.

"Everything's lost its meaning recently. They've all become icons or logos to put on shirts and bags to sell stuff for these companies. It's the companies that are immortal.

102

We're just these busy worker bees at the hives buzzing about and when one dies the rest continue business as usual. We now live in a cold, greedy society that only cares about fame, money and appearances. Morals? None of that shit matters anymore. Who gives a toss if it doesn't turn a profit? It's all a big race to beat the clock and to grab as much stuff as you can and look good while you do it and to hell with everyone else. There's no such thing as humanity or compassion anymore; they're just buzzwords used to sell products or ideas to people who want to feel superior to their bloody neighbours. Love is a cliché and sex is just another way to sell more ideas and products to people who feel inferior or insecure. Heroes? They are confused with celebrities. Can you imagine? When was the last time anyone off any of those ridiculous Big Brother programmes did anything heroic? I dare you to ask a selection of people on the tube or in a pub who their hero is and I bet you it's some fucking glamour model or footballer. Nobody cares anymore. Nothing any of us does really matters when you think about it. I have wasted so many years being this disillusioned do-gooder and for what? Human lives - our lives - are these tiny blips on life's radar. My life doesn't matter so I stopped getting out of bed. Laura's life didn't matter"

"Of course it did. How can you say that?"

"Maybe to us, but the rest of the world's still going. All the caring, worrying, protesting, believing? It's all childish bollocks."

"Don't be silly. Think of all the people who've made a difference. They leave a legacy."

"A legacy buried in the back of the Guardian obituary pages."

The waitress arrived with two greasy plates of eggs, toast, chips and beans. Elise glanced at her plate, forced a brief smile and nod to the waitress and returned her gaze to the plate.

"Maybe you just need a change of scenery or some anti-depressants."

"The world's an ugly place and no medication or long weekend in Paris is going to change it. We're all going to die and I am fucking tired of kidding myself."

"Elise, did your mum set you on a date with Nietzsche?" Kat joked in between bites hoping to distract Elise's dark mood.

Elise merely rolled her eyes and resigned herself to her food momentarily. Kat reached over the table for the ketchup and paused, staring transfixed as something outside caught her eye. She pointed outside "Hey, check it out." Across the street stood a teenaged yob smoking a fag on the corner with a roguish glint in his eye. Across from him a decrepit woman hobbled slowly into the street with a cane. As she made her way through the littered street the yob spotted her and watched. As she neared the curb he walked over and helped her up. She nodded her head and smiled, thanking him. He nodded back and returned to his corner as she slowly shuffled up the pavement.

Kat smiled triumphantly to Elise. "If that isn't humanity, I don't know what is. You just have to look for it; it's still there. Maybe you're still grieving. It's not just about crying, you know. I've read that grieving is a complicated process covering a host of emotions like anger, denial, and hopelessness. And sometimes death can leave you depressed. Come on, for once you're normal. Seriously have you thought about seeing a therapist or talking to your GP for medication?"

"Ha! That's so American, Kat!" She spread marmite on her toast and dipped it into the runny egg yolk. Elise looked older. Her face seemed drawn and the fluorescent lights of the café revealed dark circles and lines beneath her fraught and bloodshot eyes. Normally animated and buzzing with energy, she was lethargic and hollow; a sepia-toned photograph instead of a full-colour cartoon.

"I'm serious. A lot of what you're saying and doing sounds like grief or depression or both. Not to be cliché, but I'm here for you. Any time at all you can call me or show up at my place to cry or yell or to just sit and say nothing at all."

"Thanks," she muttered as a few toast crumbs fell from her lips.

"We were all worried. No one's heard anything from you since the funeral. As much as we'll all miss Laura there are a lot of different ways to look at death. In tarot cards, death can mean change; like it's a way for us all to reflect and grow I guess. And the Buddhists believe death is actually rebirth since you'll be reincarnated or reach heaven or Zen. So, how you live now affects your next life; like if you were a right selfish bastard you could return as a shit-eating housefly. Or the Christians have heaven and hell. I don't want to sound like some twee, new age tree hugger but when your grief clears, try to grow from it. Wasn't it Nietzsche who said that what doesn't kill us only makes us stronger? Let people smear all the shit they want in your garden of life; it'll only serve as fertiliser for your flowers."

Elise stared hard at Kat, snorted, bent over and coughed. Kat looked on in alarm as Elise's back rose and fell silently. She reached over tentatively and asked, "Are you all right?"

As Elise sat up Kat was a little confused to find her laughing hard and quietly. "That has to be the worst bloody analogy I have ever heard in my entire life." Kat faltered for a moment not sure whether to be offended but upon seeing Elise laughing she simply smiled back and finished her eggs.

Ophelia woke early with a renewed sense of optimism. The sun finally broke through the heavy grey concrete clouds and this was the only day each month she didn't resent the hectic London rush to work. It was payday which confirmed that she managed to survive another month; never mind that most of her pay would be gobbled up by rent and direct debits by the following Tuesday. She confidently stepped out of the flat and deliberately smiled at anyone who met her gaze. Those quick to return the smile were probably on the same pay cycle. On that particular morning she had a tangible reminder in her bank account of why she bothered showing up for her mediocre job every day. She felt that anyone who said money can't buy happiness was either already wealthy or bitter and broke. It hardly mattered that she had uttered those sentiments a few days before.

Payday was also the only day she ever bothered to show up on time. She sauntered in with a steaming cup of gourmet coffee and a maple pecan pastry ready to work or at least look busy. She rang Kat's office to see if she had skived and then worked in tandem searching for a cheap holiday destination for Christmas before completing a report. Her relationship with her family was nonexistent and there was no partner to tag along with to their family so this Christmas looked dull and lonely. She never touched on the subject with friends to avoid anyone feeling obligated to invite her to theirs for Christmas dinner.

Over the past ten years she busied herself with an assortment of activities to keep the blues away. Ophelia also learned that London is eerily still and quiet on Christmas day. It had to be the only time London wasn't teeming with people. One year she spent the whole day pretending Armageddon arrived and she was one of the few survivors. She walked all along the South Bank eating stale jam doughnuts trying to spot a bloke she would consider shagging to sustain the human race. That was a dark moment for mankind.

After a fruitless holiday search, she decided to distract herself with a bit of holiday shopping and finish her report. She could always volunteer at Shelter if she didn't find anything to do. By the end of the day she decided to do something other than going home to mope. Ophelia grabbed a paper and sat in the pub to review her options over a pint of lager. As a resident of London, she hardly ever saw any of the tourist attractions. The infestation of tourists and day-trippers kept her away but there was another procrastination: She always figured she had time to see the sights but always found herself too busy or tired to bother. Ophelia and Kat only ever seemed to go when they had friends over from the US, which wasn't often especially after September Eleventh. Elise took her mum when she visited or she went with friends to cause mischief. As the hum of happy hour intensified, she noticed the Tate Modern was open late so she finished her pint and left. The admission was free and probably less crowded which suited her perfectly.

She hardly thought about the previous night with Mark. Walking around the gallery with an old CD on the Discman, she cocooned herself with reflections. The memories of him when he first started to come round for drinks with Laura when they were both young and full of hope echoed over the music as she scanned the paintings on the walls. She was too afraid to confront him and his grief and didn't want to embarrass him about the way he acted or felt but she couldn't help but feel hurt. The nagging hurt followed her like a restless shadow as she made her way around.

One installation stopped Ophelia in her tracks. It was a shed or Wendy House that an artist had blown up and painstakingly hung each broken board, empty can and miscellany in midair with what looked like fishing wire so that it appeared that time had actually stopped at the moment of explosion. A lot of the critics had mixed views on whether or not this was art, but she found herself transfixed by it. The thought of freezing a moment seemed wonderful. And to see the fantasy realised had left her touched. She wanted so often to be able to pause in the middle of a scream and save it for later use or to display it or wear it like a badge. She could look through a thesaurus all day and never find a word that so aptly described that feeling the way this installation captured it. She thought of Mark as the shed and how over time items were carelessly thrown in like anger, disappointment, fear, confusion and grief. He was alone for the past few weeks with feelings and thoughts simmering. Maybe last night he happened to explode.

If only it were possible to collect all those emotions and find an appropriate time to ignite it with gunpowder. Or better yet, lock it away in the freezer and maybe crush it down to make snowballs to throw at people or thaw it out for a chat with an old friend over Chablis. She circled the room several times, taking in every minute detail until her stomach told her to hit the café.

Ophelia looked up to pay for her soup and was struck by the nagging familiarity of the cashier. As she fumbled around her purse for money she tried to place her. She found the coins and admitted defeat to herself as she handed the money to the woman.

"Is your name Ophelia?"

"Yes," she replied, relieved that the recognition was mutual.

"Ophelia Graff."

"Yeah, I thought you looked familiar! I'm so sorry but I'm still trying to place you."

"You went to elementary school with my sister, Caroline. I was a grade behind you."

"Marie! Yes, how are you? What are you doing in London?"

"I'm studying art at St. Martin's. What about you? How weird that we bump into each other here."

Relieved at placing her, the information flooded back –a little too much information in fact. "Oh god! I was so horrible to your sister! Please tell her I'm so sorry!" Ophelia added hastily, unsure if Marie knew that she picked on her sister for years.

Marie waved Ophelia's concern off as she took her money. "She's over that! It was years ago."

"I'm so glad. All the same, please tell her I'm really sorry. I feel terrible about the way I treated her."

"You were just kids. I bet she'd love to hear from you."

"Um, okay. Let me give you my mobile number and email address. Hey, when do you get off? Can I buy you a drink?" She pushed a fiver over the counter towards a cap-puccino or a glass of wine.

"I can join you in fifteen minutes," she replied glancing at the clock and the queue. She shook her head and she slid the rumpled bill back to Ophelia. "Don't sweat it. I get all the coffee I can handle. See you in a bit."

As Ophelia sat and waited for Marie to join her she began to wonder what Caroline was like now. She worried the childhood teasing left her a self-conscious wreck or hopefully she became extremely successful in spite of it. Maybe she had a big pile of resentment with Ophelia's name on it, or maybe she could forgive and forget. Ophelia shuddered when she recalled how she would taunt her daily. Shame swept over her, twisting her gut and blushing her cheeks as she thought of how cruel the taunts were. No one likes to think of themselves as mean or evil, but she knew too well the malice children were capable of. It's ugly, but human and even worse to recall the offences as an adult since there is more perspective and no way to take any of it back. If Caroline decided to contact her, Ophelia owed her a huge apology and wasn't sure if that would even begin to cover it.

She started to recall all the people she wronged or hurt from childhood to the present. The list wasn't huge, but it wasn't small either. If she died tomorrow, that would be something she wanted reconciled. She wasn't about to apologise to every tosser that cut her up on the motorway or kiss and make up with all the commuters she elbowed to force her way onto a packed train.

She just wanted to make amends with people she was cruel to or deliberately hurt for whatever stupid reason. If Kat could learn to drive, Ophelia could certainly clear a few skeletons out of the cupboard.

-

Kat's hands trembled as she buttoned her blouse. She assessed herself critically in the mirror and sighed. The blouse flew on to the pile of rejected items on the bed.

"You nearly ready? I don't want to stress you but we need to leave in twenty minutes." Ian called from the other room.

Kat scanned her closet, searching for something to wear. It was stressful enough having dinner with the in-laws but with PMT it was nearly impossible finding something to throw on that wasn't uncomfortable or looked wrong. Had it been two weeks ago, she would have left with the first thing she tried on. On that night the pile grew until she settled on a plain black skirt and sweater. She pulled her hair back, combing it with shaking fingers. "Okay, be right down."

Kat didn't feel hungry at all and considered feigning a migraine to stay home, but knew Ian was looking forward to seeing his folks. She just couldn't understand why it mattered if she was there or not. If anything, it was probably nicer for all involved if she stayed home. One of Dorothy's friends must have been talking about her daughter-in-law and what a great relationship they had and Dorothy needed to return the boast.

They met at a stuffy French fusion style restaurant full of people looking deliberately aloof as they scanned for celebrities with sidelong glances. Ian squeezed Kat's hand when he spotted his parents and tugged her towards the table. Kat exhaled and followed Ian to their table.

"Hello, darling." Dorothy trilled to Ian. "Katherine, my darling daughter-in-law. Did you just come from a funeral?" She smiled as she helped Ian out of his coat.

"Excuse me?"

"You're wearing all black, dear. Don't any of your clothes have colour in them?"

Kat looked down as she seated herself. "Well, it flatters my figure I guess." She replied sheepishly. She nudged Ian's leg as she pulled her chair in. Ian's father, Rhys, smiled broadly and cleared his throat to break the awkward silence.

"Don't mind her, love. I think you look fine. A woman needs a bit extra for a man to grab onto!" He wiggled his brow and broke into a wheezing laugh. Ian gently patted Kat's clenched hand.

"So how's work, Dad?" Ian asked. Kat poured a glass of wine as Ian chatted to his parents. She was careful to smile and nod at what seemed the appropriate times while she mentally made lists of chores, groceries and what she originally hoped for in a marriage when she exchanged vows with Ian.

Ian seemed to resemble Rhys in appearance alone. His mannerisms were similar to Dorothy's which worried Kat when she pictured herself growing old with him. Kat privately thought Rhys resembled Teddy Roosevelt. He had big false teeth and a bushy moustache and he favoured bow ties with brightly coloured corduroy trousers. That evening he had purple trousers with a yellow shirt, grey vest and spotted bow tie. Kat always pictured skinny, feeble accountants or piano teachers in bow ties. It made Rhys all the more surreal. Rhys had a brusque, almost domineering manner and as usual ordered for everyone. He was old fashioned in his beliefs and thought it an abomination that women had maternity leave when they should be home. He worked as a barrister. A few years ago he won a high profile case concerning some members of parliament and an S & M club in Surrey. After that he found himself working on a lot of high profile cases for a lot more money.

As the conversation continued, Kat glanced over at Dorothy. Her bony fingers were bedecked in jewels and baubles of all colours and shapes. The swelling in her face had finally gone down from her facelift – an anniversary gift from Rhys along with her new ring. Kat noted two tiny scars near her ears where the incisions were made. Dorothy was obsessed with looking young or at least a vulgar approximation thereof. Her regular Botox injections made it all the more difficult to determine how to take Dorothy's remarks. Her hair was coloured an unusual shade of red, as if it were meant to be brown and then halfway through, she changed her mind and went for blood red. She kept it fairly short, spiking it. It rather suited her, Kat smiled, very much the dragon lady. As always, she was mutton dressed as lamb. The top was silver with beads and sequins touting some expensive designer in big letters. If she had been obese they could have attached her to a bungee cord and used her for a disco ball. Her trousers were black leather which though it was the style of the moment, it suited only rock stars or anorexic supermodels and Dorothy was neither.

Ian was their only son and they were extremely protective of him. Kat was used to them ringing or popping by at least a few times a week to "check in". She often wondered if they had hoped their son would marry into a wealthy family of status where Ian could get a job at the fantasy father-in-law's firm, company or whatever while their fantasy daughter-in-law would pop out an endless stream of babies and stay at home, ringing Dorothy helplessly, wanting to know how to be a perfect wife and mother like her. Kat knew they weren't terribly keen on Ian working in theatre and even less keen on Kat supporting them on her meagre wages.

Kat felt herself finally relax after her fourth glass of wine. Her grin began to feel natural instead of forced, her shoulders slid away from her ears and she felt almost prepared to stomach the main course Rhys had ordered for her as long as it didn't involve molluscs or stinky cheese. Ian stroked her back every so often.

"And how are things for you at work?" Rhys asked Kat.

"Uh, okay. Bit stressful lately, though no more than usual."

Rhys nodded. His cheeks reddened after a few glasses as well. Kat wanted to offer more information, but knew from experience that it would be a mistake. The more vague and neutral the response, the less likely she would receive any unwanted advice or criticism.

"Are you still getting those yeast infections, dear?" Kat knew it was only a matter of time before Dorothy got to more personal enquiries. Having been married for five years now, Kat didn't blink.

"Yeah, they're gone. I found eating live yogurt helped. Thanks."

"Well do be careful. I read in the Daily Mail that too much dairy could cause Crohn's disease."

This could go all day. Kat called it old wives' tennis. Basically Dorothy would enquire about an ailment, diet or other lifestyle area and upon responding, she would offer up a nugget written in either the Mail or the Evening Standard. If you were skilled, you could then counter her advice with either some proven facts or even make something up. This would usually stop Dorothy as she gathered her thoughts or until she thought of something else to ask after and advise on. With the fifth glass of wine Kat grew bold.

"Oh Dorothy, don't be silly! That's mainly about cows' milk, which we don't use anyway. I always buy goats' milk as it's easier to digest and better for allergies."

Dorothy nodded hesitantly. 'Check and mate!' thought Kat as she smiled triumphantly and returned to her drink.

The conversation lulled for a bit. With a new bottle of plonk opened, Kat grew chatty and merry.

"Has Ian told you about his meeting with the theatre company?" She asked his parents slowly trying not to slur her speech.

Dorothy rolled her eyes dramatically. "No one ever tells us anything," she sighed. "You know Ian, Arthur Murphy said he'd be happy to have you start in his firm as a legal assistant or secretary and perhaps work your way up. I don't know why you haven't called him back yet."

Kat immediately regretted that she mentioned it as Rhys and Dorothy launched into a lecture on Ian's life and their finances. Ian always managed to stay calm and nod through these speeches though they made Kat cringe. She hated how they always censured her husband for following his dreams. Kat didn't care if they weren't wealthy nor did she care what Ian did for work as long as he was happy. Not a visit went by without them bringing Ian's career up and Kat resented it. And there Kat had practically initiated it.

As Dorothy verbally badgered into her son, Kat noticed Rhys's cheeks blossomed into a warm rouge. She was relieved that she wasn't single-handedly drinking both bottles of plonk and curious to see what Rhys was like on the sauce. Rhys appeared to be listening to his wife, waiting to interject. It didn't look like Dorothy was going to pause anytime soon, so Rhys slowly turned to face Kat. His finger pointed at her as his hand swayed like a meaty, hairy flag.

"You know, I reckon this is your fault." He confided, holding his other hand to silence her as he continued.

"Yes, you. I think that your working full-time has emasculated my son. Perhaps he'd actually be working in a firm or better if you knew your place. And in case you didn't know your place, it's in the home, making tea and having children."

116

Kat's face reddened with rage. At that point Dorothy and Ian were rapt watching both her and Rhys. "I'll have you know, Rhys, that times are a lot different now that all the dinosaurs are extinct and if it weren't for my working full-time, I think your son would be miserable in some office resenting me, you and your wife. I think it's high time you and your wife started minding your own business and left us to ours."

Kat's hands were trembling uncontrollably as she pushed away from the table and made her way out of the restaurant. As the freezing rain hit, her tears streamed down her face taking her mascara with them. She made her way to the nearest Tube station. She found herself hoping someone would try mugging her so she could punch, kick and shout at them. It was unlikely to happen in Knightsbridge but the thought kept Kat walking in the direction of the station. She seethed the entire journey home.

Kat sat in the bath as water ran down her face and shoulders. The water was scalding, but bearable by the time it reached her. The steam was thick, making everything appear ethereal and dreamy. Kat would often sit in these showers until the hot water ran out. As the water started to cool, Kat climbed out and towelled off. Feeling weary and deflated, the anger had burned down to a few embers that would smoulder for the next few days. She fumbled around for her track bottoms and top. This ensemble was reserved for sick days or after a long difficult day at the office; Kat would throw it on and stretch out on the sofa.

Ian returned home about ninety minutes later. He gently opened the door, pausing for a moment to listen for breaking glass or crying or any indication of his wife's mood.

"Kat?" he called hesitantly. He could hear the shower running as he walked down the hall. He decided to fix some tea.

Kat started at seeing Ian on the sofa with two mugs of tea. She was half expecting him to follow her but was still surprised by the tea. "You okay, love?" he enquired, laying a video games magazine on the coffee table. Kat nodded as she sank down next to him. They sat in silence together for several moments. Ian felt for her hand and interlaced his fingers with hers. "I'm sure things could have gone worse," he offered hopefully.

"Ian, I am not going to your parents' house for Christmas," Kat stated simply.

"Okay then, fair enough." Ian squeezed her hand and released it to get his tea. "What do you want to do for Christmas?"

"I want to go home. To America."

Ian contemplated the request for a few moments. Kat still stared straight ahead breathing calmly. "We can go to America on one condition." Ian looked over to see if Kat would respond. Her eyes bore into the wall as she uttered a grunt.

"If you to stop smoking we'll go to America for Christmas. I think that's fair enough."

Kat faced her husband looking as he had just slapped her. "What the hell would you know about fair? I work my bloody ass off only to have some tosspot supervisor with no social skills tell me off like I'm some frigging toddler caught in the cookie jar while you stay home chasing rainbows."

Ian attempted to stutter a rebuttal but Kat glared at him, her eyes green lasers cutting into him and her hand went up firmly to indicate that she was far from finished.

"Then I agree to be vulture fodder for the evening and have your dad making sexist comments about how it's my fucking fault you don't have a proper job or that I have a fat ass. Do you think that's fair? When was the last time I asked you to make a sacrifice for me? When have I asked you to do anything for me? Does my mother tell you that you're ruining my life?"

"Your mother's dead, Kat. Stop being vicious." Ian's spine curled as his shoulders hunched in. He looked on the verge of tears so Kat abated, already regretting the harsh words.

"I'm sorry. I really shouldn't speak when I'm angry with you."

Ian cleared his throat and turned to face Kat. "Look, it means a lot to me that you came tonight. I'm really sorry about my dad. He was a bit drunk and I don't think he meant it."

"He seemed to mean it to me. Maybe the alcohol let him finally voice his opinions." Kat added quickly keeping responsibility fixed on Rhys.

"Okay, fine. He was drunk and normally wouldn't have said such a thing. I think he felt awful that you left. My mum was really worried, too."

"About what other people thought."

"Come on. Stop. You take things so personally."

"It's hard not to."

"She isn't like that. You know my mother just doesn't have a filter so she says everything she thinks."

"You certainly wouldn't excuse me if I did that."

"You would be doing it to be mean."

This argument happened at least every three months and Kat never won. It often ended with her leaving for a few fags and a pint at the local pub or Ian would drive over to his parents' house for a few hours. Kat grimaced ruefully trying not to get roped in and decided to change the subject.

"So when do I have to quit smoking?"

"Why not start right now?"

"After the evening I've had? You have a better chance of getting the fucking queen to scrub our toilet."

"Fair enough," he conceded. "We'll have a fresh start for tomorrow then."

"Fine. I'll book the tickets online tomorrow when I would normally have my first smoke of the day."

Kat rose abruptly and sauntered to the door.

"Where are you off to now?"

"I'm gonna smoke 'em while I got 'em." She muttered as she headed for the balcony.

Kat struck the match and inhaled deeply, tasting the first drag mixed with the sulphur. She sighed as the smoke dissipated into the brisk night.

It was like kissing an old lover who knew all of her secrets and had complete control over her. She couldn't keep herself away, yet she always felt guilty after being with him. Ian would complain and she knew it hurt him but she couldn't stop herself. There was a sense of calm, of solace, whenever she kissed the tip and inhaled, mulling over her thoughts and dreams or a smoky shoulder to cry on. Kat was having an affair with the Marlboro man. Usually in a relationship or marriage when both parties were seeing the Marlboro Man or Joe Camel, it was *a ménage à trois* with three safe, sane and consensual parties.

However, if one partner was visiting Marlboro country and the other wasn't it could create all sorts of problems. The smell was abominable and for whatever reason it was always even more pungent after coming in from a brisk day. Then there was the constant hacking and wheezing and coughing up what sounded like a lubricated puppy in the middle of the night, thus keeping the non-smoker awake. The health warnings that the smoker would ignore would send the non-smoker on edge worrying how they would fit an iron lung into the living room. And of course the expense! These and many more would cause small rows or rifts in a relationship and drive the smoker to meet their beloved in secret or become defensive when confronted by the non-smoker.

Kat leaned on the balcony bidding her lover a reluctant farewell. Her cigarettes had seen her through so many hard times. She'd been smoking a lot longer than she had known Ian. She felt as if she were betraying her lover. Kat counted her remaining smokes and her heart sank -she had three left.

–

121

The train lurched forward and eased itself out of the station. Elise watched the city slip away. It felt like she was slowly sinking. As she studied the buildings and the shapes they made on the horizon, her heart felt heavy in her chest. The world seemed to slow since Laura's death, sometimes to a full stop. Seeing London sliding by in the window reminded her how fast things moved before. She absently touched her head, feeling the soft velour of her shaved hair.

She stood in front of the mirror for a good ten minutes contemplating her hair that morning. It was 3 in the morning and she woke groggily but whatever she tried sleep eluded her. Elise smiled recalling how she often shaved her hair on the number 1 setting at uni, leaving a bit of fringe or random patches of hair. She would colour them with marking pen during lectures daydreaming about living in Paris, selling her work out of galleries and arguing about art's impact on modern society at a smoky café.

She sighed as she recalled how full of hope and promise the future seemed. When she left uni, Elise grew her hair out. As she stared back that morning, she couldn't remember why. She couldn't see why she ever felt disinclined to cut it. It was only hair; it grew back. Why did it matter at all? It's not like it mattered in the afterlife. Besides, the less you had to lose, the easier life became. Elise wanted to have nothing to lose again. She held her hair out as the clippers hummed. Her hand relaxed as the hair fell over her shoulders and onto the floor.

She saw off several friends in the past year and was at her breaking point. One lost to heroin, one from a cancerous tumour and then Laura. There didn't seem to be much point in getting close to anyone if you were only going to lose them. And it wasn't just death. People grew apart or got fed up and left, or people changed. It wasn't worth the misery, she reflected as she worked the clippers around her head.

As the first rays of sun struck the cool blue and pink skies Elise wished her heart had calluses. It seemed too soft and delicate for the abuse it suffered. It would melt or stick to people who would let her down or leave her. It broke so easily and never seemed to fully mend with each injury. She wanted it to be solid, dressed in layers of unfeeling, impenetrable flesh, impervious to the bumps and scratches of life in general. She left a shock of hair in the front long enough to push to the side behind an ear if in the way or stick out under a hat when she saw her mother. She swept the hair into a pile and stuck it in a carrier bag for a later project. She felt lighter. It was then she decided to take a walk.

She walked to Waterloo across the still and sleeping city. She felt like a girl alone in a toyshop. The streets were vacant with pigeons cooing occasionally. The quiet consoled her as she crossed Waterloo Bridge, looking down at the Thames. The water almost looked blue, reflecting the infinite indigo blanket of sky. The sodium lights shimmered on the rippling current. Normally Elise would stay to see the day dawn, whether it was the sun colouring the horizon or the lighter clouds replacing the dark night sky as the street lights shrank back into their daily shells. Instead, she pressed on towards Waterloo station.

She looked at the departures board and decided to see Paris for the day, maybe even two. She longed to be faraway and alone. She wanted to just walk around for hours and make up names or identities when she introduced herself to strangers. Her depression seemed to crowd her in London like an overbearing flatmate or contagious disease. She didn't want drugs or therapy, only to escape from it for a bit. In a new setting away from everything she knew and everyone worrying was exactly where Elise needed to be. It was liberating to simply dress, throw a few CDs in her bag leave a note and go.

She looked down at the foggy condensation left by her sighs and gently tapped it with her finger, leaving tiny moist spots of clarity within the mist. Elise pushed all thoughts aside as she watched the greens and blues stretch ahead. This was exactly why she hated being awake: there were relentless streams of thought buzzing about and she was tired of fretting or feeling the dull ache of her heart breaking over and over in her chest. She only hoped the train was going fast enough to outrun the grief, anger and her self.

Ophelia sat in an office she didn't recognise. It was dark with forest green wallpaper, cherry wood panelling and a dark mahogany desk. Dust coated the rows of books on the bookcase and a pair of blood-red velvet drapes obscured the only window in the room. She was sat in big cracked leather wingback chair and her feet couldn't touch the floor, adding to her vulnerability.

Across from her sat Laura. She was dressed in the outfit she'd been buried in. She briskly scribbled some notes on a clipboard, her face taut in concentration. A small desk lamp highlighted a pair of white bony hands with traces of dirt beneath her nails. This tiny lamp seemed to be the lone source of light in the room and cast long haunting shadows around the walls. The scratch of the pen on the paper was the only sound and filled Ophelia's head, getting louder with each decisive stroke.

"Renee Massaro, kindergarten." She called as her eyes scanned the notes.

"Laura? ... How?"

"Renee Massaro." She repeated.

"Huh?"

Laura patiently placed the pen on the desk and pulled a cigarette from the drawer. Her eyes were fixed on her notes. She raised her head and fixed her eyes ahead. She lit the fag and inhaled deeply.

"Do you or did you ever know a Renee Massaro?"

"Well, yes. In kindergarten, as you said. What does she have to do with this? I have so much to say to you! I, we, Mark, everyone misses you so much. It was so sudden, you going."

"You stole from her lunch bag. And in the fourth grade you smacked her across the face at playtime when-,"

"When she called me a stuck-up bitch. Yes, I remember. What does this have to-,"

"Weren't you supposed to be a friend of hers?"

"Kids do stuff like that. It's normal."

"You think it's normal to hurt people? How can you rationalise hurting someone?"

"I wasn't rationalising anything. I, I-"

"Neil Iaucci." she said, exhaling a stream of smoke and tapping the ash onto the floor.

"I was friendly to him when no one else spoke to him."

"You pitied him! And snubbed him repeatedly after you started hanging out with Joel Casey, the bassist in that band. You even laughed while they teased him."

Ophelia grew hot with shame and hung her head. "Yes, that, too."

"And how long did Joel Casey hang around?"

"He stopped hanging out with me after I had sex with him."

"Was it worth destroying Neil's self-esteem? He went home every night and cried while he thought of ways to kill himself. Was it worth it?"

"Laura!"

"I didn't think so. Those things rarely are."

Laura nodded and wrote something on the clipboard, the fag hanging out of the corner of her mouth. She shut her eye as the smoke floated towards the ceiling.

"Laura, why are you doing this?"

"Cordelia Graff."

The name hung in the smoky air.

"I haven't seen or spoken to my sister since I left. I think about her all the time, even considered calling or writing her, but afraid it would open a can of worms."

"When you were eleven and went to the town square with her that bully approached you two. She started to taunt you and Cordelia, pushing you and tugging your sister's ponytail. What did you do?"

"..."

"Ophelia! What. Did. You. Do?!"

"I ran home."

"You left Cordelia behind. Your younger sister who looked up to, trusted you, needed you and you left her with that older girl who was clearly looking for a fight."

"Cordelia was okay! I thought she'd follow me! I was too scared to think."

"She was scared, too, Ophelia!" Laura countered evenly. "She was scared and you abandoned her!"

"When dad came home drunk, we hid together in the house and pretended we were panthers blending in the night waiting for an angry gorilla to pass through the jungle of our bedroom. I protected her then."

"What about the nights you cowered in your closet while he held her against the wall by her throat and screamed at her?"

"There were nights I got it, too! Sometimes it was best to stay out of the way."

"And when you found her wearing your favourite t-shirt you chased her into the garden and hit her so hard on the head with your mother's gardening clog, you split the skin above her brow. She got five stitches for that."

"Please why are you doing this? Stop! I'm sorry! Please stop."

"What about me, Ophelia? What do you have to say about all those times you were too busy, or too tired or just lazy? All the lame excuses and postponed plans. What do you possibly have going on in your life that is so bloody important? You have nothing. You live alone. You have no family. You hate your job. What was so important? I hope it was worth it. You have nothing of substance. You waste your time pottering about in that dingy little flat or at the pub. The sad thing is you won't realise until it's too late that your whole life passed you by and you're some lonely singleton, working late, gossiping at company dos and moping over a pint. Life is out there and you're too bloody passive to take control of it. You're too afraid to want something and then do something about it. Your life is a series of regrets, Ophelia. You've wasted twenty-seven years screwing people over or sitting on the fucking sidelines."

"That's not true!"

"Isn't it? Isn't it? You don't need to get cross with me."

"You aren't being fair!"

"Life's not fair. Stop whingeing about it and start living it. You always took the safe and sensible route and where has it gotten you? Are you happy?"

"Laura, stop. Please!"

"Are you happy?"

"Laura!"

"Are you happy?"

"....no...."

"You're less alive than me."

"Please, Laura, stop."

"It's a bit late for that now. You're not dead, Ophelia. Stop living like you are. What are you going to do with yourself?"

Panic gripped Ophelia's heart. Laura levelled her eyes to meet Ophelia's as the ceiling and walls continued to close in. The shelves tumbled to the floors scattering books, dust and spiders. Ophelia's chest tightened as the room shrank. Out of the corners of her eyes she saw the walls looming closer. Her heartbeat grew louder as the pace quickened.

"Time won't wait for the lazy, the cowardly or the indecisive, Ophelia. Time waits for no-"

She jolted awake gasping for air. Her bed sheets were sticky with sweat and tangled up to her waist. Rain pelted steadily on the window. She untangled the sheet and stretched. She rolled over and listened to the empty rhythm outside. The guinea pig shuffled about in his cage, the clunk of his water bottle sporadically interrupting the rhythm of the rain. Grateful that it was nothing more than an awful dream Ophelia tried to make sense of it.

It was the first dream she could recall since Laura died. It continued to haunt her long after waking. The bitter residue of the dream tainted her day and mood. Days like that she found loneliness a high price to pay for freedom. It always felt less daunting after sharing a bad dream with a partner upon waking. As if by telling someone the demons were set free. A partner would be there to offer an embrace or comforting words, even analysis. As she listened to the rain Ophelia felt profoundly alone. She left the radio and telly off in the flat that morning and just listened to the rain as she tried hard to analyse and resolve the bad feelings the dream left behind.

While the kettle boiled she remembered her last relationship and how she had to account for late nights out or overlook his embarrassing or irritating habits. She thought of all the concessions she would make and tried to recall him ever meeting her half way on anything. She felt selfish and hated to admit it she was content to look after herself. She knew she wasn't alone, either. Ophelia had been with plenty of selfish men. She enjoyed having the whole bed to herself, duvet and all. Her flat was cluttered but it was all hers and she didn't have to hear anyone moan about paying their fair share of groceries or losing interest and disappearing.

It left her with insecurities and worries but no one to share them with. The anxieties were like bamboo stalks that would start off as small buds in the afternoon with an email or news story and then violently shoot up overnight. She felt herself getting older, jaded, and she still couldn't put a finger on what she wanted out of life let alone a partner. She poured her coffee and leaned over the counter, staring silently at the rain-spattered window.

She thought about running into Caroline's sister the night before. How could she approach her after all those years and all those taunts? She realised this was exactly what Laura – or, rather, her twisted subconscious manifestation of Laura - had warned her against. She had to stop living with regrets and actually do something about them.

An inspired thought came to her. She would send a letter. It was more heartfelt than an email and less awkward than the phone. It would enable her to lay out all off her thoughts on paper and edit as necessary.

Ophelia was a self-confessed stationary addict. In the age of text and email she still loved to receive or send letters. Every year at Christmas she would buy some cards at Oxfam and take an evening or Sunday out to write a brief annual summary for her

131

friends across the pond detailing what she had been up to, which usually wasn't much. They weren't quite as twee as those letters posh Stepford wife types sent to their boarding school alumni complete with pictures or PowerPoint presentations in a personalised newsletter format. People may joke but every year Elise's mother received them from the inevitable double-barrelled surnames. They boasted that Charles became Board Chairman (because he blackmailed the head of the board with some uncompromising photos of him and a hooker in King's Cross); Hattie was at a swish Ivy League uni in the States dating (shagging) the head (the whole) of the rowing team; Thurston III has landed a job at a top firm in Milan (to support his drug habit and fetish for Hindu boy prostitutes) and they added a whole new floor to the house (to make room for the deluxe S&M dungeon for orgies). Kat loved when Elise read between the lines of her mother's Christmas cards. It was a tradition started about three years prior by Laura. She had wanted to introduce Kat to Ophelia since Kat was homesick. It also filled Kat's diary so she could avoid Boxing Day at the in-laws.

They had brunch at Elise's and spent the afternoon gorging on leftovers from Fortnum and Mason. Elise brought back and read between the lines of all the newsletters. Ophelia confessed she had sent similar newsletters written by hand but added the excuse that the stationery was always great. Ophelia's smile faded as quickly as the memory materialised realising their Boxing Day ritual wouldn't be the same without Laura.

Ophelia tried to gather fresh resolve and drew a warm bath while drafting an apology. She positioned the telly to see it from the bathroom and hope to catch the last of the Saturday morning cartoons before braving the high street for stationery and a paper.

Kat emailed Elise and Ophelia to meet up for lunch on Thursday at Melati, a Malaysian restaurant tucked away on seedy Peter Street in Soho. She stumbled across it by accident and noticed a bunch of working girls' "offices" upstairs from the gentlemen's clubs and sex shops directly across the street. Melati gave her a cinematic view of the comings and goings of the oldest institutions and their clientele. Ever since she enjoyed staring, pointing and laughing at the unfortunate johns that milled in and out of the doorways advertising models of all ages, shapes and persuasions. When they were seated that afternoon, Kat excitedly pointed at a sad red light bulb dangling in one of the windows. "Come for the hookers, stay for the food!" She beamed after they took their seats.

"I can't believe he said that! What a cunt." Elise muttered in disbelief.

Kat replied eagerly thrilled to finally be able to talk the evening out with someone willing to see her point of view. "They came over last night to apologise but in true in-law fashion skated around the whole subject and tried to turn it into me not wanting to be part of their lovely little family."

"Family of jackals maybe." Ophelia had handled too many tearful calls from Kat regarding Ian's parents that she now dismissed his parents as monsters and found it hard not to dislike Ian.

"Rhys seemed genuinely embarrassed over it, though I think he was more sorry that he said it to me, though. I think he really feels that way. Dorothy was touchy-feely and brought me some tacky designer knock-off handbag. To ease the awkwardness I made the mistake saying how I felt bad about walking out. Then Dorothy pipes in, 'and so you should after making such a scene, and there of all places! You ruined the evening for everyone. I am not walking on eggshells to protect anyone's feelings. This is how we are and you're simply going to have to get over these neurotic sensitivities of yours, dear.' I nearly walked out then."

"You didn't ruin anything." Ophelia hissed. "You're married to that vampire and she's complaining?"

Elise cocked her head. "Vampire?"

"Yeah. Vampires sponge off you emotionally or financially, zombies are the ones you keep dumping and they keep coming back, and the wolf man has a nasty temper. Everyone's been with at least one monster if not all of them. Those are the most common but there are others."

"Fucking hell, do you have some manifesto you're writing based on past experiences?"

"Elise, it's not just me. Look at Kat."

"Ophelia! Ian's not a vampire!"

"Kat you held down two jobs last year to buy his crass and nasty parents gifts while he played video games and worked on some script the BBC never used."

"It was shortlisted."

"Ophelia's right. You nearly got assaulted working on that perfume counter." Elise feebly interjected.

134

"And remember when you complained about how he moaned when you asked for a ride because he was about to move up a level?"

"His heart's in the right place."

"Only when it's convenient for him. Why doesn't he ever stick up for you?" Ophelia countered.

"I don't know."

Elise waded further in and tried to mediate before a Paxman-style interview grew out of a friendly lunch. "Kat I'm saying this as your friend. Every relationship is a balance of power. Whether it's friends or siblings or spouses. The balances aren't completely even in every area but that's because we all have strengths and weaknesses. As far as I can see you're iron and he's feathers; the scales of your marriage are totally uneven."

"He just needs to find his niche."

"He just needs to find his job or at least a spine." Ophelia flagged the waiter down for drinks.

"Feelie! Easy tigress! Kat, she's just worried about you. You're so stressed."

"I know. It's hard but you can't throw away a marriage based on one problem."

"You can if he refuses to compromise and it is affecting your wellbeing."

The waiter finally came and took their orders. Kat sat thoughtfully thumbing the dog eared menu. "Every time I tried to defend myself Ian tried to change the subject, worried I was going to upset them, but after his folks left we had a huge row. I told him if that's how his mother feels she can go fuck herself. I'm not dealing with that woman anymore. She's a fucking barracuda. I told him she shouldn't worry about walking on eggshells. I just won't see them anymore. I've had it. And after all this, they basically excused me from enduring another mind numbing outing."

"So, did Ian have anything to say?" Elise asked.

"What could he say? That was the straw that broke the camel's back. I mean, I can't possibly be nasty to them after all they've done for us and I know if I were to ever say anything to Dorothy, it would hurt Ian. But I am not going to let them make me miserable any longer. Life's too short." Kat forced a smile and began to order.

Ophelia turned her attention to Elise. "So how was your weekend?"

"Nothing much." She mumbled as she scanned the menu.

"Come on, Elise. Your hair says a different thing entirely. Were you abducted by a mob of beauty school students? Join a cult? ...the first to fall asleep at a party?" She teased.

"I just got tired of it, I guess." She shrugged.

Ophelia wasn't convinced.

"Oh wow! Look how nasty that old pervert is!" Kat chirped as she pointed excitedly. An older man furtively slipped in the doorway advertising a young Swedish girl who was eager to please. Kat cackled. "I bet he's out before we finish our lunch."

She checked her watch as Elise and Ophelia ordered.

"Seriously, Elise, is everything okay?" Ophelia continued.

"I'll be fine. I went to Paris for the weekend for a change of scenery and the haircut seemed a good idea." She managed a crooked grin to back up her claim.

"I've been thinking of you this week," Kat said to Elise as her eyes intermittently scanned the street. "And I just think maybe you need to be inspired again. You know, take on a big project to get you back on track or at least keep you busy. Pimp!"

A sedan with tinted windows drove up and a man in a tacky suit got out and headed in to the flats. Sadly there was no feather hat or platform shoes. Elise considered Kat's advice. Ophelia began watching the pimp.

"Yeah, that might not be a bad idea. I know you've got the gallery show in a few weeks and -fucking hell! Look at that!"

Ophelia was in awe. Kat and Elise looked over at the sex shop following Ophelia's gaze.

"What?"

"That's Clara Bitchy!" She said in disbelief. Sure enough it was her office nemesis busily dashing through the coloured ribbon curtain in the doorway. "She's that absolute prat who's always grassing me for coming in late. I can't stand her."

"Well it looks like she's got a bit of a kinky side to her. Unless she's a PA doing someone's dirty work?" Kat mused as she craned her neck.

"I hope she's running a personal errand."

The three women sat fixated on the doorway like cats ready to pounce, tails twitching in anticipation. Their meals were set in front of them but they were too absorbed to notice. Clara tried to casually step out onto the pavement when Elise suddenly rapped on the window. Clara froze and slowly turned, sensing their eyes on her. She met Ophelia's gaze and her mouth dropped in shock for a second and a dark shade of crimson flooded her cheeks. Ophelia's face twisted into a smirk almost involuntarily as she demurely waved at her. Kat broke into a throaty laugh, pointing in Clara's direction. Clara lowered her eyes and ran down the street out of sight.

"Wow, that was random," Kat managed as she returned her focus to the table.

"A high point to my day." Ophelia conceded.

Elise smiled. "You two are incorrigible."

Ophelia returned to the office after a defiant two-hour lunch break. She decided to conduct an experiment to see if Clara would dare say anything. It also enabled her to do a bit of holiday shopping. As she sauntered by the desk, Clara stiffened almost imperceptibly.

"Enjoy your lunch?" Ophelia asked casually.

Clara folded her hands together in her lap. "Um, sure. Thanks."

Ophelia relished how the tables had turned.

"My lunch was full of surprises." She purred, settling into her desk and enjoyed a pleasant, empowered afternoon.

-

Fruit sellers hollered their selection of fruit and vegetables in the market stalls. People bartered over costs and quantities. The smell of sandalwood and patchouli loitered in the doorway of the bong shop. Elise exhaled as she passed the fishmonger and inhaled as she passed the crepe stand. This was a skill acquired after a few walks in this part of Soho. She had nowhere to be and nothing to do.

This could be refreshing although today it only served to reiterate her lack of purpose. Elise felt adrift in a vast, cold sea of smoke, concrete and closed faces. She longed for an anchor or lighthouse but knew that it had to be of her own doing. She was idle for so long that Elise wasn't sure she had the strength to head for shore. She was too far out to anchor herself. The horizon ahead seemed daunting and uncertain.

Elise wanted to return to the world of smiling, chatting, creating and actually living instead of existing by default. She ambled past the animated café and bistro tables of Old Compton Street and felt detached from everything she saw. She was the burglar outside the window looking in, resenting and coveting their easy contentment. She tried to figure a way to break in.

"Hey! Elise, right?"

Elise spun round trying to place the voice, mentally sorting through a catalogue of memories.

"It's me, Sara. You bought me dinner a few weeks back."

Elise nodded in recognition. "Hi."

"Thanks for that. I was famished. It had to be one of the best meals I had."

"It was nothing, no worries." Elise forced a quick smile. She felt a huge store of energy being used to exchange a few words.

"Listen, I managed to get quite a bit of change today, why don't I treat you to a coffee to say thanks?"

Elise paused, wanting to refuse and flee while simultaneously craving the company. She realised she should have been touched by Sarah's generous offer but her heart was too heavy from the weight of her mood.

"Well, how about a pint?" Sara tried.

"Okay, sure." She managed a genuine smile and they headed to the Crown and Two Chairmen.

Elise stared through the window waiting for Sarah to return with drinks. Sara poked her face in the line of Elise's vision and gently waved. As her focus returned to the table, Elise shook her head and grinned absently.

"Everything okay?" Sara asked.

"No, actually. I've been in a bit of a rut lately." Elise confided.

"Better now than the summer."

"Huh?"

"Well, the winter's a good time to sort emotional stuff since everything else slows down. You get lots of rainy days to ponder over bowls of soup or long nights to sit under the duvet on the sofa watching telly. Can't do that in spring or summer; you'd be wasting all that sunlight. It's hard to get distracted or down when gardens are in bloom. That's why Christmas is in the winter; to keep people from offing themselves."

Elise laughed. "It's more surprising people aren't offing themselves because of it."

—

"Hey hon, what's for dinner?"

"Amphetamines. I didn't feel like cooking and this way you wouldn't be hungry." Kat called as she hung her coat. Kat laughed to herself as she tugged her boots off.

"How was your day? The airline tickets arrived. Did you have any cigarettes?"

"I wouldn't give Dorothy the satisfaction," she called as a flash of resentment rumbled through her. Kat quietly padded into the kitchen and hugged her husband. "Do I smell like I've been smoking?"

Ian turned, brushing his nose past her hair and along her neck. "No, you smell like overpriced perfume."

Kat smiled, kissing him on the nose. "See? So have you told your folks that we'll be doing our own thing this year for Christmas?"

Ian turned and walked towards the living room. "I will." He called.

Kat leaned against the wall and slowly slid down to the floor. Her muscles tensed slightly as she felt the cold tiles through her skirt.

"You've got to tell them. What are you so afraid of?"

Her back was flat against the floor warming the tiles beneath her as she lazily moved the magnets on the fridge door with her stocking-feet. She twisted a few stray locks as she listened for Ian who seemed to be deliberately immersed in his gaming. She could hear his fingers manipulating the controls and a wave of frustration flooded her. She only wished he tried to understand his wife the way he did his games. When they were with his family he never caught any of her signals for help or early exits. And when they were alone in bed he might as well have worn boxing gloves when he touched her. He could manipulate those tiny controls almost intuitively and when he had trouble would research it or get a magazine, and yet Kat gave up on passion thinking marriage was about stability and friendship instead of ardent desire. She also knew marriage was about equal partnerships and after working all day she didn't feel up to thinking of what to cook for dinner. She tried to push her friends' lunchtime ob-servations out of her mind.

"I wonder if it'll snow this year," she mused.

Over the last few days she grew increasingly excited about their first Christmas alone. She yearned to establish traditions that were hers and Ian's alone. Kat's anxieties faded about the upcoming holidays knowing she would be on the other side of the Atlantic. Ian's family were very formal about the holidays which added more strain for Kat.

She was quite happy to spend Christmas at Ian's parents the first couple of years. It quickly became another obligation. Kat always started her shopping early to stagger the expense and found that she had to start even earlier since she had Ian's parents, aunt, uncle and cousin. Ian never had any money to contribute nor was he much of a shopper so Kat would make the list, save the funds and do the holiday shopping. Along with the additional presents for Ian and his family came additional anxiety. The worries weren't necessarily unfounded, either.

The year Kat and Ian first moved to the UK finances were tight. Remembering Dorothy had complimented the scent of her hand cream, Kat decided to get some for a gift. She hoped Dorothy would appreciate how Kat remembered she liked the scent and it didn't hurt that the cream was from a high street pharmacy instead of a designer scent from Harrods. Pleased to have completed her holiday list well under budget Kat decided to drop by her in-laws' home to see if they needed any groceries on her way to the shops. She noticed the same exact bath salts and hand cream in a gift basket on the table that she had gotten for Dorothy.

Kat tried to sound casual as she asked, "Who got you this?"

Dorothy glanced at the basket. "Oh that! It's for Tracey, the cleaning lady."

Cold dread struck Kat dumb as she smiled and nodded. Ian later tried to assuage Kat's fears that Dorothy would feel insulted by the gift reasoning that his mother would understand that money was tight for them and appreciate the thought.

Instead, on Christmas morning Dorothy opened the gift and grimaced with disgust trilling to Kat, "Oh Katherine! I won't be using this."

That one gesture had spoiled the entire day for Kat and she reminded Ian each time he asked her advice on buying his mum a gift. It was one of many stones in the well of Kat's love for Ian. She found with each insult from his parents, or his refusal at a job opportunity or favour he forgot he promised the pile got bigger and weighed heavy in her heart mired deep in disappointments. She always reasoned that he cared about her – and Ophelia would assert that he cared about his parents more - or that he would eventually get a job – Elise even found him a spot in her father's firm but Ian refused, stating that he studied theatre at university and it was the only industry he would work in. She wished she could find the words to tell him how she secretly hoped he would just be considerate or appreciative rather than entitled or lazy. Some days they had a great time laughing or joking in their secret language full of refer- ences or gestures from their shared history. On those days he was her best friend and confidant. But on nights when she wanted strong arms to defend her, hold her or ravish her she was left frustrated. She was stuck without family or roots in a foreign country with no family back in the states. She often joked to Ophelia that they were trapped on Gilligan's Island but secretly she worried sometimes she really was ship- wrecked and stranded.

It always seemed impossible to get out of going to the in-laws for holidays but their recent disastrous dinner out had finally granted her a much needed pass. Ian seemed enthusiastic about the holiday and Kat agreed to pay as a Christmas gift for Ian and her. All they needed to do was pack and break it to his parents.

144

"Did you book the driving lessons?" Ian was eager to change the subject as he saved his game.

Kat rolled onto her stomach. "I have my first one Saturday. I can hardly wait," she sighed.

Ophelia was in the middle of compiling data for the end of year reports. In an effort to stay busy she collected data for the last three years and organised it by revenue, performance and geographic location using a pivot table. She was surprised at how interesting the project was after she found the initiative to use all of her experience and knowledge despite the brief being vague and basic. She found it satisfying to see the impact her time and efforts actually had. She managed to add some graphs with summaries and even added strategic recommendations. She was amazed she managed to accrue all this knowledge as if by osmosis over the last few years.

She was about to add a competitor summary when John suddenly materialised at her desk.

"Ophelia, can I see you in the upstairs boardroom in ten minutes?"

"Sure."

As he walked away she wondered what he wanted. She realised after looking at the overall performance of the company on her year-on-year graph that they had to make some cuts to outperform last year by more than 5%. Then she realised that Christmas was around the corner and the sword of Damocles' was hanging over her. She fumed thinking that she spent four days on that document and over three years at that office. She realised she was going to be out of a job in ten minutes to calm the chairmen because some bloody shareholders got their shitty knickers in a twist over profits. Didn't those greedy bastards understand that she needed that job to pay her rent? She would finally be rid of that monotonous bore of a role once and for all but at such a high price and nothing in place to go to. There was bound to be a redundancy package but Ophelia wasn't sure how long it would last or how long it would take to find a new job.

As the thoughts raced around her head she wondered why not go out in style? She had three years worth of data and intelligence at her fingertips and it would be a shame for it to go to waste. She saved the report and quickly emailed all of her files and contacts to her web-based email account. She deleted all emails, binned all business contacts, renamed and hid all relevant files on her drive, deleting some and doing a few fun find-and-replace on others hoping that Clara would have to take on her work once she left. She stuffed all her papers into her gym kit bag that never made it to the gym and headed to the boardroom.

Satisfied with a departing gesture of anarchy and spite she made one last coffee and headed in. She was met with two sombre faces from the H.R. department as well as John. John held the door for Ophelia. She tried to hold her head high and maintain an air of impassive dignity. She knew she had slacked off a good deal over the past few years, taken sickie for hangovers and hadn't made any effort to advance her role. She still didn't see how it warranted the outright loss of her role. She was hardly alone in her hands-off approach to work and she was fairly careful not to step on toes so wasn't sure why her head was on the chopping block. She sat down and grinned at her executioners. Slightly baffled at her gallows smile the two women exchanged brief glances and commenced.

It was the usual apologetic speech about how times were tough and they wanted to keep everyone but the business just couldn't afford to continue as it was. She did her best to look serious and suppress any emotion. She was tempted to ask if they decided by drawing names in a hat or if it was more of a silent popularity auction. In a way she was relieved the decision had finally been made for her. She fantasised about leaving for a while but was too frightened to leave on her own. She now had the impetus and three months' paid time to figure out what she actually wanted to do with. A small part of her felt rejected and worried but there was a strange freedom in the redundancy.

It suddenly dawned on her why the death card was sometimes a good sign when Elise did her tarot. This was a chance to break free and start fresh. It was equally exciting and frightening but there was no choice. She never had to catch Clara watching what was on her computer screen. She never had to worry about someone nicking her sandwich in the communal fridge or have to do another presentation that John would take credit for.

She managed to maintain her composure until they offered her counselling at the end of the meeting. She started giggle and soon was laughing uncontrollably. John looked alarmed and the women pursed their lips as Ophelia's laughter faded into an awkward cough.

"I'm sorry. I'm a bit surprised is all."

"Everyone reacts differently. It's rather a shock when it happens. If you do find you need to talk or have questions we'll be here and also offer a support scheme."

"Thank you."

The company had been thoughtful enough to let her go before 11 on a Friday morning. Ophelia was finally free to make good on all of skive fantasies and had a long weekend as well. She hurriedly piled her things into a box as a security chap stood by her desk and stared impassively towards the exit. She left the building with her professional life haphazardly thrown into a small cardboard box. It was weird to see the past three odd years summarised in such a small space. It felt like there should have been a more significant accumulation to reflect the time. Instead it seemed to merely reflect an empty, miserable existence filled with Far Side clippings, stress balls and a chipped Mr. Messy mug.

Instead of throwing a pity party at the redundancy local she made her way to Elise's. The bus was full of shoppers looking vexed and claustrophobic. A few seemed to be on the verge of tears. She carried her box to the off licence for some port and grabbed some take-away en route. Ophelia was surprised to find Ian answering the door.

"Oh, hey Ophelia, how are you?"

"I just got sacked actually. What are you doing here?"

"Working on a script with Jo."

"Really?"

"Yeah, I saw her show and had a great idea."

"Cool. Is Elise around?"

"Yeah. Oh hey, come in."

As Ian led her in she almost didn't recognise Jo. He was dressed like Joe in a scruffy unshaven face, denims, rugby jersey and trainers. He seemed shy and somewhat reserved as he waved. She knocked tentatively on Elise's door. After a moment she heard a muffled voice.

"Come in!"

"Elise?"

"I'm in the wardrobe, hang on a second."

Elise came out wiping her hands on an old faded t-shirt. "Hey Feelie, what brings you round so early?"

"They made me redundant."

"You're certainly taking it well."

"I'm actually okay. I'm finally out of a job I was unhappy in. I'll get paid for three months while I look for something better and I got an early start to the weekend. Can't complain, really."

"Fair enough." Elise shrugged with a smile.

"What have you been up to? I've not seen you in ages."

"I'll show you." Elise looked happier than she had seemed lately. Or rather, she lacked the expression of angst that seemed to veil her since the funeral.

She lead Ophelia to her studio. In the centre of the room lay a Scalectrix set amongst a small-scale model of London. In one lane was a double-decker bus full of plastic green army men and, oddly enough, farm animals. In the other lane was a Mercedes sports car with one figure in the driver's seat. Elise shot Ophelia a proud and mischie-vous grin.

"Go on, take your pick."

Ophelia laughed, feeling about 10 years old again. She pointed to the flashy sports car.

"I suppose I can afford to side with the capitalist pigs since they've just given me a three month paid vacation."

Ophelia's controller had a neon pink £100 note glued onto it over a frantic collage of logos from fast food retailers to superhero emblems. Statistics in newsprint were dotted about citing toxic emissions in China, child labour in Asia, and the global warming. She scanned the controller for a few moments then craned her neck to see Elise's TFL control pad. On it was a neon green Tube ticket over logos for the NHS, London transport and other public services. There were facts about Thatcher's refusal to fund improvements or maintenance for the London Underground.

"So, we're going to race or are we gonna navel gaze?"

"Okay. You put so much on these controls."

"Ready?" She arched her brow.

"I guess. Are these like the classic Scalectrix?"

"Sort of. Steady."

Ophelia nodded.

"Go!"

The sports car sped off, sparks crackling behind while a high-pitched humming noise followed it around the track. The track itself was a wild assortment cardboard buildings pasted over in newsprint. Headlines with car adverts from magazines were pasted all over. The London Eye was an old tricycle wheel while Tower Bridge had two milk cartons plastered with car ads and petrol station logos.

Elise's bus crept along clumsily like a fat and sleepy red caterpillar. After the Mercedes streaked past the bus a fourth time, Elise looked over.

"Want me to show you the second part?"

"What? Do I get a trophy for kicking your arse?"

She pointed to a seemingly identical set next to it. The tracks and controls were similar to the first except that the bus had three figures in it while the Mercedes was boxed in by several others identical in all but colour and passenger. The passengers were similar to the ones the bus contained in the first part, so there a few farm animals behind the wheel.

"The rule is that you have to use the same vehicle as you did before."

Ophelia took the controller knowing that this race was lost.

Elise's bus hummed forward only slightly quicker than before while the Mercedes' wheels spun in place, screeching against the metal tracks. The other cars were gridlocked as the bus happily chugged past.

"I've been secretly hoping this piece doesn't sell." She confided. "I'm having too much fun with it."

After several futile races, Elise showed her a few of her the pieces in the studio. There was an old medicine cabinet with a red velvet curtain where the mirror would be. Inside were plastic amber American-style prescription bottles. Plastered over the labels were tiny film posters and album covers of various celebrities who met their demise through prescription drugs.

"I had Kat get her mates from the US send over their empty bottles. It's shocking what some of them are on." Elise clucked.

The next medicine cabinet had a mirror. When opened, the shelves were empty. Instead there were articles from magazines about supplements, cellulite cures, weight -loss drugs, wrinkle remedies, information on depression, stress as well as adverts for medications.

"Too bad you didn't do more like these. You could have dressed up like a nurse for the opening."

"They're part of a series. I'm still working on the last three."

Ophelia was startled by the life-sized wax sculpture of Margaret Thatcher. It was jet black and dusted with a black powder to appear as if carved from coal. Thatcher was seated and her legs crossed demurely. She was reaching down with a handkerchief in Union Jack print, poised to wipe off the sole of her shoe. The bottom of her feet were covered in red paint and dolls' body parts, furniture and clothes had been scattered onto the ground beneath her as well, creating a macabre throne.

"Thatcher as Godzilla?"

"Practically. I'm really pleased with it. Took bloody ages!"

Beyond Maggie was Joan Crawford. With a menacing grin, the figure was clad in a 1940's housewife dress of Dorothy's newspaper clippings.

"I even matched her shoes!"

Sure enough, her heels were streams of advice on PMT, housekeeping, weight-loss and casserole recipes.

"Has Kat or Ian seen this yet?"

"Nah, I won't show her until the opening I reckon."

"This is great."

She nodded vaguely. "Hey, how about you? What have you been up to?"

"Aside from getting the sack today, not much, really."

"Just two weeks until my show. I'm so excited. This will be the biggest exhibition I've ever done."

"Well if you need help or anything, I now have time on my hands."

"Cheers. I may take you up on that offer."

The take-away was lukewarm but edible. Their cheeks grew rosy with port. When that was finished they finished some brandy Elise found under her bed. They sat on her floor, chatting and searching the radio dial for a decent London station, taking the piss out of the presenters and their crap play lists. After finishing the partially congealed food, the sky grew darker with the approach of late afternoon.

"I always feel cheated out of time in the winter." Ophelia sighed.

"I know. The days are so short. And the weather's shit so no consolation there."

"The weather's rubbish all year round. It's just in winter we're holed up in our offices or houses or the pub like Morlocks. No wonder you're all so miserable."

"If we're so miserable, why do you Americans come here and then stay?"

"Why does anyone stay in a miserable situation? Whether it's a go nowhere job or crap relationship or rubbish location, people just get stuck. Frogs get boiled alive because they don't notice the water heating up. Maybe we're just frogs."

"That's depressing, Feelie."

"It may be but it's the truth. How often do you hear some twat moaning how they're so miserable and then do nothing about it? Most people just wait for change. They just bide their time moaning. Look at me. If I wasn't let go I would have just continued there."

"Maybe you can go with the momentum and change anything else you're unhappy with."

"I suppose. What about you? You're always doing stuff."

"Yeah, but not necessarily everything I want. Everybody holds stuff back for one reason or another."

"Where's your bin?"

Elise looked around her room. "I can reuse the takeaway boxes and the bottle can be recycled. Hey, want to go now?"

"Go where?"

"Recycling. It'll be fun."

Feeling merry with port, Ophelia humoured Elise. They lugged two bin liners full of jars and bottles to the local dump and managed to blag their way in as it was closing for the day. The bottles clanged as they rolled around in the bags.

They clambered up the steps to the skip and peered in. Shards of glass glittered in the moonlight like a sea of green. Magpies called to each other noisily in the distance. Steam puffed out of their nostrils and evaporated into the cold night air. Elise rummaged about in the sack for green bottles. She set the bottles daintily at their feet.

"We've got to be quick. Those chaps are dying to go home."

Elise handed her a bottle the picked up a wine bottle for herself and drew her arm back. She flung it into the glittering abyss making a resounding crash that echoed across the night sky, silencing the plotting magpies. Elise looked over to Ophelia. She exhaled and threw her bottle against the wall of the skip. It shattered and settled. It left her both startled and exhilarated.

A succession of crashes followed. Elise threw the bottles and cursed loudly as they crashed. Ophelia found her cheeks streaked with tears. The glints of light grew blurry as the tears continued to fall freely. She didn't have to explain anything to Elise who was in her own world bleeding her anger and frustration with every shot. Their voices rose like screeching banshees accented by the smashing of the bottles and jars filling the dump with a devilish cacophony that frightened the men who let them in. When the last shards of glass hit the skip, Elise felt lighter. She breathed in the cool night, exhaling warm little clouds. They stared at each others' agitated state dumbly for a moment before erupting into laughter.

They picked up the remaining sack of cans and headed to the last skip. Still giggling they sang carols, replacing words with curses laughing as they dropkicked the cans into the designated skip. After they emptied all the sacks they scurried out singing manic thanks to the men at the gate. With their green reign of destruction over, they headed to the bus stop and staggered onto the first bus to pull up. They fumbled up the stairs to the top deck and fell into the empty seats in front of the window.

"Where does this bus go?"

"Dunno." Elise smiled.

"Where are we hoping to go?"

"No clue. Wherever it is, I hope it's fun."

They scanned the streets as the bus hummed past, jerking to a stop every so often. Centrepoint glided into view. Elise's face lit up and she motioned for them to get off. The bus streamed past in a red blur. Ophelia looked at Elise quizzically.

"There's a great Lebanese place on Greek street. We can sit, eat, drink and plot the evening's activities."

"I'll get the bill for this, then."

"Don't be daft. You just lost your job."

"I insist. No worries. Besides I may need you to buy me dinner in three months."

"Fair enough. You know, if you don't find anything I may be able to help. I know this solicitor, Steve. He's a family friend and is always looking for help at his office. He's a bit, uh, eccentric but a really decent chap."

Ophelia eyed Elise sceptically. "I'll keep it in mind."

Kaslik looked small from the street but felt big and opulent once they walked in. They snuggled into a corner and ordered a bottle of wine. Elise scanned the menu absently.

"A few years ago I was dating this guy, Arsehole Pete. He once told me that souls travel in packs. You think maybe Laura's in our group?"

"We can only hope, I guess. Have you had any dreams of Laura?"

As Elise explored the depths of her wineglass Ophelia yearned to hear a similar anecdote of Laura fiercely interrogating her. Elise looked up puzzled, and shook her head. Ophelia's heart sank. She wrote several letters on Saturday owning up to being a twat, bully, bitch, etc and sent them off the same day. So far she had heard nought and in a way was relieved. She hoped the apologetic confessionals were lost in the post and that was the end of the matter. The other scenario was that most people had forgotten her sins altogether and binned the letters assuming it was an obligation for AA or for a bet. No one ever seemed to remember what they had for breakfast, never mind some random jerk in grade school. Ophelia prised her attention away from neurotic worries and returned to face a thoughtful Elise.

"Arsehole Pete?"

Elise looked up, surprised. "Yeah, he was a complete arsehole. I was only with him for a few weeks in uni, but even now, we all call him Arsehole Pete. Everyone who met him thought he was an arsehole, or that's what they told me. And they were right. A complete bastard."

"As in grumpy sod bastard or love rat bastard?"

Elise rolled her eyes. "Nah mate, then he would have just been 'that bastard'. He was so rotten that arsehole is his title. For example, I was in bed with a high fever, hallucinations, sweats, the works. I didn't want to ring for an ambulance but needed to go to A&E. Nobody was around and Arsehole Pete had a car so I rang him and explained that I needed a ride and couldn't move. He tells me he can't do it because he's doing his laundry and that I should call a cab."

"Wow, title earned."

159

"Exactly! So, how will you be spending your next three months of freedom?"

All the things she whinged about wanting to do materialised with mocking grins. It was strange to have a wish granted. She was thrilled to be rid of the crap job, but the future seemed uncertain. She had no choice but to move on but was scared about finding nothing or finding something that was worse.

"Look for another mind-numbing job?"

-

Smoke danced seductively across the table teasing Kat with the familiar scent. Music from someone else's youth boomed in the dark cavernous wine bar.

People throughout tapped their feet or bobbed their heads smiling in recognition. It didn't sound familiar to Kat. A few of her colleagues at the table were singing along to the chorus, giggling when someone else forgot the words. Others traded stories about school discos or rah-rah skirts. Kat knew this feeling all too well; the island castaway who, upon discovering the local tribe, is allowed to sit in as an honorary guest and observe local rituals and customs. Even after five years she felt alien sometimes, especially in big groups. Not always, but on occasion an old catchphrase or theme-tune or political reference would come up and Kat would be reminded that she wasn't from around these parts. It made her feel isolated like when she was out with Ian's family. No matter how much she practiced her accent or watched nostalgic programmes or listened to Capital Gold she would always be an interloper with her own culture, references and childhood.

A girlie night out with the women from her office was unusual. Kat dreaded work drinks. She often feigned exhaustion or begged off citing fictitious plans but knew that if she never went it invited animosity or suspicion. With the in-laws on her all the time she could do without the extra headache. The last thing she wanted was to be at the bottom of the pecking order. She learned the hard way how crucial support was in the office.

After her mum died Kat was deemed unsuitable for foster care after a fire damaged her room when she fell asleep smoking. She spent three years counting down to her 18th birthday in a residential girls' home. The girls at the home bickered and gossiped constantly although the topics were never about dates they went on, school exams or television shows. They gossiped about each other sleeping together after lights out, argued about morning bathroom schedules, bummed fags off each other, or compared juvenile records. When Kat finally left the home, she feared girls. She found them manipulative, ruthless, vindictive cats purring to your face and scratching you to ribbons behind your back.

She was wary of roommates stealing from her so found the cheapest studio flat for rent in a grotty area and waited tables. She kept to herself and away from fear. It often gave the impression Kat thought she was better than everyone when really she was ashamed of her past. Kat had been at the company for two years and wanted to have friends at work rather than acquaintances but still felt like a square peg in a round hole. Laura was the first friend she made inside the workplace in the UK. Laura was so open and friendly. She was considerate and had amazing comic timing. Kat was in fits of laughter whenever they went to lunch. She never seemed to get embarrassed which Kat envied and admired in equal turns. Laura could laugh at herself, which made it impossible to embarrass or talk about her.

After a particularly boozy Christmas party Laura took centre stage on the dance floor. It was crowded and hot in the hall and an old disco song had come on. Laura started to shimmy and tease her dress off in the middle of the dance floor. The sales department egged her on and the marketing department stared in shock. Kat had been coming out of the loo and saw Laura swinging her dress like a lasso above her head.

She ran over and clasped her free hand and danced her over to coat check in her bra, knickers and stocking feet. She threw her coat over her giggling friend and bundled them into a black cab. The next morning Laura walked into the office with her head high, brandishing a pork pie hat insisting the sales team tip her for the previous night's performance and gave Kat the 50 quid in the hat to repay the cab ride. If it had been Kat she wouldn't have ever returned to the office.

Kat hoped Laura knew how much she inspired her. It wasn't as if an opportunity presented itself to tell her before she died. Kat thought of Laura as indestructible and still found herself wanting to ring Laura at times after a row with Ian or ask advice about work. Her heart wrung in despair each time she reminded herself Laura was gone.

That night found Kat nodding and smiling over a plate of bangers and mash as her co-workers nattered on about an EastEnders storyline Kat knew nothing about. Admittedly, it was a small price to pay to avoid disapproving stares by the office tea kettle. Having survived a month of desperate or downright stupid enquiries about lumps and rashes or the odd piss-take by giggly kids, Oufie was out with them for dinner and drinks. She recently quit smoking as well and kept casting jealous glances at the smokers.

"Here's to Oufie's first month!"

Debs, the senior office manager crowed. The others cackled and clucked as they raised their glasses. Alone, women were harmless, nice even; but in large groups they were a volatile mob of vultures that gladly feasted on anyone who appeared to be getting too big for their britches.

Kat played it safe and took the neutral route. With an office that was largely female this proved the best tactic. She was desperate to ask if anyone else had any nasty run-ins with the eagle eyed manager but wasn't sure where anyone's alliances lay.

"So Kat, any plans for Christmas?"

"Actually I'm flying back to the States."

"Wow, that's great. To see family?"

"Uh yeah. I've not been since we moved here."

"How long's it been then?"

"About five years now."

"How exciting. With the exchange rate just think of all the shopping."

Kat wasn't thinking of that at all. As the women rabbitted on about clothing labels and American shopping malls, Kat retreated into her own private worries about whether Ian would tell his mum about Christmas or if he would ever find a job. Paying for the flights would make expenses even tighter but she had to go home. She wanted to go six months after moving to London but couldn't afford to. Ian never understood yearning; when he was stateside his parents flew him home once or twice a year and were always available to cater to his whims. She worried he would never have the impetus or drive to do anything. It was a luxury she couldn't fathom after years of bringing oversized handbags to all you can't eat buffets to smuggle food home or stealing loo roll from the local McDonald's when she ran low. Ian could never understand struggle; he never needed to. All the women at the table seemed to have partners or husbands from the same social class and seemed content. Kat smiled at the table while turmoil

brewed deep within her heart.

Elise slid on a pair of bug-eye sunglasses. Her wellies spattered lead coloured water from the puddles on Camden High St. when she stomped through them. James eyed her disapprovingly as he popped a flapjack into his mouth.

"I can't believe I agreed to go with you today," he muttered. "I certainly wouldn't have done if I had known you were planning on going in your pyjamas."

"What? They're flannel pyjamas, mate. Besides I wore a coat."

"Elise darling, you're wearing my old tweed coat which is three sizes too big and your pyjamas happen to be covered in cartoon sheep. To complete this ensemble you're sporting a red kerchief and with those ridiculous space goggles. You look like Jackie Onassis on crack. The charity shops probably won't even charge you."

"You're so cruel, James. I've got a beastly hangover and here you are trying to give me fashion tips. It's Saturday morning in Camden. No one gives a shit, dear."

One Saturday a month Elise would tour a different neighbourhood around High St. She would target charity shops for material to use in her work mainly, although it was also a great way to get acquainted with an area by looking at what the locals cast off. The wealthier neighbourhoods boasted designer clothing that had obviously been purchased on a whim and never worn with the price tags confirming this. Hammer-smith had an epic collection of records and books whereas Shoreditch, Brixton and Camden had great clothes hidden amongst the racks. James had just finished his porridge when Elise staggered into the kitchen for a cup of tea before embarking on her monthly expedition. Eager for an excuse to avoid sitting at his desk fraught with writer's block he volunteered to join her. Elise rummaged through the toys carefully as James looked around at the books.

"Do you look for anything specific?"

Elise examined a stuffed koala closely before setting it down on the shelf.

"Sometimes. Or I just get inspired by something. I guess it just depends. How about you? Where do you get ideas?"

"I haven't had an idea in ages."

Elise smiled at an Action Man figure and placed it in her shopping bag.

"Maybe you need a muse?"

James chortled dryly. Elise faced James and took off her sunglasses to reveal a tired, pasty hung-over face.

"When was the last time you were really able to sit down and write?"

James stared back at his housemate and searched for an excuse or reason. Elise took the toys, a few dog-eared books and a peacock blue dress to the till.

James exhaled, "months. It's been months since I've been able to write anything more than a grocery list. Every day I sit at the desk and the moment my arse hits the seat my head's empty. My motivation's completely sapped. I should just surrender to the fact that I will never finish this bloody book!"

"Maybe you need a break from it?"

"Tell my agent that."

"Maybe you need-"

"You need a fry-up, Elise. You look like death warmed up. I don't know what you were drinking last night but it's not doing your complexion any favours. Come on."

On their way to a café they wandered through a labyrinth of market stalls. Being a Saturday they were teaming with tourists, crusty punks that looked as if the 90's never happened, day-glo club kids wandering around still high from the night before, junkies shivering as they waited for a fix and elaborately decorated Goths eyeing one another with sneers or coy smiles. Racks of Doc Martens, t-shirts sporting maxims, patterned tights and handbags lined the stalls where people haggled over prices.

"I can't remember the last time I spent a Saturday at Camden market," James mused as he examined a shirt.

The café was tucked away towards Chalk Hill, providing a quiet contrast to the bustling markets of Camden. Elise tucked in to her bubble and squeaked as James held up his hand solemnly.

"You'll never lose that hangover without any brown sauce," he admonished. He furrowed his brow and proceeded to cover her eggs, beans and toast with it.
A few tables over a girl periodically glanced over at James and Elise. Elise caught sight of her and registered the face as familiar but with the hangover her brain worked twice as slowly trying to place where she knew her. After several fruitless seconds of trying Elise abandoned her mental search and returned to her breakfast. As she shov-

elled the runny eggs into her mouth the girl rose to her feet and strode over to grab a handful of serviettes from the counter before gaining the confidence to digress over to Elise's table.

She squinted at Elise affecting to recall her name before asking.

"Elise? Elise, hey."

Elise slowly turned and nodded trying to deny her headache and curdled stomach.

"Hello."

The girl rolled her eyes and revealed a haughty grin before sighing with impatience.

"Mara Chase-Worthington. We both featured at the exhibition together in Brick Lane at the Brewery a few years back."

Elise nodded as the name clicked. She would have never placed the name in the labyrinth of memories muddled further from last night.

"Oh yes. How are you, Mara?"

Mara feigned surprise. "Don't you read the Guardian? I've been short-listed for the Turner Prize. Isn't that exciting? I'm also going to be on News Night Review in two weeks' time. So, how about you? What have you been up to?"

A smile played at the corners of her mouth as she watched Elise chew her eggs deliberately.

James motioned his fork towards Mara.

"See? Didn't I tell you that if you gave anal you'd go further regardless of talent?"

Mara's face froze in horror, silenced by the surprise counter-attack. James set his cutlery down and smiled at Mara.

"You'll have to excuse Elise, dear. She's got a rather nasty hangover and breathing your dick-breath all over our food isn't helping."

A red-faced Mara slowly retreated to her table with her napkins and managed to maintain composure while she finished her tea. James chortled to himself.

"You've no idea how long I have been gagging to use the term 'dick-breath' in a sentence. No pun intended."

Elise found herself laughing despite the hangover. Her head throbbed as she chortled weakly.

"James I don't know why you don't just write those trashy novels like Jackie Collins. You're just as catty and have better insults."

"Then what would I have to agonise over? Besides; those sorts of books stopped selling after J.R. was shot."

"Well I owe thanks to my chivalrous queen. Remind me to polish your pink sceptre later."

"Oh come on. Your stuff is obviously just as good as hers if she had to come all the way over here to boast. If anything your work is probably better for her to have to even bother telling you what she's been doing."

"True, I suppose. It doesn't make it any less irritating, though. The last thing I needed this morning was her coming over and boasting while I tried not to hurl."

Elise spooned the remaining beans onto some toast and sighed to herself. "I was actually picked as one to watch in art school."

"And you've succeeded. Your work's going to be exhibited at the Zee Gallery in a week's time."

"James, the gallery's run by a friend and the show is very small."

"Well, why not go for something bigger after this?"

"I couldn't possibly. You wouldn't understand."

"Sure I would. Go on darling, indulge me."

"It's really not as easy as you think. I can't just call around and ask a gallery to put together a show for me. If it were that easy don't you think I would've done it by now?"

"I wonder."

"What's that supposed to mean?"

"All I meant was that you could do anything you want to, tiger girl. No need to take my head off."

"And I could also make a spectacular fool of myself giving people like Miss Sodomy over there the satisfaction. No thanks."

-

Ophelia slowly opened her eyes. It took a moment to recall where she was and how she got there. Much to her relief it was her flat. She looked around to see if she remembered her purse and sure enough it was upended in the corner.

"Thanks for remembering my hand bag, drunk me."

Sadly her drunken self failed to remove her trainers before getting into bed. The sheets were streaked with mud and other unthinkable elements found on floors of London buses. She bundled the bed sheets together with yesterday's smoky clothes into a pile and threw on a robe. She fumbled around the cupboards for tea and recalled that she was made redundant yesterday. She would have to get the Guardian and see what other crap jobs were out there.

Taking her tea and some digestives into the living room she noticed the answer phone light blinking. She waited for the break in between cartoons and checked the messages.

"…Hi Ophelia, it's me, Mark…Sorry I was in such a mood that night…um, you know how it is. Anyway I wanted to say thanks. If you're around some time maybe we can grab a drink or…or something. Thanks."

Her heart sank feeling regret and petty for getting so cross with him.

"Hello. I'm calling for Ophelia Graff. This is Caroline. My sister gave me your number saying you wanted to get in touch so here I am."

Ophelia fumbled for a pen to write the details down on the back of her gas bill. She was surprised and thrilled to hear from her but also nervous since it meant she would have to own up to all those shitty things she did and said to her. It was easy to write a letter and drop it in the post box but a live dialogue was a scary prospect with countless unknown variables. She reasoned that Caroline sounded friendly enough on the phone but still wasn't looking forward to admitting that she was a complete bitch to her.

Ringing Caroline actually seemed the soft option at that point. Ophelia remembered she was five hours ahead of Caroline and was able to put it off and return to the cartoons and some programme with a posh fox puppet.

-

Kat was up early to her surprise. She vaguely recalled vomiting outside the train doors before they closed on her coat. The rest of the evening came to her in flashes. She looked over at the clock and was amazed to realise she wasn't feeling ropey. She leapt out of bed and went down to make coffee. Kat felt as if she'd cheated death; she managed to avoid a hangover. She got the paper at the door and thumbed through it as she finished her coffee. About half way through the third page a dark cloud of nausea crept in. Within a half hour Kat's head throbbed and her stomach lurched with every movement. Betrayed by her own body she searched her refrigerator shelves for yoghurt. Ian came down to the kitchen and chuckled as he watched his green-faced wife try to make a smoothie with shaky hands.

"Wild night on the tiles?"

"Hardly. I was held captive at the pub with work colleagues."

"Did you have a good time at least?"

"No. I got trolleyed while I listened to them cackling about who knows what..."

"Aw, you poor thing. What are you looking for?"

"Some yoghurt to settle my stomach."

"I'll make you a fry-up. That'll help."

"Cheers, sweetie. You're so good to me."

"What time's your driving lesson today?"

"Oh fuck. I completely forgot about that. You don't seriously expect me to go in this state, do you?"

"Well we would still have to pay for the lesson and last I checked we aren't exactly rolling in money, are we?"

"No but if we both worked full-time-"

"Do you want me to add rat poison to your fry-up?? Now, you still need to learn to drive so you should go. Next time book the lesson mid-week."

"Thanks a lot, butt munch."

"What? I didn't go out on the lash last night knowing I had a driving lesson today."

Ian set the fry-up in front of Kat and grabbed a plate for himself. "So what time is the lesson then?"

Kat thought wearily and groaned. "Shit! Less than an hour."

After they finished eating Kat retreated to the sofa for a kip while Ian did the washing up. It seemed like she only just closed her eyes when the phone rang. Kat groped around for the phone and answered in the fiercest tone she could muster.

"Hello?"

"Hi. I am looking for Katherine North. Is she available?"

"This is she."

"Hello. This is Mr. Saloush from the driving school. I am waiting outside your house. Are you ready?"

"I guess. Hang on."

Kat slipped on her trainers and a baggy jumper. She couldn't understand why he hadn't simply knocked on the door. Kat kissed Ian and trudged outside. She saw a

174

man sitting in a trance-like state in the car outside her house. She approached the window and tried waving at him in vain. After rapping on the window he slowly turned his head towards her. He had eyes like an owl and wore a beige suit that blended seamlessly with the interior of the car. He held a finger up to the window and proceeded to put on his socks and shoes.

"I prefer to drive barefoot so that my feet are closer to the earth."

"Ummm, okay."

Kat waited until Mr. Saloush put on his socks and shoes and slid into the driver's seat. Mr. Saloush smiled and began to explain how she would need to be at one with the car in order to be able to drive it. Even without the hangover Kat wanted to run over Mr. Saloush. The entire lesson continued with a similar theme; Mr Saloush giving spiritual advice and Kat looking at him as if he just attempted to fornicate with her guinea pig. Kat had been driving for nearly ten years and was still uncomfortable with the concept of driving lessons. She had learned to drive in a supermarket car park with her friend's beat-up pizza delivery car and if that was good enough to get her licence then she didn't see why she should have to pay some flaky knob for lessons.

Every time she stopped too short or turned a corner too sharply, Mr. Saloush would lecture her on the importance of attending to the car's needs. Kat began to refer to him as "Mr. Slushy" and was even more amused when he didn't seem to notice. As they pulled up to Kat's street Mr. Slushy informed a rather green and poorly Kat that she would need a further five or six lessons before booking her exam. Kat looked at him incredulously and curtly nodded before hurrying in to throw up.

"So how did it go?"

175

Kat wiped her mouth with the flannel. "The guy was a complete flake! I can't believe we spent thirty quid on him. And get this; he reckons I should have another five lessons before I take the bloody test! The cheek!"

"Well, he probably knows what they'll look for on the test and wants you to succeed."

"A likely story! He probably just wants to get as much money as he can out of me. Bloody thief."

"Have a think at least. You can always shop around."

"Whatever. Why can't I just book the frigging test?"

"You can do that but it's about seventy-five quid a go and you want to be sure you get it right?"

Kat rolled her eyes as she flopped down on the sofa next to Ian and watched him playing on his game console.

"Have you told your folks about Christmas yet?"

"I will."

"We leave in three weeks. Don't you think you ought to let them know sooner rather than later?"

"I'm nearly finished with this level, love. I've been trying to get here for days. Can we please talk later?"

Kat gazed at her reflection in the window. She was heading back after attending a course on "soft skills" in Birmingham. It seemed ironic to send a large group of staff out for a two-day seminar on efficient time management though Kat wasn't about to complain about the break from Norman, Dorothy and London. As she peered at her face against the passing night sky she noted her cheeks were filling out again. A patch of acne along her chin taunted her. The GP insisted the breakouts were hormonal but Kat suspected stress. She was already fretting about the next driving lesson. The last thing she needed was some flaky weirdo criticising her. She was on edge all week anticipating an irate call from Dorothy about Christmas and how Kat single-handedly ruined it for everyone. Her absences from her desk were scrutinised to the point that every time she returned from the loo, two beady eyes would slither out from behind the monitor then quietly slink back and her overdraft was almost used up. She hadn't finished Christmas shopping plus she needed her money to pay the gas bill and get food before her next pay cheque on the 25th.

As the train pulled into Paddington Kat gathered her things and tried pushing her worries out of her head so she could focus on things like if there was anything in the house to make dinner with. As she tried to mentally picture what was in the cupboards she was surprised to see Ian on the platform waving at her.

"What are you doing here?"

Ian rushed up to hug her and took her bags. "I am taking you for dinner, wife."

"Cheers. To what do I owe this?"

"I'll tell you later. How was Birmingham?"

177

"We had to act out all these lame scenarios about teamwork. I felt trapped in an episode of Sesame Street. Things like, 'How can Andy get Emma to work more efficiently when Emma-"

"Only has one arm?"

"If only! It was far less funny. And the food was crap. One of the women in finance even got food poisoning. One pair was caught doing the nasty in the lifts and someone blew off the whole second day after a heavy drinking session the night before. Same stuff that always happens at these things, really."

"The train journey back okay?"

Kat checked her watch. "Only a half hour late so I guess. Have you been waiting long?"

"Nah, I grabbed a cup of tea and worked on that play I've been doing with Joe."

"Cool. So where are we going to eat then?"

"I figured we could go for Thai?"

"Sounds good."

The restaurant was nearly full as they sat down. Ian had made a reservation the night before. Ian ordered a bottle of wine. He smiled excitedly as his hands fidgeted about the table. Kat sighed and focused her attention on Ian. She was trying to mentally organise her chores and schedule for the week. Ian poured her some wine and waved a hand to bring her attention back to the table.

"Okay, now we're seated and have wine. Tell me the big news."

"Get this; Joe has some friends in Toronto that loved the script. They want to do it in Toronto next summer."

"You're joking!."

"I know! They're going to give us a nice bit of dosh, travel over there and everything."

"Ian, that's great! So are we going to Toronto for the summer?"

"We'll be there for at least three months, though they reckon it will probably run for at least six, maybe more."

"What about the house?"

"We can rent it out or something. Who knows, maybe we'll like it so much we'll end up selling it and living there."

"So this is that top secret project you've been working on with Joe? I thought maybe you decided you liked wearing my knickers or something. So can you tell me about the play now?"

"It's actually a musical about a brothel and we've called it 'Clap! The Musical!' It's very blue, but Joe reckons they'll love it in Toronto. Joe did all the songs. He reckons if it does well in Toronto we could even get it in San Francisco and Sydney. My head's spinning at how quick it's all happening. I only just got the call this morning and thought I'd surprise you. This is it, Kat! I've finally got my foot in the door! We'll probably want to head over to Toronto in June and since you are my lovely missus we should have no trouble getting you working papers. So, what do you think?"

"Wow. That's great! You've finally hit it with your writing. Joe must be thrilled."

"He is. Normally he only ever does music and cabaret banter but he was great to work with."

"And you knocked that script together in no time at all. That's fantastic."

Kat fell in love with her husband all over again. She thought she gave up hoping after years of disappointment and was surprised to have all the old feelings flourish over dinner. After years of support and encouragement every time he was told they'd call him, she felt vindicated for her perseverance. They laughed and joked like they used to. The meal managed to wipe clean the dusty surface of their marriage, the resentments and frustrations. They managed to recapture that elusive feeling of when they were young and optimistic and in love.

After dinner they went for pints and drank enough to think that dancing would be fun. They made their way over to the Borderline for sloppy dancing and tequila shots. The lights, smoke and playlist made them feel ten years younger. At two in the morning Kat and Ian laughed at each other covered in sweat and out of breath as they stumbled on the night bus. They shared a bag of chips with fried chicken on their way to the mini cab office in Leyton. While they waited for the driver, Ian grabbed Kat and kissed her hard on the mouth. Her whole body lit up with a new sensation as if it were a handsome stranger instead of her husband. Kat swooned when Ian put his arm round her in the cab. She leaned over clumsily and whispered with a slur, "I can't wait to get you home."

They woke in the middle of the afternoon. Clothes were littered about the hall. Kat rolled over and snuggled into Ian's chest. The sun slipped through the curtains. She wished every night could be as perfect. She pattered down to the kitchen and switched on the kettle. She decided to surprise him with a nice eggs and sausages for breakfast. Ian rubbed his eyes as she brought the tray in.

"Wow, cheers love."

Kat shrugged modestly as she set it down on the bed. As they sat up, Kat looked over at the wardrobe.

"Where are the big suitcases?"

"Hmm?"

"The ones we used when we went to Spain."

"Ah, they're in the Wendy house."

"You mean our garage?"

"Yeah."

"I should get them out this weekend. I can't believe we're finally going! That reminds me. Did your mum take it okay over dinner on Tuesday?"

Ian fell silent and paused uncomfortably as he picked at his eggs. Her blood ran cold. She could feel a lump form in her throat and a wrench tighten a valve in her heart.

"Did you wuss out again?"

Ian grew red.

"I'm afraid not. Actually, I wanted to tell you last night but a good time never presented itself."

Kat felt sick.

"Tell me what?"

"I told my folks about how we were probably going to Canada this summer and that we'd probably be away for at least six months and my mum was heartbroken."

"Heartbroken she'd have to meddle over the phone or the internet? Heartbroken you finally have an opportunity to be happy and successful in your career? Or heartbroken that she's lost control over you since you've grown up? If that's the case she shouldn't worry. Getting married didn't seem to change anything, did it?"

Ian dismissed her comment. "She looked really gutted. I just couldn't bear telling her that I wouldn't be home for Christmas. She would've gone to pieces. I'm her only son, she's got that chest thing so she's quite frail and her brother and his family are in Lapland with their grandkids so she would be alone with dad this year. I couldn't break her heart, Kat. I knew you'd be with Beth and your friends and have loads of catching up so if anything I thought I'd be in the way. I was going to change my ticket so that I'll fly out after Boxing Day on the 27th. I know it's last minute but this play just came up and they were keen in Toronto, which changes everything."

"Maybe for you. But what about me? We aren't all just supporting roles in the theatre of your fucking life. It isn't always about you. You know what? Don't bother with the ticket. I don't want you there at all. And since I paid for the tickets I'd have to sort it." Tears of anger and disappointment welled in Kat's eyes as she tried to make sense if what Ian was telling her. "I can't fucking believe you."

"I know you're upset, but I hope you can see how important it is to my parents. I know you guys don't get on but they are my folks and I love them. There will be so many more Christmas days for us. My parents aren't going to be around forever."

Kat's eyes became daggers and her lip trembled. She could feel that familiar pit in her chest of disappointment and resentment glowing red and black like coal.

Ian grew exasperated. "This is hard for me, too! I want to spend Christmas with both of you and it's just not possible. Have you ever thought about how hard this is on me? It feels like you're always trying to get me to pick a side and I just can't do it."

"I see." Kat calmly got to her feet and stalked off to the shower. She grew angrier as she sat under the stream of water. The betrayal felt sharper after such a great night. Her tears mingled with the suds as she reviewed her options. She could hear Ian walking around outside and then the front door close. She heaved a sigh as she stepped out and towelled off. After dressing, she went and got her luggage and threw in everything she could think of.

She ignored the phone ringing knowing it was probably her driving instructor or Doro-thy, which was the last thing she needed. She went out and grabbed two suitcases.

She tried to fit as much stuff as possible in them. After packing, she grabbed a sheet of paper and wrote a quick note to Ian:

"Ian, I am going to stay at Elise's before leaving for the states. Don't bother coming to the exhibition. I'd rather not see you. I'll ring you when I get to Boston.
-Kat"

She rang a taxi and waited.

-

Ophelia thumbed through the jobs pages of the Guardian carelessly as the train lurched forward. She was meeting Kat at South Woodford to help her bring her baggage to Elise's. As she scanned the jobs on offer it occurred to Ophelia that she really had no idea what she wanted to do next. Anxiety grew and she folded the paper into her bag. She reasoned that with three paid months off would give her plenty of time to figure it all out. The unknown seemed exciting and full of options that wouldn't normally be available. She could look into working for a charity or even changing fields altogether.

Passengers gradually trickled out between Mile End and Leytonstone. The sky was thick with grey. Formations of birds seemed to be hurrying to warmer, sunnier skies to escape the grotty and worn Christmas decorations grimly hung on the lamp posts. The train pulled into the station and Ophelia caught sight of Kat leaning against the wall beside two large suitcases and a rucksack. She looked small and nervous next to the oversized luggage. She scanned the crowd and gave a weary smile when she spotted her friend.

Ophelia nimbly cut through the crowd and embraced Kat in an encouraging hug.

"You okay?"

She mustered a tearful nod and fished for a tissue.

"Look, it'll be fine. Honest."

They dragged the cases onto the train carriage and sat.

"Can you imagine how often Dorothy would've called if you did take Ian? Seriously the holiday would have sucked."

"Now I get to go alone."

"Kat, I can take the spare ticket if you like. I never have plans for Christmas and so much time off at the minute. I could rent a car and drive to Buffalo or take the train up."

"Really?"

"Yeah. With the exchange rate it's probably cheaper anyway. When do you leave?"

"Week and a half?"

"Great. I'll ring the ticket agent at Elise's and arrange a transfer. Piece of piss."

"Really? That would be great! I'm so out of pocket now."

"My pleasure. I've a few people I was hoping to see so it works for me. Then I can put off job hunting to the New Year."

"Thanks so much."

Elise woke with a start. Twilight purples and pinks glowed against the broken slats on the blinds. She was surprised to be up so early after staying so late at the gallery fussing her exhibit. She walked through the doors several times trying to see the pieces with virgin eyes. She rolled over to face the window. Elise was determined to don a mask of apathy concerning the show but over the past 24 hours the mask would slip to reveal genuine excitement. When Zee approached her about featuring in the gallery she had shrugged and mumbled a cool assent. After she received the floor plan and noticed her work would feature as the central part of the show, a small yet stubborn seed of enthusiasm took root.

Elise tended that seed like a cactus, feeding it as little as possible and keeping a safe distance. She was petrified that something would fall through at the last minute or go pear-shaped as things often do. Or worse, Zee would change his mind and go with an edgier or more provocative artist. Only after she gingerly placed the double-decker bus on the Scalectrix track in the actual gallery did she dare breathe in the intoxicating bouquet of exhilaration. She stepped back and allowed herself to finally admire her ideas and dreams on display. The physical manifestations of late nights, inarticulate furies and passions under spotlights with placards bearing her name sent a chill down her neck.

Viewing her finished pieces Elise was suddenly struck by how much she missed Laura. Laura could have been there to help her set up, suggesting different angles or chiding Elise for not doing the show sooner.

Tears fell on the gallery's wooden floor as she recalled how often Laura encouraged her to organise an exhibition.

"Here it is," she mused aloud.

She fished around in her pocket and found a pen. She walked through the two rooms looking at all of her pieces on display and stopped at the medicine cabinet of fallen idols. The iconic faces beamed out of medicine boxes and bottles all gone in their prime. She scrawled "For Laura" on the placard and headed home.

As she lay in bed reviewing the layout in her head, apprehension crept in the dark corners of her room. She could see everyone hating the exhibition or just not showing up at all. The latter left her petrified. She cringed at the notion of waiting for everyone in an empty gallery with Zee trying to appear unruffled, sneaking sheepish glances at her. Unable to bear that situation, Elise rolled over and groped around the floor for the box of pastries she had the foresight to grab last night.

Sweet dark patches indicated where the frosting or jam had collected while she slept. There was no middle ground with day-old baked goods; either they were absolutely scrummy moist and sticky or insipid, dry and impossible to bite into. The iced fingers were delicious. Elise tried to retrace her route to the bakers so that she could go again after a night on the tiles while she licked the cream from her fingers. After finishing a half-eaten Bakewell tart, Elise reluctantly checked her emails. She dreaded all the last minute cancellations peppered with weak excuses or insincere apologies.

There always seemed to be a huge drop-off in the day or hours before an event. This always happened without fail in London. It could be a birthday party organised at Nobu or even a launch party for a film or magazine and a handful of supposed mates would meekly beg off or simply not show up at all. She reasoned that an early notice was better than expecting all and seeing no one. She already knew her parents wouldn't be there. This broke her heart.

They were on a cruise someplace or other. After her father went into semi-retirement her parents were determined to see the world via luxury travel. They seemed to be on the run from time or eluding the ageing process. Elise would often joke, calling them time fugitives. Inevitably they always returned tanned and slightly more wrinkled than when they last left. They'd ask her to repeat what she said or squint at the Telegraph crossword puzzles. And they never seemed to take an interest in her life or passions. She felt bitter in the knowledge that they would've happily taken an active role in a lifestyle choice made to reflect their own.

She was disappointed despite being emotionally prepared for the inevitable. They had defended their absence claiming that the trip had been booked ages ago and that the Worthingtons were depending on them. Elise nodded and thought ruefully that they would have cancelled their trip if she were getting married to some well-bred ponce with a double barrel name or if she were speaking at a law congress or baby baptism if she ever decided to have a baby.

None of those events had ever remotely interested Elise. She tried convincing herself that it didn't matter much, but deep down it mattered more than she cared to admit. Her parents always asked after her work and offered to invest but never managed to make it to any of her shows or openings that her work featured in. Even at university her parents seemed to stay away. It was almost like they were punishing her for choosing a path they couldn't understand.

Her father seemed so sure she would go into law after her "rebellious patch". And if not as a barrister than surely as a PA. Her mother thought she would just marry a lawyer, have babies and move close by. At first they humoured her decision to get an arts degree. At 27 it wasn't funny anymore. Part of Elise wanted to please her parents and earn their approval but everything that would make them happy would have driven Elise mad.

190

She scanned all the "good lucks" or "something's come ups" and wondered what sort of flowers they'd have sent to the gallery. She tried to hint at how important this particular exhibition was to her. They would probably send a really extravagant bouquet of some type of rose she never heard of. Flowers depressed her. They died within a week. Then they grew mouldy or furry as a final insult. A nice box of chocolates or bottle of wine would be more appreciated. Her parents actually showing up and expressing their approval would be ideal.

She scrolled through the messages and was surprised to see only a handful of cancellations. She wanted to relax but then worried that not a soul emailed to say they would be coming, either. She forced her features to maintain an outward calm or apathy in preparation for the big event. Mahesh would tease her about her seeming aloof. He'd come out of his room and cross his arms over his chest and tilt his head saying, "Whatever! I could care less!"

This was always said in a musical Hindustani accent. Elise loved to hear him speak. His voice was one of the reasons she had chosen him as a housemate. James thought it crazy when she had told him but after three months without missing any rent or utilities and delicious meals, he ate his words.

Elise scanned piles of clothes on the floor and in her wardrobe. She wanted something happy and shiny. She wanted to have already picked out an outfit but was afraid if she planned ahead it would have jinxed everything. Her eyes caught sight of a silver shimmer and remembered picking up a sequinned tube dress in Shoreditch. There was electric blue hair colour that she saw yesterday in Camden and figured the ensemble would go great with her knee-high combat boots once she polished them.

Elise drew a bath and made a pot of tea. She grabbed the newspaper from the door-step and took the supplements upstairs. She threw in some bags of chamomile tea to the steaming water and willed herself to relax. Her shock of hair sat under a small freezer bag covered in blue. The best thing about early Saturday mornings was the absolute silence in a house normally populated with telly, radio, show tunes, scream-ing and laughing. Everyone was either asleep or still hadn't come home. As one of the loudest residents, Elise was surprised how delightful the quiet was.

By 11a.m. Elise shimmered and her shiny boots reached her knobbly knees. She grabbed a warm pullover and crept to the kitchen for some food. Joe lumbered through the door with his feathery boudoir slippers and kimono scratching his nether regions, yawning.

"Today's the big day, innit?"

"Yeah."

"And you're all kitted out for opening night. You scrub up well, love."

"Cheers."

"At least now I know not to wear the same dress. No sequins, I promise."

"I reckon I could take you in a catfight if you show up in the same thing."

Joe erupted in a merry laughter.

"Pah! Someone's jealous. I weigh twice as much and make grown men faint in my sparkly frocks."

"I somehow don't think it was the frocks."

Joe smiled slyly and hugged her.

"Where are you off to?"

"Just going to run some errands and head straight to the gallery. Might have a kip there before we open."

"I'll see you there tonight. Just give me a bell if you need anything."

Elise shrugged on her big green army coat and whispered her thanks before slipping out into the brisk grey of November.

-

A brief flurry of sleet swirled in the yellow glow of the streetlamps. Winter had officially arrived with the promise of a frost to leave the grass coated like sugar and stain-glass crystals across the windows in the morning. Ophelia vainly hoped the snow would settle so she could stay in and fix hot chocolate like she did in Maine when she was twenty years younger. Instead she wrapped up and headed to Elise's opening. Being redundant freed her up to help Elise, watch talk shows and sleep a lot. Most mornings she slept until 10 or 11. She figured everyone did this after they stopped working. The first few days were heaven. She lounged about, did her nails, touched up the paint in the hall, took an afternoon yoga class and downloaded a complicated torte recipe off the internet. She was more than happy to help Elise and give herself some purpose or direction.

Convinced nobody would bother showing, Elise opened one of the bottles of wine her parents sent down to use for the opening in their absence. James laughed and assured her that he and Jo had both personally promised sexual favours to all of their press contacts. Ophelia and Kat assured her that since there would be good plonk they'd be turning people away. It was odd to see Elise nervous about anything as she was normally confident or apathetic about everything. Had anyone else been anxious Ophelia would understand but was surprised about Elise. Ophelia couldn't stop thinking of how Elise paced and fretted while she waited for the tube.

It never ceased to amaze her how appallingly bad the Underground was. It didn't seem to matter if you travelled during rush hour or the middle of the day. And the weekends were full of delays like signal failures or partial or complete line closures for track maintenance. The passengers were aggressive and it was expensive. It was a cruel tease to have so much happening in the city and unreliable means of getting anywhere. She hoped that it being a weekend would make the journey more pleasant but it was crowded in the carriage and fraught with delays.

It was foolish of her to assume the Northern line would actually be operating a smooth running service, especially on a weekend. They were stuck in a tunnel for a good twenty minutes. The tunnel was probably next to the earth's core since it was the archaic Northern Line and sweltering despite the carriage being half full. There was no way for to her to assure Elise she was on her way. She began to remove her scarf and gloves resigned to the situation. It took a few moments to realise that while she was vexed, she was still a lot calmer than she'd normally be. As they sat in the carriage the lights flickered, reflecting the passengers' waning hopes of making their engagements in a timely fashion. Passengers shook their heads, or rolled their eyes. Some supped lager from cans to ensure that they'd be on equal ground with their mates waiting at the pub.

194

Having no lager or novel Ophelia reflected on her free time and grinned, thinking that she was being paid to sleep late, watch Richard and Judy, eat biscuits and loiter about the flat. It was a bit disappointing that the only thing she managed to do was update her CV and clean her flat. She used to spend hours at her desk begrudging the job for keeping her hostage from more important projects like making a short documentary, redecorating her flat, repairing the airing cupboard, learning Spanish or even getting winter clothes out of storage. Instead she procrastinated. She resolved to make a to-do list next week and set the alarm for 9am every day. The train staggered forward and slowly made it to the next platform. Everyone gave a sarcastic cheer which was followed by a jeer when the conductor announced the train would be terminating at the station.

Ophelia made a beeline for the station exit and headed out to hail a taxi. It was a surprisingly clear but cold night. As they drove up Charing Cross Rd she saw groups of women in feathers and horns on hen nights, blokes already pissing in doorways, couples with linked arms weaving slowly through the swarm of theatre-goers and clusters of people heading to parties or piss-ups with cold white wisps of breath sneaking through woolly scarves. The queue at the cash point was peppered with the usual suspects of a Saturday night. Clubbers, families, uni students all standing around waiting to get money out to spend, lose or have taken from them in what they hope to be a memorable night out.

Ophelia made it to the gallery a mere twenty minutes after she promised to be there. Elise didn't see her arrive. She was busy nodding with wine glass in hand at some bloke gesticulating excitedly. He wore an intense expression to match his suit though the pile of dreads sitting atop his skull seemed incongruous. The place was by no means full but there was certainly a decent crowd for that time of night. She hoped Elise was happy with the initial turnout at any rate although it was hard to tell as the gesticulator was now turning red and appeared to be tracing doodle in the air for his captive's benefit. Ophelia was tempted to intervene but wanted to see if he would start doing charades next.

Ophelia made her way to the wine table, following the exchange with her eyes until an elaborately dressed man minced by on shiny pink stiletto heels. The shoes were actually the most conservative part of his ensemble, her gaze discovered. He appeared to be sporting a floor-length ball-gown made entirely of doll shoes. She was captivated at the detail. Shoes in pink, black, blue and silver reached the floor in a fairy-tale train. The bodice hugged his hairy chest alluding to many hours wiled away at the gym. He had a blue bee-hive wig with a few pairs of Barbie and Cindy shoes dotted throughout but for some reason he decided to keep his handle-bar moustache. He caught Ophelia's gaze and waved coquettishly as she waited for her glass of wine.

"That is a beautiful dress."

"Cheers. I made it myself."

"Wow. It must've taken ages."

"It wasn't too bad. Lucky I have a friend who works with toy companies."

"Ah. Are you here for Elise's exhibit?"

"In this get-up? Darling I'm exhibiting here tonight as well."

"Ah. I see. Is this your first show then?"

"No, I've been around for ages. Is Elise a friend of yours then?"

"Yeah. It's her first big show."

"Really? I would have figured she'd been around judging by the size and spectrum of the collection."

"I think she just puts things off."

"Well, do check out my work. If you like the dress, I'm sure you'd enjoy it, sweetie."

"Cheers."

He turned heel and scurried over to a crowd of people emerging from the coatroom. Ophelia sipped the wine and was surprised at the quality. Usually whenever wine was free it was certain to resemble drain cleaner or be watered down. She surveyed the room and noticed a subdued Kat coming out of the coat check.

"Have you heard from Ian?"

"Nope. The airline rang back and asked if you would mind flying out on the 18th instead of with me. They were oversubscribed but it does save you on fees so you're just paying the airfare."

"Sure. I'm easy. How are things at Elise's?"

"Good. Glad the show's doing well."

"I know. She was so nervous about the opening night. So he hasn't called at all?"

"Nope."

"Aren't you worried?"

"He's probably stuck on some level of a video game or at his parents' house being spoiled rotten."

"How are the driving lessons?"

Kat rolled her eyes. "The instructor is a complete donut. I find it ridiculous that I've been driving for over ten years without incident and this knob seems to find fault with everything I do."

"If it makes you feel any better, I didn't pass the test until the sixth attempt."

"If the frigging test is so bloody hard, why are they such bad drivers?"

"They're no worse than Boston drivers."

"All the stupid cars with lights under them, blaring out noisy bass thumps, driving down residential streets like they they're on the fucking M25."

"I think that has more to do with you living in Essex, dear. It just so happens that Essex is the boy racer capital of England."

"How is the wine?"

"Surprisingly tolerable. Shall we get trolleyed on Elise's parents?"

"Hmmm, sounds like a plan. Let's see her exhibit over our first glass so we have clear heads, though."

"Good idea."

Despite having seen her work at her house Ophelia was still impressed by the layout as they walked in the first room. She could've easily seen these pieces in any of the museums. She was really moved by the pride she felt for Elise as they surveyed the room. People pointed and debated over her work and she felt a warm flutter in her chest for Elise.

"Oh wow." Kat murmured as she caught sight of Elise's homage to her friend's mother -in-law. "All of Dorothy's clippings…," she mulled as she bent down to admire the shoes and surreptitiously peeked to see if there were indeed clipper knickers (there weren't). She smiled slyly as she scanned all the clippings that she had accumulated over five years. It was satisfying to see them put to use.

"Hey, I thought I saw you both come in."

They hugged Elise and babbled praises to her. Ophelia playfully ran her fingers through Elise's blue shock of hair.

"I was going to say hello but you were busy being talked at. By that guy in the suit."

"Oh, him!" Elise laughed it off and focused on her Joan Crawford sculpture. Elise gestured at the steely, provocative glare and perfectly formed brows. "What do you think?"

"It's amazing! Thank you so much for taking the clippings! I can't think of a more perfect use for them. I absolutely love it!"

"It's yours."

"Fuck you! No way!"

"I insist."

"You'd fetch loads for it."

"You have it. No one else I know would appreciate it quite like you will, I'm sure."

Kat eyed her sceptically. "I couldn't possibly."

"Kat, it's nearly Christmas. Consider it a gift for the yuletide season and say thanks, you ungrateful bint."

Kat fluttered her lashes, clearly touched. "Thank you."

"Everything looks really great." Ophelia raised her glass.

"Cheers, Feelie. I'm just glad there was any turnout at all. Oh, Steve the solicitor is here tonight. I'll have to introduce you. He mentioned that he's been quite busy lately so if you start to tire of the idle life..."

"Erm. Thanks."

"I've got to say hi to some people that just arrived. We'll catch up later?"

It was a great night especially since the bar seemed to have an infinite supply of wine. Ophelia busied herself throughout the evening with trips to the bar topping up hers, Kat's and anyone else who seemed to be running low on drink. It was on one of the trips that she ran into Elise and Steve.

"Ophelia, this is Steve."

Steve smiled. He was wearing a suit and had to be at least ten years older. Ophelia smiled and mumbled a greeting as she groped for his hand to shake. She regretted drinking all that wine as both her head and tongue felt thick and fuzzy. Steve seemed nice enough from her slightly blurred vantage point. On closer inspection his teeth were a bit wonky and he seemed almost cartoonishly bashful. As Elise receded into the bustle of the crowd Ophelia smiled and stiffened in an admittedly drunken fashion. After a few awkward moments, she relented.

"Elise tells me you're a solicitor."

Steve smiled and nodded. Ophelia tilted her head to the left and asked "So what do you think of it?"

He looked startled as he pointed behind her. "That?"

She turned to find a large canvas full of naked people missing limbs with mouthfuls of bloody flesh and began to giggle uncontrollably. Steve relaxed and joined her laughter. They turned to the painting and continued to snigger as others looked on with concern. Steve seemed more at ease as he asked her all sorts of questions about herself, current affairs and modern art. She reckoned it would have been stimulating conversation had she been sober.

After the gallery began to empty Ophelia went in search of Kat and finally found her having a kip on the sofa. She was curled up and her heels dug into the fabric. A light flashed and she turned to see Elise lower a camera. She teetered over and thanked Ophelia for coming.

"It was a fab opening. I wouldn't have missed it for anything."

"Yeah, I guess life surprises you sometimes."

"I'm not at all surprised."

"Thanks."

"How long has Kat been sleeping here?"

"I think Steve was a bit smitten with you," Elise sang. "I reckon he'd pay you just to take him to lunch."

"Right now I'm happy watching daytime television, but I'll keep it in mind. Did you sell any pieces tonight?"

"Yes. The medicine cupboards are all going to loving homes. The Scalectrix set is being featured in the Guardian and the Ecologist magazine."

Kat stirred gently so they bundled into a cab. They drove past clubbers waiting for night buses, couples rowing outside of cars, yobs vomiting over kerbs and crowded kebab shops with lines snaking around the corner. Kat sighed as she kicked off her shoes and sank into the sofa. Elise found some crisps and a box of Jaffa Cakes in the cupboard.

"Shall we have these with wine or tea?"

Kat squinted at the tray of junk food and opted for wine which they had plenty of. Kat produced a pack of fags that she found in the gallery. She lit two and handed one to Ophelia. Elise poured some wine into some mugs and set them down. Kat eagerly inhaled.

"Thanks again for letting me stay over. Do you think I'm over-reacting about this?"

Ophelia sat across them and waved the smoke away with a magazine. "I'd be upset. It's hard to say since I'm not married and hate Christmas."

"It just seems so cowardly. He accused me of forcing him to choose when I've done no such thing! I've spent every fucking Christmas at his parents' since we've been married. Now I finally get tickets -two tickets that I paid for!!- to America for Christmas and you'd think he'd be okay with coming with me. Like it's not as important because I don't really have family. What the fuck?"

"And he hasn't called. Or has he, Elise?"

"No. Nothing."

"This year meant so much to me. I'm not even sure I'll still be married to him next Christmas."

"You've been so supportive to him. What's one Christmas?"

"Or I'm finally realising his parents mean more to him than I do."

"Maybe he's more scared of his mother than he is of you?"

"Feelie, it shouldn't be about fear."

"I may go and not come back."

"Elise! Phone for you!"

Jo sang up the stairs. Elise reluctantly trudged downstairs trailing her duvet. She had been spending the nights at the galleries or making up lost time with friends and then sleeping all day. She was still feeling depressed but figured getting out at night was betting than not going at all.

"Your majesty, the phone awaits." Jo bowed and presented the receiver. Elise snatched it with a tired sneer.

"Hello. Elise? My name is Lorna and I'm ringing from the Opti-Level agency. We saw your pieces in the Guardian and were hoping you might be free for a chat?"

"Um, okay. That sounds great. When did you have in mind?"

"How are you fixed for this afternoon, perhaps 3.30?"

Elise looked around for a clock and found she had five hours. "Sure." Elise groped around the desk for a pen and scrap of paper to take he address details down. She replaced the handset in its cradle and felt a small rush of exhilaration. To have any response from the show was good and a meeting was even more encouraging. Apprehension loomed but Elise blocked it out of her mind as she looked for clean clothes and laid them out. She reasoned they simply wanted to purchase a piece and wanted to negotiate a price. She lay down and set the alarm for 1.00.

She dreamt of a red balloon floating through Brick Lane. The sky was a vivid blue and the street was deserted. The buildings and shop fronts were awash in grey. Elise chased the balloon which maintained its distance. Faster and faster her legs pumped yet further and further the balloon drifted. She swung her arms in rhythm with her feet and gracefully alighted. As if it were the most natural thing she treaded the air in pursuit of the red balloon. She glided past the gherkin and around St Paul's Cathedral as the balloon casually soared ahead of her.

The wind tickled the stubble atop her head as she followed the red balloon to the top of the OXO tower. As she flew closer, she noticed a figure sitting on the tower waving. Laura was there waiting on the ledge above the "X". Her bare feet dangled over the side as she reached out and grasped the white string of the balloon. She smiled as she handed it to Elise who landed lightly on the ledge next to her. Laura kissed her on the cheek as she wrapped the string around her wrist. Elise hugged Laura then held out the balloon and stepped off the ledge. After a sharp dip the red balloon carried her high into the sky above the city. She felt giddy watching the buildings and the Thames shrink gradually from sight and be swallowed by the vibrant blue sky that seemed to stretch for infinity.

She woke to the faint buzzing of the alarm and was a little sad to have left the dream. Her flight felt so real. She showered quickly, watching the water turn blue from her fading lock of hair. After digging around under her bed, she finally unearthed a portfolio and threw in some of the brochures from her exhibit as well as some socks. She dressed hastily to avoid fretting or changing her mind and dashed downstairs for some toast.

Elise caught the bus to the Tube station. The red stood out at her as she fondly recalled the giddy feeling in her dream. The only free seat was across a man holding a sleeping toddler. The toddler, a girl, looked about 3 and was curled up on her father's lap secure and warm in a think pick coat and moonboots. Her face had been painted like an exotic butterfly with sparkling gold and purple hearts and stars. Elise smiled as she watched the girl sleeping soundly while her father read a Chinese newspaper. She yearned to be that girl for that moment or to even have a moment like that in her own memory for reference so that she could always return to it when she was lonely or depressed.

Elise thought of that girl throughout her journey on the bus and the District Line until she reached St James's Park. After that she grew nervous. Her suit suddenly felt ill-fitting and she worried about being too cold in only her scarf and hat. Her portfolio looked old and dirty from its hibernation under her bed. She looked at her watch and knew she simply had to press on and meet Lorna.

When she reached the door, Elise reminded herself that she didn't really need any-thing from the agency and if they weren't happy with her they could just as well sod off for all she cared. She threw her shoulders back and approached the reception desk. The receptionist asked her fill in the guestbook and gave her a mug of tea.

Elise looked around the waiting area. The sofas were a bright lime green and seemed cartoonish against the shiny white walls and matching floor tiles. A big screen broad-casted music videos above a shelf showcasing awards Elise had never before heard of. The pictures framed on the walls were advertisements Elise recognised from the Tube and billboards. She blew in her tea and warmed her hands on the sides of the chunky orange mug while she sank into the sofa. A middle-aged woman strode in wearing layers of monochromatic grey knits.

"You must be Elise. Hello, I'm Lorna. Thanks for coming on such short notice. Our Creative Director loved your work."

Elise clutched her mug as she rose to her feet and shook her hand. "Cheers."

Elise followed Lorna down a corridor and into a board room. A bloke was sitting at the table roughly ten years older than Elise poring over some stills. He waved as they came in and stood to greet Elise. "Hi, I'm Marcus Stephens, creative director. Thanks for coming on such short notice."

"Thanks for inviting me."

Lorna gestured for Elise to sit. "We saw the review in the Guardian and Marcus popped over to view your work at the gallery. We were keen to see you today since we currently have an account that looked like it might cleave nicely with your talents."

Elise nodded as she sipped her tea, unsure how to respond. Lorna continued after a few moments.

"Basically, one of our biggest clients is the government. They commission us to create, manage and distribute most of their public service campaigns. This particular account is sensitive and could use some new creative talent behind it and we are also trying to expand the teams. When Marcus saw your work he was quite keen to have you come in and meet us. How does this sound so far?"

"Great. Although I'm not sure what you're proposing?"

"To start, we'd give you a small project on a freelance basis. You'd come in a few days a week, work with myself and a few others on the account and then we'd go from there. Does this sound like something you'd be interested in?"

"Sure." Elise was utterly dumbfounded. The idea of having a brief and a deadline seemed both thrilling and suffocating. Marcus smiled.

"It'll give us both a chance to see how a long-term contract or permanent role would fit. The initial project will be for 30 days."

Lorna then cut in and began to speak about the agency and campaigns it managed previously and the work involved. Elise had a hard time taking all of the information in. She had no idea at all that is was a job interview. The idea of working at an agency never interested her although working on a government account seemed a noble enough cause as opposed to doing ads for some lager or leisurewear company. The idea of doing respectable work involving creativity seemed attractive. As they reviewed the brief with Elise, she took down some notes and met some of the other people working on the account. Elise agreed to come in on Monday to get started. On the bus ride home she realised that it was the first serious job she ever had. Her blood ran cold and the fear set in.

-

Kat looked out the small oval window trying to make out how much had changed since she left five years ago. The muted light for the seatbelt sign blinked off and the passengers swelled up en masse to retrieve their luggage from the overhead compartments. Everyone seemed to be full of anticipation, relief, anxiety or some emotion that would get them off the plane as soon as possible. Kat looked over at the empty seat beside her and felt waves of rage, disappointment and resentment wash over her numb emotional shores. She resolved not to think about Ian for the duration of her trip and focus on enjoying herself.

She watched others file past and began to worry that nothing would be as she left it or that all her friends would have forgotten her, letting the busy every day of their lives fill the gap she left moving to London. As the last few OAPs trudged off the cabin a sterile quiet filled the space. It made the white, slushy scene outside the window seem like a snow globe that she could turn upside down. A tired stewardess spotted her and marched over swiftly. Kat noticed as the stewardess progressed down the aisle her drawn and tired expression transformed before her. A smile blinked as quickly as the no smoking light and her shoulders fell back giving her more height. Kat admired her ability to adapt – or at least appear to- for small tasks and wished she could ask what her secret was. It had to be part of the airline stewardess training or something. Kat wondered if prostitutes and politicians had to attend similar seminars.

The stewardess seemed to glide towards her without making a sound. She cocked her head slightly and gingerly placed a hand on the headrest before her.

"Are you all right, ma'am?"

Kat winced at the title she had been addressed with as if the flight had suddenly aged her.

"Yes, of course. I just thought I'd wait a few moments before gathering my things."

She got to her feet and stretched before gathering her bags. Kat stuffed a wave of bitterness deep within her chest thinking of how she would have to laugh off coming to Boston alone to all of her friends. She hadn't decided whether to make up a story or just tell everyone the truth. Either way she knew they would all side with her immediately and she would worry that she was painting an unfair picture of Ian.

Logan airport seemed almost provincial despite being a busy destination in its own right. The halls were vacant with familiar tiling on the floors she remembered from grade school. Flags hung limply depicting various countries and cast long shadows. As she waited in line at customs she reflected on the state of her marriage. Obviously there were issues but it wasn't until she had lugged her suitcase through Heathrow by herself that she realised how much ill will had built up within her. She had been smothering her discontent for so long that the recent tear enabled it to seep out at an alarming rate. Ian loved her and treated her well enough. He never yelled or laid a finger on her, which was an achievement when she compared him against some of the jerks she had dated. On the other hand, Ian hadn't earned much money or respect in all the time she'd known him and often seemed to accept defeat without a fight. And for whatever reason he never seemed to defend her against his parents. She juggled these sentiments as she watched the customs line shrink.

Focusing on the row ahead of her she was surprised to see so many Americans returning from other countries. Admittedly, most appeared to be on business but she did spot the odd fat tourist who had exchanged their teddy bear pullover for a Union Jack one. The accents that surrounded her were a comfort in their familiarity. Recognition perked her ears at phrases she used years ago being spoken behind her. As she reached the desk she noticed the officer was about her own age and was surprised how much younger she really was when she left. He scanned her passport and looked at her.

"You live over there now?"

Kat smiled and reviewed her stock of excuses for leaving America. They would always come in handy when a fellow American would sneer and accuse her of being unpatriotic.

"Yes, sir. I'm visiting family for Christmas."

He smiled and shook his head.

"I don't blame you. I'd move out, too."

Kat smiled and nodded to cover her shock. He waved her through and she scurried towards the baggage reclaim. As the cases and bags paraded past like jaded beauty pageant contestants Kat felt lonely. Ian would often provide funny commentary about the carousel as if it were a NASCAR race in slow motion or a surreal catwalk full of deformed spacemen. She recalled a long weekend they had taken with Elise and her one-time partner, Aaron, to Prague. Elise suggested they attach letters to the baggage that passed by more than once. Ian happily grabbed a pen and paper to scribble desperate notes like "I thought you'd never come! Hold me!" or "I feel abandoned and think I need a hug or therapy." They all fell about laughing as Ian gleefully attached the letters to the baggage. Kat smiled before she spotted her luggage and reverted to her angry setting.

After finding the shuttle to the rental car company she finally was in the parking lot and was told to pick from a selection of cars in her price band. Kat had to remind herself to get in on the other side of the rental car and took a few moments to review the interior of the vehicle. As she familiarised herself with the features and lights she dialled home on her mobile. Part of her was keen to leave the call a few hours and make him worry but was also keen to hear his voice despite her feelings. The phone rang once.

"Hello?"

"Hey. It's me. I'm just calling to let you know the plane didn't crash."

"Did you have a good flight?"

"Eh. The food was rubbish but the films were good."

"Isn't that always the way?"

"Did I wake you?"

"No, just going through some edits."

"Good."

"Yeah. Where are you?"

"In the rental car lot."

"Did they give you a nice car?"

"Yeah. I just hope I remember how to drive it."

"You'll be fine."

"Well I'd better let you get some sleep."

"I miss you."

"Well, you didn't have to."

Kat hung up quickly and switched her phone off. She opened the window and lit a fag to will herself not to get emotional. She took the hurt and folded it like an origami crane. She tucked it away deep in her heart among all the other disappointments and vowed to enjoy herself while she was home. The wind spread the wells of tears over her cheeks as she pulled out of the lot. The road signs seemed at once familiar and foreign as she tried to figure out which turning she needed to reach Beth's house. Beth had lived around the corner from her parents' house when Kat was little and was the only person who stayed in touch when she went into care. She would send letters or ring to see how Kat was and send books to her whenever she arrived at a new foster home or girls' home.

When they were older, Beth visited Kat or would sign her out for a day on the weekend and they would take the train into Boston to visit the Tea Room or rummage through clothes at the Garment District or walk up and down Newbury Street in search of job openings at the nice boutiques. Beth was roughly her size so Kat always got her cast-offs since Kat had a tiny budget as a ward of the state. Beth stayed in touch with Kat after she moved to London and was the only friend who had come to visit her in the UK. As Kat managed to negotiate her way out of the Big Dig, the highway grew more familiar. Nostalgia returned with each mile she put behind her. She recalled wild nights with friends or group outings on weekend with her residential homes or even family trips to the Stone Zoo as a girl.

She turned the radio on hoping Massachusetts remained in a vacuum while she was away. She didn't recognise any of the bands or songs although the voices of the announcers were the same in their accents and catchphrases. Kat was surprised at how easily she found Beth's house after five years. Kat could never figure out how Beth's house was worth the same as Kat's in Essex and be three times bigger. All of the houses in the block were generously spaced out with big garages and identical front lawns. Beth ran out of the house and hugged Kat close to her.

"You look so European!!! I'm so excited you're here!"

"And you look just like an American housewife in your track suit! I've missed you so much!"

Beth laughed at Kat and grabbed one of her suitcases.

"Fuckin' A, Kat! How much shit did you bring? Where's Ian?"

Kat looked at her feet and Beth went quiet.

"He's spending Christmas with his parents."

"You've got to be shitting me. Jesus Christ, Kat. I'm so sorry. Look, don't feel too bad. All me and Joe ever fight about is his mother. She's one of those nutty, overbearing Italian mothers from Revere and since he's the baby I will never be good enough for him no matter how many fucking ravioli dishes I can make or how often I clean the frigging house. He's probably having lunch over there right now. Serious! Most women worry about their men sleeping with a woman at the office and I get to worry about mine at his mother's!"

A baby's cry echoed through the house as Kat set the last of her luggage down in the guest bedroom.

"Blimey, I always forget how much bigger your house is than mine!"

"Don't be silly. You live right next to the train station close to London. Of course your house is smaller. Better get Andrew before all his toys are out of the crib. You can stay here and get settled or see why I'm back on the pill?"

"Oh come on, he can't be that cranky."

"He's a tyrant. Only 18 months and already I can't wait for the terrible two's to be over!"

Kat followed her friend into Andrew's room where he stood shaking his fists and screaming. His face was red and mottled with curly tufts of hair strewn about his head. As predicted there were soft toys all over the floor. His face lit up as he saw his mother walk in and he began to franticly babble

"I wanna get up ma, wanna get up!"

"Okay, Andrew, but no screaming. You're gonna give your auntie Kat a headache. How about we get some juice?" She lifted him out of the crib and fingered his locks into something less savage while wiping his nose with a tissue. "You get so messy when you have a fit, Bee-boo. Isn't that better?" He sniffled and nodded as he got his breathing under control. Kat tried not to look too horrified or disgusted at what was supposed to be her god-son.

Beth poured some apple juice into a sippy cup and sat Andrew in front of the telly where a giant foam dinosaur jumped and danced with deliriously happy kids. Beth turned on the coffee maker. The fragrance of coffee filled the kitchen. Kat instantly recalled how much she missed afternoons like this. No matter how close she was to Elise or Ophelia, they never shared the years Kat had before her 20's or the shared ritual of coffee makers in big kitchens. Kat poured her heart out to her oldest and dearest friend. From her frustrations with Ian's lack of ambition and work, her in-laws that never seemed to even make an effort to understand that she was culturally differ-ent, or the Jekyll-Hyde line manager at a job that offered nothing more than a regular pay cheque now. By the end of it, Kat had used half of Beth's tissue box and most of the coffee.

"I had no idea you were so miserable over there. Why didn't you say?"

"How could I? Just ring you up and tell you that leaving the country was a bloody mistake and that I had no idea what to do?"

"You could always come back here."

"And lose my National Healthcare or go back to working my arse off in a call centre where I get five days holiday after a whole year? No thank you."

"Did you just say arse?" The two descended into giggles until Beth was summoned by Andrew spilling juice all over the sofa.

-

After seeing Kat off at Heathrow Ophelia decided to continue the momentum and do some job hunting. She went into the Borders book store on Charing Cross Road since she could peruse the paper over a coffee for free in a comfy chair. It would probably be available at eleven in the morning since most of the job hunters didn't rock up to the book store café until about three. Luckily someone had already been through the jobs pages in the coffee shop so she didn't have to get the paper from downstairs and try to casually walk it up to the first floor.

Feeling festive she ordered a mocha and a gingerbread man. As suspected, there was nothing on offer so close to Christmas so she caught up on her texts. She had a generic text thanking her for attending Elise's opening and then curiously a message from Steve about how great it was to meet and whether she was free to come in one or two days a week to work at his. After a discouraging look at the flimsy jobs on offer for the rest of the month it seemed an offer she couldn't refuse.

She texted Steve and told him she'd be happy to come and work for him. Within moments, the phone rang.

"Hey, it's me Steve."

"Hi. Thanks for the offer."

"Not at all. My assistant cut his hours so I could use the help. Are you around tonight at 6?"

"For an interview?"

"Ish. I'll show you the office along with the stuff you'd be doing."

"Sure."

"We're on Kennington Park Road so it's pretty easy to find. I'll text you the floor and the address. Now that you have my number you can ring me if you get lost."

"Erm, yeah. See you for 6."

If only every job interview was that easy. Having secured part-time work without the jobs listings she moved onto the Times crossword while the rain poured down outside. She had enough time to take in a film and a pint after lunch to get to her "interview" with Steve.

Around 5.00 Elise sent a text asking where she was. Ophelia explained she was heading to Steve's office. She was in a bus that was half empty with jaded pensioners

218

and weary young mums with cranky toddlers. The phone rang and she walked to the top deck to take the call.

"An interview? Seriously?"

"Yeah, he texted me and it would be nice to fill the time before I leave for America."

"Are you around after? I have great news!"

"All right. I'm on the bus but should be free after seven."

"Okay where shall I meet you?"

"I can meet you in Camden or Old Street? Why, you sound ready to burst."

 "Feelie!! You'll never guess!! I got a proper job!""

"Really? Where now?"

"They rang this morning after someone saw the exhibition so I went in to meet with this agency and they offered me a contract working as a creative on this government campaign to end human trafficking. I'm actually quite excited. I go in Monday to meet the rest of the team and get started. I may start on some ideas now so I have a lot of samples and ideas to bring them next week."

"Wow that's great! I'm so happy for you! Where's it based?"

"St. James Park. And I get to work from home as well. I just have to make sure I don't fuck up somehow and lose it."

"I'm sure you'll do fine. You've got loads of great ideas. Just think of all the trouble you caused at Nike. The government should be a piece of piss. What agency is it?"

"Opti-Level?"

"Yep, someone at my old company did some stuff with them. Can't remember what they did but were a nice agency to work with so that's a good sign."

"So what is this interview for then?"

"He sent me a text after I met him at your opening and he asked if I'd be free a couple days a week to work at his firm."

"That should keep you busy."

"And give me extra cash until I figure out what the hell I'm going to do for work next year."

"Not more of the same then?"

"I'm not sure. Part of me thinks that it would suck to jump right back into the same miserable job in a similar but not identically boring office full of petty arse kissers doing the same rubbish but if I start off in a new field I'll have to take a huge pay cut and start all over. I wonder if I'm too old at this stage of the game to go entry level and live like a student to find out it's the same kind of headache with a different title."

"Fair enough. If you could pick anything you wanted with no worry about salary or experience, what would you do?"

"I honestly don't know. I never really thought about it. Even now after being made redundant, I haven't given way and imagined a dream job."

"Why not? You've got three months with pay. If there's ever been a good time to dream surely it's now?"

"I guess. I am either worrying that I'll never find gainful employment again or that I'll end up in the same unhappy situation. Those seem my only two realistic options."

"Fuck realism. Do what you want."

"Cheers, I'll use that as my new Maxim."

"Seriously, Feelie. The only limitations in life are the ones you set yourself."

"Not with my rent, utilities and transport expenses. I need to make sure all those things are covered or I'm screwed. I know the dole won't cover my expenses and my savings will only get me so far."

"That doesn't mean you can't get a job that makes you happy. Unless you're happiest asking if they want fries with that."

She laughed and hopped off at her stop. Steve's office was on the 3rd floor and a lot smaller than expected. There were mountains of files and papers everywhere. Steve ushered her in and made a cup of tea.

"It's the last clean mug. You should be honoured."

"Uh, I am. Thanks!"

"Thanks for popping in. As you can see I 'm in serious need of assistance. These cases need organising, these papers and files need filing plus some data entry of new cases and closed cases. I can give you fifty quid a day twice a week. Mondays and Wednesdays would be ideal but we can switch it around if need be. Interested?"

"Sure. Sounds good. When would you want me to start?"

"Monday? Around 9?"

"Okay. Do I need to bring anything?"

"Just yourself and enough determination to stay awake until lunch."

"I think I can manage that."

"Did you want to pop out for a drink?"

Ophelia knitted her brow. "Hey, are you chatting me up?"

Steve laughed and blushed. "Not at all, I swear. I always get a drink on Wednesdays. It seems like the best way to toast surviving the middle of the week."

She surrendered to Steve's reasoning and was lead to South London Pacific which was a Tiki bar incongruously open in a very urban part of south London. He ordered them two colourful drinks complete with umbrellas and they sat pretending it was a tropical island they were stranded on rather than a gloomy one.

Kat and Beth ran onto the train carriage giggling.

"Can you believe it's been a good six years since we've been on this train headed for Boston?"

Kat smiled at the thought, awake but still fuzzy after adjusting to the time difference.

"Has it been that long?"

"At least. I don't think we've actually bothered with the trains since we were teens."

"Where are we off to then?"

"Now that we can afford it, I vote we hit Newbury Street and maybe stay for dinner? After that why not check out some old haunts for a game of pool at the Cambridgeport Saloon. Then maybe go dancing?"

"I'm in, mate!"

Kat hadn't spoken to Ian since she arrived. He could easily ring her at Beth's house but was obviously too busy stirring the Christmas pudding at his mother's house to bother. If Kat rang him she would be conceding defeat and she was not about to give in first and she still wasn't sure how she felt about her marriage. She didn't want to miss him anymore and knew that if she heard his voice she might break down and ask him to come to America or she may just decide to throw in the towel. At that point she wasn't ready for either. Over the past few days she kept herself as busy and distracted as possible.

Beth kept her busy; taking her Christmas shopping, to have Andrew's photo taken with the mall Santa and to meet all of her neighbours who seemed to be far too friendly not to be on medication. Kat was excited to see her old stomping grounds, eager to run into old faces and tell them how well she's done for herself. For every small-minded person that laughed at her, scorned her or wished her ill, Kat was dying to tell them how many places she'd been and seen or that she was living in one of the most exciting cities in the world. Even if she did hate it there and the people were rude and the trains were rubbish.

Snow was piled on the streets they passed, stained with exhaust and dog piss. Kat felt like she was finally home for Christmas and was determined to have a great time. Beth called home to check on Andrew and returned her mobile to her purse.

"I can't believe how calm Joe is. I bet he's frantically calling his mother every five minutes or already has the old battleaxe over there."

"Still, it was nice of him to give you the night off so we could go out on the piss."

"On the piss?"

"Drinking. You and I are gonna drink for England tonight."

"I can't get over how British you sound now. You've grown so much since you left, Kat. You're so much more confident and you look great. I know you were really upset yesterday and things can't be great all the time but you do seem to be doing really well. When I think of how we were and where your life was going I think you were right to go. Leaving was probably the best thing you could do for yourself."

"Yeah, the last big run. Beth, I always just ran away from everything."

"No, you took some space and sorted your life out. I think what you did was really brave. You left everything you knew and went to some foreign country."

"Come off it. I had no roots here. No family. Well, you're like my family. You know what I mean. I didn't really have anything left for me here and I just didn't want to turn into some sad townie working at a collections centre or worse. You should see what happened to some of those kids in the homes I was in. I think I got lucky. And England is hardly foreign when you think about it."

"I think you got a chance to become the person you always were deep down. You're more daring than me."

Beth lead the way down Newbury Street explaining what became of the shops and cafes that once lined Mass Ave and were now the same storefronts seen in any city in any country. It was like a tour of evictions, bankruptcies and buyouts. Kat asked about her favourite record store in Cambridge end Beth shook her head grimly.

"No one buys records these days. If buildings aren't owned by the universities then no one can afford the rent except for the usual suspects. Who knew we needed so much frigging coffee and khaki-coloured pants."

"Trousers," Kat absent-mindedly corrected.

"Nearly all the personality seems to have gone from here. A few small pockets still exist but who knows how long that will last. A shame, but I guess that's progress."

Kat was disappointed to find the places that housed countless memories were gone, as if a good part of the trip had been in vain since she was not only looking to see old friends but see familiar places and recall old feelings. Most familiarity seemed to be wiped or faded away in the five years she'd been gone. Her favourite spots for a Saturday afternoon were replaced by a Starbucks or Gap. She had wanted to take in the smells of mouldy vinyl record sleeves left behind by someone headed for New York, LA or the suburbs. Kat wanted to be 18 again.

-

The lights throbbed blue, purple and red as the music pulsed, powering the trembling bodies on the dance floor. Numbed by drink Kat allowed her senses to be overwhelmed as she watched faces in the crowd, leisurely scanning for recognition. She realised suddenly that she felt like a stranger in a place she once spent most her free time. One face emerged and seemed to loom closer every time she blinked her heavy lids. She involuntarily returned the smile the face flashed as he approached. Suddenly the face disappeared and she felt a hand on her shoulder.

"Hey there! Where have you been? I haven't seen you in years!"

She slowly turned and tried to scan her memory for a name. He looked so familiar and yet she hit a brick wall trying to think of who he was. He eyeballed her and laughed.

"Jesus Christ, Kat! How can you forget me?" He seemed to pause more for effect. "Or are you that shitfaced?"

Kat giggled and shook her head.

"Sorry. I live in a different time zone now and the drink's not helping."

He exhaled a throaty laugh and raised a hand to flag the bartender. "It's me, Ed. I didn't gain that much weight or get that many tattoos."

Ed! Of course! Kat harboured a crush on him in her teens. She saw him at countless parties where she laughed at his stories and antics. When Beth threw a party for her 21st they shared a drunken snog and fumble. Then he seemed to disappear. Looking back, it was probably for the best since realities never seem to meet the expectations of a crush. The longer someone is admired the more virtues they seem to acquire until they're on a pedestal so high that any real encounter would result in nothing but disappointment. Ed reached over and hugged her, resulting in a curious heat spreading from her chest to her fingertips. He ordered two Pearl Harbours which impressed Kat since even she had forgotten it was her favourite cocktail years ago.

"Well, where did you go?"

"To London."

"What? Seriously?"

"Yeah. Almost six years ago. What about you? I haven't seen you since Beth's 21st."

"I ought to drink both of these to catch up with you. Who are you here with?"

"Beth. She's off in the other room with some friends so I've been drinking and people watching. What have you been doing with yourself these days?"

"I deliver packages for UPS. The brown uniform used to chafe but now I kinda dig it. I am fully down with the brown! How bout you? Lemme see your teeth. Do you still have all of them?"

Ed pried her lips open and examined her mouth. "Ah, good. Just checking. What do you do in London to stay busy?"

"I work at a call centre answering questions about flu, sex diseases and dick cheese for the National Health Service."

Ed paused and burst out laughing. "That's fucking hilarious! Serious? You're frigging serious?!"

Kat nodded and began giggling and telling him about all the shitty calls she fielded. The longer they spoke, the closer they sat and Kat felt at home for the first time that day. She couldn't recall exactly what attributes she gave to fantasy Ed but she was definitely enjoying reality Ed. His presence had an electric charge about it and soon enough Kat found herself dancing under the strobes against him and laughing wildly. There was a vague guilt as she thought of Ian that was quickly replaced by resentment. She reasoned that she probably wouldn't even be at the night club if he actually had the nerve to stand up to his mum and accompany her to Boston like he originally promised.

The night sped by and soon last call was announced. Kat and Ed staggered to the bar and ordered a few drinks each exchanging conspiratorial glances. Beth appeared next to Ed and appraised Kat curiously. Kat responded with a blush.

"Hey you, I was wondering where you were," she playfully poked Kat and then turned. "Hey, Ed. How've you been?"

"Beth! How's it going?"

Beth smiled at Ed and returned her suspicious glance to Kat. "We've gotta head in a few."

"I'm getting a cab back. Where are you two headed?"

"We can take the T, don't worry about us."

"I insist. It would be my pleasure."

Kat's eyes pleaded with Beth who cautiously agreed. The night air chilled them as they looked around for a free taxi. People poured out of the night club. Sensing the inevitable futility of hailing a cab right away, Kat suggested they get a pizza.

"Is Hi-Fi still open or has it been replaced by Pizza Hut?"

"It's still there and still open." Ed clasped her hand causing Kat to go warm in the icy wind.

Beth found a table in the corner and Ed brought a pizza over with some drinks. They settled into the seats and began the ritual of peeling off scarves, coats and hats. The pizza smelled heavenly as the hot steam rose from the centre. As they ate, talk turned to catching up on old friends.

"Remember Chad? He's in rehab now. Oxycontin."

"What happened with Michelle? Did she marry that guy from Austin?"

"Every time I am in the DMV Steve seems to be at the desk. He's starting to look like his dad. No joke!"

"Did they lose their house in the end?"

Kat watched the tennis match of local news between Ed and Beth while she took bites of pizza. Sadly the pizza taste wasn't able to live up to the smell or the memory although the flavour of disappointment was becoming a recurring theme.

With warmer hands and full bellies the three set out to hail a cab. Snow was falling in thick flakes settling in slushy patches on the streets. The cab slowed cautiously to the kerb as they negotiated the slippery pavement. Ed gallantly took Kat's arm while he opened the door for her and Beth to climb into the back. He fell in heavily next to Kat. Beth and Kat laughed as they bounced on the seat. He gave the driver Beth's address and ordered him to drop them first.

Sleep's black velvet net pulled Kat in. Her head bobbed lightly before resting on Ed's shoulder. He stroked her hair from her face and squeezed her shoulder. The soft hum of conversation faded along with Kat into the dark depths of sleep.

She fell in deep, swimming further away from the murmur of voices and the gentle rhythm of the engine. Shadows and silhouettes danced past her whispering playfully in a tongue understood only in dreams. Her movement was graceful in its weightlessness as she stepped lightly over starfish and crawling infants soundlessly moving at the bottom of the ocean floor. The sea grass undulated lazily as she made her way towards what looked like her childhood home. In the foreground was an ultraviolet treasure chest opening every few minutes to release pearly bubbles containing guppies and sea horses floating towards the hazy light above.

The house seemed smaller and somehow softer as if it would gladly yield to the touch. She remembered that house tucked away near the Schraft's building in Charlestown. There were two other families living there; one above and one below. She would ask her parents to tell her about the candy Schraft's used to make in that factory every time they drove past. The bright pink neon sign fascinated her, making a small part of her child's mind certain that if she were to turn up alone and have a look around she would find that they still manufactured candy buttons and were waiting for an industrious girl like her to take over the building and resuscitate the business.

Under the ocean her house looked small and isolated as the bubbles danced about. As she neared the house a fear overtook her. She wanted to go in and pass her hand over the dirty embossed wallpaper on the stairwell and take in the familiar scent of leather shoes, cat litter and gas stoves. But a part of her was afraid her mother would be passed out on the sofa with the smell of gin on her bathrobe and her father angry that she had come noisily up the stairs. The pull was too great and she found herself passing the treasure chest regardless. The railing felt squishy as she padded up the steps. The three steps took all her energy and she found herself exhausted as she reached her porch. The sun bleached sit-n-spin sat in the corner that she remembered leaving behind when they moved away. Seeing it there comforted her. She sat on the top step watching jellyfish swim past flashing pink, violet and blue.

"Hey, Kat! Wake up. We're here."

Kat felt his breath on her cheek and realised she hadn't been stroking Ian's leg at all. Her hand froze as her eyes opened wide. It took her several moments to focus her vision and slowly the dirty nicotine scented upholstery reminded her she was far from home. Ed grinned softly and tucked her hair behind her ear and grabbed her handbag. Beth opened the door and took her wallet out and Ed shook his head insisting he was happy to see them home safely.

Beth took Kat's bag and held the door for her. She sleepily turned her head to Ed and smiled. Lurching numbly for the seatbelt she searched for the words of thanks and good evening in vain. She heard the click of her seatbelt release as she watched Ed pull the belt back. She managed to form a clumsy thanks with her heavy, swollen tongue.

Kat giggled dumbly as she turned toward Beth and felt Ed grab her hand. She felt him lean close and turned to meet his face. He kissed her awkwardly and within a moment she had found herself kissing him back. She surrendered utterly for a second before reality pulled her back. She looked down and Ed uttered an apology under his breath. She gave his hand a squeeze before throwing herself into Beth's arms. The door shut and she felt Beth waving with her free arm as the car disappeared into the white snow globe lit by the streetlights.

Kat woke up with a thunderous headache and fuzzy feeling in her gob. She heard a baby's frantic screeching tear through her foggy sleep before remembering where she was. She slowly pieced together most of the evening but was distracted by waves of nausea. She hated herself absolutely at that moment for mixing her drinks and drinking too much especially knowing the inevitable menace of hangovers. She missed having Ian there to tease her, share in her misery or to make her tea and toast.

Then a feeling of shame and regret dawned as she recalled the kiss. She buried her head under the duvet and tried to force time back. The guilt and regret seemed to exacerbate the hangover. After a while she sheepishly crawled out of bed and made her way to the kitchen. The baby's cries were now a disgruntled whimper as he sifted through his O-shaped cereal. His face was troubled and mournful. Beth mirrored Kat's hangover in both posture and expression before grinning haplessly and muttering that they were too old to be staying out all night drinking so much.

Kat sat across from Andrew and tried to meet his eyes. Knowing she was watching him brought a coy grin to his face and he self-consciously turned his head, checking back periodically to ensure she was still watching. She smiled dumbly before being struck by an overwhelming sickness. She lurched to her feet and ran to the bathroom. She clutched the loo with trembling hands. Her eyes watered and she hoped all of the hangover would leave with whatever was erupting from her gut.

She was shipwrecked and assaulted by several violent waves. The room began to spin as her stomach relentlessly contracted at irregular intervals. Her mouth burned as the sickness subsided. She reasoned that she fully deserved it after betraying Ian. It wasn't just the kiss but the infatuation she felt almost immediately after seeing Ed again. It wasn't love in the least and she wasn't interested in seeing him again in that

233

capacity. It was more the lightness she felt in letting go of her recent mistakes, mundane daily life and return to that thrilling feeling of being 20 where she wasn't worried about mortgages or in-laws or happiness. She also worried that she was just putting on a brave face and in fact really did want to end her marriage. Kat felt weary as she lifted her head and groped for the sink.

She realised she couldn't pinpoint what made her unhappy, either, but knew she hadn't felt happiness come as easy as it had the night before for many years. She was always worried about money or listening to Ian worry about money, even though he did nothing about it. She hated their flat and his parents' constant meddling. Most of all she was petrified that Ian was content to let things continue as they were indefinitely. She felt trapped and leaned into the sink to be sick.

She got her breathing under control and tidied the bathroom. As she walked out she was startled to see Beth in the hall. Andrew was slung on her hip, smiling at Kat as a few bits of cereal clung to his chin and forearms. Beth stared anxiously as Kat wiped her face.

"Are you all right?"

"Yeah. Must be a hangover or some dodgy food."

"Or alcohol poisoning. Let me ring my doctor and see if we can get you looked at this morning."

"Beth, honestly. I'm sure I'll be fine after some toast and coffee."

"It's no trouble. He's right down the street. Seriously."

"All right. Cheers."

-

Kat sat across from Dr. Khalil as he looked at his clipboard and then at her. He smiled warmly.

"You're not looking so great, dear."

She tried to smile but had to focus on keeping her toast down. She shivered and grabbed her cardigan to wrap over her hospital nightie.

"You don't have fever and it isn't food poisoning. It would appear from your urine sample that you're going to be a mother."

Kat paused and tried to place the last time she had to frantically search the bathroom cupboard for sanitary towels and froze as she realised it had been nearly two months. Dr. Khalil smiled sympathetically as he read the shock and subsequent horror register on his patient's face.

"I'm afraid that you'll probably have a few more mornings like this where you feel sick but it should go away after the first trimester. In the meantime you will want to stop drinking alcohol and get as much rest as you can. After the baby's born you won't sleep nearly so much."

She shuddered at the mention of trimester. The idea of pregnancy seemed utterly foreign.

"Are you sure? Could there be a mistake? Maybe a mix up of samples?"

He paused as if realising for the first time that not all pregnancies are planned.

"I'm quite sure. Can you tell me the first day of your last period?"

Kat thought back.

"A couple months ago, I think. I've been on the pill. I missed about four days after leaving them in my bag at the gym but after the fourth day I started my period so just waited until I stopped before starting the pill again."

"I'm afraid that sounds more like breakthrough bleeding instead of a period. It can happen when you suddenly stop the birth control pill. You're actually quite fertile at that time."

He looked at her awkwardly and tried to smile.

"I can give you some leaflets with resources and options if you like? I will also give you a list of obstetricians in the area under the various health plans."

"That's okay. I don't live around here now. I don't even live in this country now."

"I'm afraid the only thing I can suggest for the sickness is some saltines and ginger ale unless of course you're craving certain foods. Then go with those."

Kat struggled to take in the news as she dressed. Surely she would have known or felt differently. She wasn't sure what to do next or even what to say to Ian. The thought of enduring Dorothy through a pregnancy filled her with dread. Besides, she wasn't even sure if she wanted a baby at that moment in her life or ever. Her head swam as she navigated the sterile halls of the hospital. Beth was threading chunky colourful beads along a matrix of tubes with Andrew. She explained what the doctor had said while Beth tried to keep Andrew from mouthing the beads.

"No fucking way! Were you two even trying for one?"

"No."

Kat stared at her hands while Beth made her way out of the hospital car park. Beth fidgeted with the radio and heating as she searched for something to say.

"Um did you or he plan to have kids anytime in the near future?"

"No."

"Are you gonna keep it?"

"I have no idea. I still haven't decided on whether to call Ian and tell him."

"Aw come on, Kat. He's your husband."

"Exactly! And he hasn't rung once since I got here."

"That was just a spat. This is something else entirely."

"I'm still taking this in myself. It was completely out of the blue. I don't even know the state of my marriage; forget about throwing this in the equation. And then of course last night I snogged Ed."

"I know! I wasn't going to say anything since really a drunken kiss doesn't count. You don't have feelings for him or anything. Do you? I mean I can remember how pissed off you were when he blew you off and-"

"Then I moved to the UK. No, I don't have feelings for him now. I mean he's sweet and all but no. Ian would be really hurt if he found out."

"About a drunken kiss? Just don't say anything. Though you do have to tell him you're pregnant."

"Yeah but that means I'd have to call and he's at his parents. The last person I want to talk to is his mother. And how terrible to have to tell him over the phone. I'd much rather tell him in person."

"I don't think that's an option. Besides it'll give you a better idea of where things stand. I bet he'll rush over."

"Doubt it."

"But now things have changed."

"He hasn't. If he was capable of change he would've come with me. "

-

Kat lay on Beth's sofa enjoying the silence of the empty house. The outside was a monochrome scene of white. The fluffy snow continued to fall against the dove grey sky. She managed to fall asleep after Beth took the baby out to his playgroup. Watching her friend pack for this short outing she thought of how this ritual could very possibly become a regular part of her own repertoire and decided to block out the overwhelming anxiety with a nap.

She was tempted to turn on the telly but knew she would be assaulted by a selection of holiday themed programmes or nappy commercials. She decided to make some tea and try to ring or consider ringing Ian instead. As she made her way to the kitchen she was startled by a burly silhouette at the door. She yelped at the knock and fumbled with the knob.

"Ed!"

"Hey. Sorry if I startled you?"

"Oh, no worries. Was just about to make some tea. Want some?"

"Ooh, I say! Cheers!" He laughed and attempted a British accent.

"I just wanted to make sure you got home ok."

"You were with me, Ed."

"Yeah, but I really couldn't remember so I thought I'd come over and check."

"Awww. Cheers! That was awfully sweet. Did you get back okay?"

"Well, I woke up on my sofa and still had my wallet so I think so."

Kat felt like she was underwater as she looked through the cupboards for tea. Her hangover seemed to be receding but only just. Nothing she ate or drank seemed to help. She rummaged through Beth's cupboard and found a box of animal crackers.

"Whoa, I haven't had these since the third grade. Nice one!"

Kat smiled as she reached into the box and pulled out a handful of circus animals. Ed smiled as he watched her bite the head off a monkey.

"Look at us. Can you believe how we turned out?"

"If anything, I used to think you'd end up living abroad writing or snowboarding. I didn't think I'd ever escape New England. Thought I'd be working at Cumberland Farms until I was 40! I still haven't a clue what I'm going to do with my life."

"Yeah, but didn't you go to college? What did you study?"

"Community college. And I didn't finish in the end because I met Ian. What does that matter? No one ever seems to do what they set out to at uni anyway. Unless it's law or accounting or business. And then usually their families or circumstances force them to."

"You think accountants never stare at their spreadsheets and sigh, wishing they ran off and joined the circus?"

Kat laughed as Ed performed his best impersonation of a wistful accountant. He reached out and held her hand. Kat froze as the confusion and shame about last night blossomed across her cheeks.

"I'm pregnant."

Ed's hand froze. Kat slipped hers out from underneath and hastily patted it.

"No, nothing to do with last night. It's just that I only found out this morning."

"Was gonna say, I don't remember much but I would hope that if I had impregnated you I would have remembered."

"Thanks."

"So . . ."

Tears suddenly spilled over her cheeks.

"I haven't told my husband. I don't even know how I feel about my husband or my marriage or my life. I don't know what I'm going to do yet! Oh god, I'm so sorry!"

Ed got up and stroked her back and cradled her, hushing and soothing her.

"I'm so sorry, I don't know why I'm such a basket case."

"No you aren't. You've got a lot going on. I'm no Oprah, but I think if you tell your hubby what's going on it may help clear up what you want to do next. Things probably seem so much bigger and impossible to handle 'cause you've not talked them through. "

Kat felt small and helpless as Ed held her. There was a safety and confidence in his arms that she hadn't felt for a long time and it was a selfishly comforting indulgence

241

she really needed. Her life suddenly seemed out of control, boiling over everywhere. She just wanted to crawl back under the duvet while all the questions needing answers just faded into the background to find satisfactory resolutions on their own. Instead she was confronted head on and had to make decisions whether she felt ready or not.

"I feel so lost."

"I'll bet. I know everything seems overwhelming, but you'll be okay whatever happens. You're a tough cookie. You have to just take stock and think about what you want, what you need and why. No matter what you decide, life will continue to move on regardless. And remember you can always change your mind. No one can tell you how your life should be, Kat."

Kat nodded at this thought.

"I just don't even know what I want or where to go or anything. I don't have any family, just my husband and my friends. I just don't want to do anything. I wish things could stay static until I was ready for change."

"So does everyone. So do I. Time just ain't that flexible. If it were, I could have gone back to that week after that party and called you back. It's probably for the best I didn't in some ways. My life was a mess back then. Not exactly perfect now, really. I mean I'm not sure things happen for a reason but if things didn't just happen to us how could we ever learn about new things or even from mistakes?"

Kat sobbed harder.

"Come now, I didn't mean it like that. Just think of all the places you've been and things you've seen just 'cause you went to college. You coulda stayed here or moved to Quincy even and took a shitty job you hated and became a townie. And who knows, maybe you will love being a mother or, um..."

"I don't even know if I'm having it. I haven't talked to Ian since I landed."

"Well, maybe you should."

Ed stayed and fixed some hot chocolate for them as the snow continued to fall. There was marshmallow fluff in the cupboard so they put huge dollops in the mugs as they drank. The sky grew vivid with pinks and violets before surrendering to a deep blue night. Streetlights contrasted the flakes. They stared out the window watching the snow fall like sands through an hourglass.

As he finished his drink, he looked at his watch.

"I ought to head out; I'm on the early shift tomorrow. Did you want me to come around after I get back?"

"I'd like that, thanks. Let me see what Beth has planned first."

"Okey doke. Here's my number. Not trying any moves, honest. As a friend it would be great to see you before you head back."

Kat smiled. "Thanks."

Ed gave her a big hug and kissed her forehead before slipping his work boots on and heading out into the night.

She watched his car fade into the snow and walked over to the phone. She still flinched at ringing his parents so she tried his mobile.

"Hello?"

"Ian, it's me."

"Hey, how are you?"

"Where are you?"

"At the flat, actually. My mum hates the gaming so I snuck out for a bit saying I needed to see some mates. How about you?"

"I'm at Beth's. Listen, I have some news."

"What's up?"

"Ian, I went to the doctor this morning and it seems I'm pregnant."

"..."

Kat's heart thumped in her chest waiting for some response across the Atlantic.

"You sure?"

"Yes, very."

"You'll have to get an abortion."

"What? Wait, why?"

"Kat, we don't have the money-"

"Because I'm the only one with a job."

"Kat, please. And what about Toronto? I finally got this gig and-"

"Are you serious?"

"What? Kat, we don't have the money or the resource to take care of a baby. Besides when we got married we both agreed we didn't want any kids."

"Ian, that's not the point. Do you have any idea what it's like to have an abortion?"

"I'd be there for you. Just think, if you had a baby my mother would never leave you alone."

Kat could feel her pulse quicken and her chest tighten.

"Okay, Ian."

"Want me to ring the GP for the appointment for when you get back?"

"I won't be coming back. I'm leaving you."

Ophelia made her way to Steve's office as the cold rain pelted her mac. She was relieved to actually have a specific reason to get out of bed, dress and have a whole day occupied with tasks. Sending CVs around was futile since London had already begun to settle into the Christmas season of parties, hangovers and forwarding crap emails so the month of December was destined to be a slow one. She arrived twenty minutes early and stopped in to grab two coffees at a nearby café. She strode up to the door of the office and stopped short.

A makeshift camp had been set up by a man who resembled a mucky Father Christmas with a nicotine-stained beard. One of his shoes was held together with packing tape. His legs were red and raw in spots with one sporting a soggy-looking grey sock. The other leg had a naked swollen ankle that fed directly into the worn leather mouth of the taped shoe. His trousers were a collection of stains and grime and appeared to be a bit small for him. A tatty duvet topped with layers of free newspapers formed a shelter from his knees to his shoulders. Ophelia watched this area closely for the rise and fall of breath and relaxed slightly after seeing some shallow movement.

She realised it was past 9.30 and guessed by the rough sleeper that Steve hadn't arrived yet. As the minutes ticked by she stood there staring blankly with a hot cup in each hand as the heat bled through her woolly gloves. The odd drop of rainwater leaked through the awning and onto her shoulder. As people ambled past she stood there rooted with this unexpected discovery and surprised to find herself comfortable in the stillness of the moment.

"For fuck's sake!"

"Pardon?"

"What are you staring at?" The dozing figure snarled as he opened a rheumy eye and looked her over irritably.

"Umm, I need to get in to the building."

"You can't!"

"Excuse me?"

"It's locked. The guy doesn't turn up til 10 most days."

"But he told me 9.30."

"Don't shoot the messenger. Looks like you should have gotten those to drink in. They'll be cold by the time he rocks up. Might as well give one to me."

She set the cup down and stepped back again.

"Cheers, love."

Ophelia tipped her cup in response. It didn't seem worth moving since Steve would probably be along soon. She decided to stay there as the considerably less merry Father Christmas clone finished Steve's coffee.

"You his secretary or something?"

"Erm, yes. Sort of."

"Better ask for a key then. He can sometimes be as late as eleven. Don't know how he manages a bloody office. Mind you I shouldn't complain since I get to sleep later on those days."

"Cheers, I'll do that."

She watched his morning routine commence as the rain rattled across the pavement. He began by meticulously folding each layer of newspaper before placing them in a battered green Harrods carrier bag.

"Nothing but the best." He joked as he gestured towards the bag.

"Have you been here long then?"

"Where? Here as in the streets of London or this patch in particular? London, three years, maybe four? And this doorway has been my bed for a few months now. Since your boss is a bit shit about waking up in the morning I get to sleep later here and it's dry." He took the duvet and rolled it before stuffing it into a bin liner. He then scrambled to his feet and had a good, loud stretch. The smell was overpowering. Ophelia discreetly inhaled the steam from her coffee to buffer the stench. He set the bags in a pile and sat down to start on his coffee.

"This is a nice coffee. Too bad you didn't think to get a bacon roll to go with it."

She noticed Steve's figure about a block away. Her companion did as well and began to gather his things.

"Best be on my way. He told me he'd call the filth if he saw me sleeping here again."

She waved as he trudged up the alley. He called behind him.

"Next time bring some food."

Steve smiled as he drew closer.

"Wow, you're prompt."

"You said 9.30."

"Yes I did. I said that thinking you'd show for 10."

Ophelia was puzzled. Seeing her confusion, Steve explained.

"Always ask for more than you want as you'll inevitably always need to settle for less. If you were at an interview, you'd naturally ask for more than your current salary, right?"

"I guess."

"Or when you throw a party no one ever shows up at the time you specify do they?"

"I guess not."

Noticing the rain and her shivering, Steve fumbled for his keys then ushered her in from the rain. He took her coat and turned the lights on.

"Make yourself comfortable. I'm going down the road for a cheese and marmite toasty. Can I get you anything?"

"Marmalade on toast would be nice, thanks."

"While I'm there can you go through the emails and phone messages? The password for the PC is C-H-E-W-S-H. CHinese Elf With Shaved Head. The phone code is in the diary. Put all the messages on the yellow pad with the blue pen. Ta!"

And with that he bustled out the door. After an eerie moment of silence she turned on the PC and listened to the sleepy machine start-up. She rifled through the desk drawers to see if Steve had any method of organisation. Aside from a lot of coppers, a few pens and a tube of red lipstick there wasn't much so she went straight for the phone to check the messages. There were 43 messages. They varied in voice and gender but were mainly the same desperate enquiry about their case and asking why they hadn't heard from Steve in ages. Some even asked why he hadn't shown up for a court date and one was threatening to pop in and give him a Glasgow kiss. After writing these messages out Ophelia resigned herself to a long day.

-

"Have you ever had one of those bizarre moments of clarity and just looked around wondering what the fuck you were doing somewhere?"

Elise sipped the head from her pint and began to cross her eyes so that she looked like a rabid zombie, the stout's head frothing out of her mouth. Ophelia regarded her expecting either get bitten on the neck or to hear where Elise was going.

"That's exactly what happened to me in this meeting today. I was struggling to stay awake as they were droning on about P&L, KPIs, ROI, blah, blah, blah-dee-blah. I was tired already but this meeting should have been videoed or used as a book on tape for insomniacs. Who the fuck manages to regularly stay conscious for these sorts of things? My head kept snapping back and I was hoping nobody noticed since I'm new. Maybe I should have my GP write me off as narcoleptic? You reckon they'd buy it? They may even give me my own napping area."

"Elise, you just started! Give it a chance. It's always hard to stay focused on things you're not familiar with."

"Anyhow, after the third head snap I just looked around and wondered what the hell I was doing there. I didn't get up to leave or anything but the situation seemed a bit absurd or foreign. I just wondered if that sort of epiphany was common for grown-up job types such as yourself."

"Erm. I no longer have a job. Though if I did, I can assure you that I have those moments regularly. Often following a night out too late while my hands trembled and I tried to look busy. Or just randomly. Though, that may just be us as opposed to everyone. I suspect some people are quite happy or content."

"Like the way cows seem content chewing cud?"

Ophelia tried to suppress a grin since Elise knew full well her own day was nothing short of bizarre. It may have been Ophelia ringing desperately on her mobile from Steve's office begging she come to Kennington for a few pints after the day finished.

"Or the way Steve seems perfectly content with all his clients phoning him up to yell at him for doing a rubbish job. He is easily one of the worst solicitors. Well, from what I've seen on telly or read in the papers. And I've never heard so many irate people in one day. I was tempted to start drinking at lunch. They would ring up crying or screaming or cursing or all three."

"What does he do when you're not there?"

"I imagine he lets the voicemail sort it out. I'll let you know when I next go in. How about you? What's it like at the agency?"

"Aside from the dull and seemingly irrelevant meeting it was fine. The team are nice."

"Who knew human trafficking could be such a laugh, eh?"

"The campaign itself is pretty neat. I think Kat is going to be asking for the samples when she gets back. We're setting a micro-site up and phone lines and at first they're just putting the cards in phone booths all over London. I actually came up with the idea about the cards and was surprised they used it. I'll be doing a lot of design work for the site and the cards. The cards will show teenagers with some info on the whole real cost of prostitutes. Then they're rolling out an ad campaign and TV commercials. It's quite nice to be able to do it for a good cause instead of selling crap to people they don't need."

"Will they make you do that, too?"

"I'm not sure. The team I'm on seem to have mainly public sector and charity clients. If I ever got someone like Shell, or Esso, or Nike I'd see if they could get someone else. So now you will have to keep your eyes peeled next year for my hooker cards. I should see if I can get Kat to model for one of them! She'd do it in the hopes that Dorothy spotted the card while at the theatre or something."

"When is she due back?"

"Think on the 6th of Jan? When are you leaving for there?"

"The 18th."

"Just over a week then."

"Still seems a shame she's there while her husband's here hanging with his parents. I know it seems like I don't like Ian-"

"You don't like Ian."

"That's not true! I just hate to see Kat get so stressed and he just adds to it. I really don't see what she gets out of that marriage."

"You're harsh! For all we know he could be very attentive and caring?"

"In the bedroom? Hmm. A rent boy would be cheaper."

"Aw, who are we to say what makes a marriage work? It's not like either of us are even close to that yet. I don't even know if we're cut out for marriage. We seem to change and grow so much through our lives how are we supposed to expect someone else to keep up?"

"It may just be more expectations we have on us. Seriously. Did your life turn out as you thought it would after you did everything you thought you were supposed to? And for any relationship it's a give and take. And it seems like she gives and he takes and she's just going to get hurt. Is she worried that there's no one else out there or did she just settle for him? I would feel cheated if I got married to someone who seems determined to stay 13 forever."

"I'm just amazed I lived past 25."

"I'm being serious. I feel like there's hardly any options to do anything worthwhile. The rules of the game are the same but the game seems to have changed dramatically over a few generations."

"There are certainly more players and I guess it's nice they let women on the pitch. Though I see what you mean. Still what are we supposed to do about it? Go hungry or hope to have a trust so we can be bone idle or while away hours on vanity projects?"

"I'm just worried a bit. What if I wake up at age 60 and realise I got it all wrong?"

12 DECEMBER

Ophelia stuffed the Christmas cards in the post box trying to force them down among the others. She had a heap on her table back at the flat that people sent. It was probably too ambitious to think they would arrive in time this year but the fact she sent them at all was an achievement as far as she was concerned. She noticed a lot of people opted to go green or cheap and email Christmas wishes. She really longed to lose herself in the holiday magic that decorated shop windows and even the shoppers weaving in and out the doors full of festive shopping bags throughout the streets. It just didn't feel like Christmas for her. There was no hope or anticipation. She really wanted that joyful happiness but instead felt heavy and blue, dragging Jacob Marley's chain round her ankles.

She finished most of her holiday shopping and was genuinely excited to return to the States but still couldn't shake the indifference. She rang Caroline and arranged to meet up with her after she arrived in Boston. She even decorated her flat in tinsel. Ophelia supposed being alone didn't help. There were no nieces or nephews, no familial obligations. When she thought about her days as a moody teenager and how her father was out on the lash every night, both she and her sister would still feel hopeful and excited about Christmas. It felt optimistic as if anything could change even though it never really did. Their father would manage to stay dry from Christmas sometimes until the afternoon of New Year's Eve but then before the New Year had begun he was hollering or slamming doors or girl skulls against floor boards.

She thought about when she was with Grant, her last long term partner from three years ago, and how there was always a certain magic or anticipation near the holiday season. They would be trying to hide gifts from one another in a pokey little flat or drinking apple cider and watching stop-animation cartoons. Perhaps being alone was exacerbated by Christmas. It didn't help that there were no office dos to look forward to, either. She had nothing to get dressed up for, plan for, feign excitement or dread over that holiday season.

At the same time she wasn't consumed with worry over her lack of gainful full time employment but knew she couldn't work at Steve's forever. The office was depressing and having clients phone up every day calling her an incompetent slag could be demoralising even if their demise had nothing to do with Ophelia. She thought she'd love the freedom of showing up whenever she felt like it but instead found she just turned up really late every morning which did nothing to help feeling lost and aimless.

She kept thinking about contacting Cordelia. After her letter to Caroline was so well received she felt optimistic about getting in touch with Cordelia. She recalled their last encounter and reminded herself to remain cautious but hopeful nevertheless.

The easiest way was probably just be to send her a card though that seemed too impersonal for a sister. She had to send a gift. It had been over 10 years and she had no idea what would be appropriate and didn't want to get it wrong with some impersonal toiletries or a scarf. Since it was Thursday she had the day to brave the west end shops armed with the cash Steve insisted on paying her. It was early enough to miss the after work crowds and late enough to miss the lunchtime shoppers.

She got off at Bond Street and decided to work her way east. She managed to last thirty minutes before the crowds proved too much. She passed through House of Fraser, Debenhams and John Lewis but more to avoid the crowded pavements than anything else. It struck her that she didn't know Cordelia at all. She knew as a young girl Cordelia loved ponies and hot sauce, hated vegetables and ballerinas but Ophelia had trouble picturing her as an adult contemporary. She wondered if she should just try and imagine how Cordelia turned out but seeing that she had as much chance of becoming a CEO as a stripper it didn't narrow it down. She fingered racks of clothes as she passed realising that she didn't even know what size Cordelia was, whether she was fat or thin. Cordelia looked tall from what she remembered but she may have stopped growing when Ophelia left.

She was in Topshop at the sweets corner looking at the Pez dispensers when it came at her at an overwhelming speed. She recalled the worst Christmas she ever had when she was 9. Her mother was just gone and her father was hitting the Jameson with a vengeance. Cordelia was playing with her new game. It was, appropriately enough, one of those tipping point games where players had to add items to a donkey without it bucking up and scattering the pieces about.

She might have been too young to notice the tension and bile brewing in her father or was just too thrilled with the new toy to care. She was whining and begging Ophelia to play with her but Ophelia was too preoccupied with her mother's disappearance. She had left suddenly in the night in August of that year, leaving only a manic scroll in lipstick on the bathroom mirror. It was their first Christmas without their mother to keep the peace, run interference and ensure money was spent on gifts instead of alcohol.

The game was a gift from a neighbour and one of the few they had to open on Christmas day. Ophelia pushed her away but she was relentless as only a child can be. After a few minutes she had shouted at Cordelia to get lost and their dad calmly rose to his feet, walked over in measured, deliberate steps and stomped on the game, crushing it completely. Cordelia went white and silent out of shock or fear. He crushed her spirit as well that day or at least gave it a sound kicking. She gravely collected the shattered pieces and gingerly placed them in the skirt of her night gown and shuffled into her room as if leading a funeral procession. Ophelia suspected Cordelia kept them for a good couple of years thereafter since she remembered coming across them at the back of her wardrobe once while searching for her allowance stash.

Ophelia knew their mother would have played the game with her if only she'd been there.

Ophelia headed to Hamleys. On Regent Street bubbles streamed out of the entrance and she could see it was heaved with weary shoppers and cranky children in frantic chaos. Demos being given on remote controlled planes and some sort of foam boomerang where happening out front of the shop. A few scruffy wind-up pigs and cows and dogs squeaked or toddled mechanically towards a plastic barrier in the store against a huge backdrop of various species of soft plush animal toys. It struck her as funny that they squeaked and toddled in place once they hit the barrier and sincerely wished she had that determination. Normally when she hit a barrier she fixed a drink and sank to the floor.

After weaving through a crowd of restless teenagers she managed to find the floor games were on and negotiated the sticky, snotty crowd. She was relieved they still made Buckaroo and even had the same design on the box she remembered, or at least the "Retro Edition" did. After waiting an insufferable eternity in the queue she had it gift wrapped and beat a hasty retreat through what she was certain had to be the closest approximation of hell on earth she had ever encountered. She went to an internet cafe and made a few searches online. She found her name and photo on a business site. Cordelia appeared to be the events organiser for a women's charity near Boston. The site even had a photo of her. She was startled to see her little sister in a smart navy blazer staring confidently into the distance.

Ophelia hastily addressed the padded envelope and affixed a book and a half of stamps before she could change her mind. She opened a card and gave Cordelia the dates she was in the States along with her UK postal address, mobile number, email address and the words "With love and apologies, Ophelia". She wanted to write so much more but didn't know where or how to start so she used the momentum to take her to the post office.

-

The Quality Street tin made its way around the office amidst chatter and cheap mulled wine. Elise was dreading its arrival at her desk. Normally at offices or jobs she happily participated in secret Santa since she wasn't invested in the job and was just there for a laugh or subversion. She was slightly surprised to discover she enjoyed her work in the short time she had been there. She even came in on days off to help with other accounts and other teams. Elise eyed the tin and tried to return her focus to her drafts. She still hadn't gotten everyone's name down and now she would have to try and get them something for the office Christmas do. Her colleagues were witty, friendly and funny yet she was haunted by fear. She felt like an interloper or con artist who somehow managed to pull off the mother of all scams and ended up happy.

Her fear of being exposed as a fake or told simply that her work was substandard would greet her in the evenings when she arrived home. It loomed over her as she drifted off to sleep as a mocking hourglass hissing with grains of insecurity. Perhaps they were wrong to ring her after all. All the feedback was positive and everyone seemed thrilled with her ideas but it nagged at her that she missed out on the neces-sary steps or rites of passage that her peers seemed to endure. It was almost as if expectations were too high and there was no way she would ever be able to meet them. Elise couldn't simply tell everyone she wasn't as good as they had hoped her to be yet she dreaded that moment of realisation when her new colleagues realised she was a complete mess and quite possibly overpaid.

One of the web designers came over and placed the tin on her desk.

"Take some of the chocolate along with the names."

She had a thick South African accent. Rebecca was her name. Thankfully she had her name in gold round her neck. If only they all had their monikers on a necklace or name badge or even tattoo then Elise wouldn't feel so thick fumbling to recall names whenever she was approached. She silently vowed to hand out badges or possibly dog collars if she ever ran an office.

She picked a name out while mulling over office dog collars. She unravelled the paper scrap and read the name Tim. She wasn't too sure who Tim was but could easily ask the ladies at reception and hopefully get an idea of what to get him.

There was also the Christmas do in a week that everyone had urged her to attend. She debated making excuses about prior engagements but James insisted it would cheer her up and help her get to know people at the office. Jo suggested she remain sober the entire night and watch anarchy descend once everyone's had too much to drink. Elise thought about going for a quick glass of bubbly and then sneak out unnoticed.

After the tin made the rounds and the mulled wine was finished she headed home. Elise opened the door to hear the phone ringing. She stopped short with the door ajar listening to the muffled hum of James's greeting and then a pause.

"Elise? Is that you?"

He stepped into the hallway mouthing that it was her mother. She paused and then slumped her shoulders in defeat.

"Tell her I'll be there in a second."

James nodded and she could hear him laughing politely. She shut the door and peeled off her rain sodden coat before making her way over to the phone.

"Hello, darling! How is the new job?"

"Lovely, thanks. How are you and pa?"

"Doing well, though we were starting to worry a bit since we hadn't heard from you in a bit."

Elise hated speaking to her mother over the phone. Her mother would often soften her with questions or small talk before trapping her daughter into a promise or obligation necessitating Elise to be on guard throughout the entire conversation.

"Mother, I couldn't very well call you while you and pa were on the cruise. I did however ring the morning you were due to arrive and Katja answered. I told her to phone me if you and pa were even a half hour late getting back."

"Why didn't she tell me you rang?"

"I specifically asked her not to mention my calling since I knew you both would be exhausted from travel. You mustn't be cross with Katja."

"Well it doesn't help that she failed to dust the crumbs behind the toaster again. I say, she can be so careless at times. I do miss Adetola."

"How was the opera?"

"Lovely as always. Winter is far more preferable than summer in Venice. It was a lovely escape for the weekend. Now then, I'm about to draft the master list for the holiday shop for Jack. Are you still insisting on no meat?"

"Mother, I've been vegetarian for over ten years. It's unlikely to change…ever."

"Yes but it can't be healthy. What sort of impact will it have when you decide to marry and have children? Talking of which, did I tell you that June's daughter just had a boy last weekend? He's absolutely precious! You must come see him when you're here. I went before we left for Venice and he's such a good baby. So quiet and Louise looked so healthy. She was positively glowing."

"Perhaps they gave her some nice drugs."

"Don't be silly, darling. Now, was there anything you had wanted specifically? I could get you a nut roast. Will you be bringing any suitors with you?"

She always sounded so hopeful when she asked this that Elise could not help but delight in telling her no.

"Well, you mustn't fret, dear. I know several that would be delighted to partner you in our parlour charades."

The mere mention of parlour charades caused Elise to flinch recalling her cousin Rupert's vulgar interpretation of the Karma Sutra and his furious gyrating and thrusting at her poor bewildered Aunt Eunice.

"Mother, I'm not sure I'll be able to make it this year."

"Don't be silly. You must. We always have Christmas together as a family. Your father is really looking forward to seeing you."

"I've volunteered for Shelter this year and they need me on Christmas day."

"Jack can easily drive you there and pick you up."

"Mother, I'm not having a driver in a Bentley escort me to and from a homeless drop-in centre."

"Perhaps you're tired after a long day at the office. I imagine it must be quite a shock after spending so many years idle."

"Or perhaps like you and pa I've made other commitments that simply take priority. How about I send you some flowers and a case of wine in my absence?"

Her mother tersely excused herself as politely as possible and hung up. Elise felt so angry with her mother for not understanding why she was so upset with her. Her parents seemed to have no interest in Elise's life. She was frustrated at having to smile and suppress her interests at her parents and make forced conversation with all of their friends. She just wanted her parents to make an effort to get to know Elise as an individual as opposed to an extension of themselves. She often stayed close by her paternal grandmother who seemed genuinely interested and proud of her. After her gran passed away a few years back Elise found family visits unbearable.

She started as she turned to face James offering her a Jaffa cake.

"Cheers."

"The kettle's just boiled. Want some tea?"

"I would love some tea."

"So have you had a change of heart, Ebenezer?"

"Huh? Oh, no."

"Aw, it'll break her shrivelled old lady heart, Elise."

"She'll find the strength to carry on, I'm sure. I just don't feel
terribly up to being jollied along by them and I'm still really cross about the gallery
opening. What about you? Seeing your mum and Mittens?"

"Yes. Back to Yorkshire to have mum dote on me and Mittens drool all over me. He's
a bit old for a St Bernard but still bounds around like a pup for sausages. I'll just have
to leave all my nice trousers at home to spare them being covered in fur and drool. I
think Gemma's popping over or we're driving to hers on Christmas day. With the two
babies it'll be easier to head to theirs."

"No one would believe this is how the author of countless saucy- no, hardcore porno-
graphic- short stories is headed north for a quaint family Christmas! Is Joe going anywhere?"

"You'll have to ask him. I think he may stay here and entertain. With
mostly everyone gone to stay with family it is nice to see someone making use of the
big dining room. I think we may even get a tree this weekend and see if
anyone fancies decorating it while getting pissed on mulled wine and stuff ourselves
with mince pies."

"What a fab idea. Count me in. I need to figure out what to get this chap for the office secret Santa. Any ideas?"

"Elise, you can't seriously be worried about something so trivial."

"It's the trivial details that people remember, James. Besides I really surprised myself at how much I enjoy working there."

"Get you. And here I thought this was another one of your missions."

"I'm actually hoping they keep me on board. Some of the projects are really interesting. I'm as surprised as you are. If you told me I'd be doing this six years ago I would have told you that you were full of shit."

Ophelia sat sweating in her suit. She arrived five minutes late and was then made to wait an additional fifteen minutes. It seemed a bit petty but the job paid well so she wasn't about to leave. Much to her surprise she found that she thrived on the daily structured routine. And hated though it was, that hellish tube journey in the morning marked the start of her day. Perversely, she missed all those familiar strangers she sat with on the crowded carriage every day. She wondered vaguely if they had noticed her absence on their journey for the past few weeks.

Although she really didn't think she could ever return to her old office she realised she wanted to find a roost among a new set of colleagues. She knew they would spend the majority of their time on meaningless projects but was beginning to think that was the point. Just as school felt like a purgatory where they busied themselves colouring, reading, revising and testing, her career was more of the same. It was never meant to be her holy grail of purpose or source of happiness. It was one aspect of her life that she had the power to invest as little or as much as she felt compelled and then reap what was sown. Her happiness wasn't something to be found or purchased. It was a conscious decision. She could be happy or content anywhere she was but the responsibility rested solely on her shoulders.

She wondered if the parcel reached Cordelia and obsessively checked her mobile and email for a message saying she was glad to hear from her sister. Ophelia felt compelled to smell her jacket for sweat but knew her luck was so crap that the interviewer would walk in at that moment and smirk throughout the entire interview thinking she was either a pervert or some fiendish cretin with hygiene issues. Either way, it wasn't worth the risk. It was better to get through the interview with a confident posture and smile to indicate that the smell was emanating from the interviewer's armpits and not hers.

Her mind wandered to the surreal moment in Steve's office the night before while she organised the last of his filing cabinet. She felt his presence behind her forcing the hairs on her neck stand on end. She slowly turned to witness his eyes boring into her. He seemed startled to meet her gaze and tried to recover with a friendly but furtive smile.

"Thanks for sorting the filing."

Ordinarily this would be infinitely creepy but there seemed to be an unmistakeable chemistry as they stood facing each other under the harsh fluorescent lights. She froze with a shocked smile as the faint buzz of attraction resonated through her chest and belly. She managed to mutter that it was no trouble and returned his gaze. They stood there in awkward deadlock until her mobile tore through the silence with a tacky jingle. With the spell broken she hurried though her handbag to see that she missed Mark's call. Her care, concern and patience had completely subsided with resentment and anger taking up residence. She knew it must be tough losing someone but alienating himself was a choice he seemed to make.

With the intense moment receding into the past, Steve busied himself in the nook of a kitchen. It was basically a basin with a kettle and a few crusty cracked mugs. Ophelia decided to finish off his inbox before heading home.

He looked a bit put out when she left. It seemed on the tip of his tongue to keep her there with work or a drink but where she wasn't sure was how she felt. She thought it best to go and clear her head. She still wasn't sure how or what it was she felt but had to admit whatever it was it left her intrigued. There wasn't necessarily an immediately obvious physical attraction but she found his sense of humour charming and really enjoyed their time together. Something was willing her to explore the unknown and to let it go further though she wasn't prepared to initiate it herself.

A chap strode up to her briskly. He was wearing a brown suit and a pink shirt which matched his cheeks and nose.

"Ophelia? I'm Tom. You were late."

"And so were you."

She stared him full in the eye not entirely convinced she wanted the job and was not in the mood for games. He stared back and nodded curtly. Tom spent most of the interview interrogating her as if trying to catch Ophelia out on her CV. She had nothing else planned for the morning and loved a good game of ping pong for the quick witted. She smugly sipped the tea he made her as he questioned her accomplishments, methods and experience.

She certainly was not going to be asked back but was enjoying the practice at the very least. Had it been a perfect role at a company she was desperate to work at she would have been more cautious but since she didn't really give a monkey's ass she was free to be as honest and tenacious as she pleased. It felt good to not care or have anything to lose. In that moment she envied Elise's ability to turn that attitude on at will.

She fixed a steely gaze on her temporary adversary and then looked at her watch.

"Well, it's been a pleasure but I'm due at another interview in Victoria and as you know it is poor form to be late. I expect the agency will let me know and all that lot."

She flashed a quick smile and gathered her things. He paused and looked as if he was debating about moving from his seat so she assured him she'd see herself out.

She left the meeting room with a full bladder and an unwavering smile. There was no way they'd ask her back and she was quite happy with the bad impression she left. If only she always felt so confident at interviews.

She had to stop into Steve's for a few hours to do a bit of work and collect her money. She had an hour to kill and still needed the loo. She regretted leaving so quickly after the interview. The sky was nearly blue and shoppers crowded the pavement, spilling out of shop fronts weighed down with bags. Sitting in the top window of the double-decker she watched the city unfold below in a colourful woolly collage of reds and blacks and browns and greys. She felt all the more removed from the happy faces laughing into mobile phones confirming wish lists and sizes

Her mind returned to Cordelia. She tried to picture her among the throng of shoppers. She wondered if she was married or had children, whether she still saw their father for Christmas or like herself, left one morning and never came back.

Cymbals crashed as a parade of Hare Krishnas threaded through the road dancing and chanting. She remembered Foyles in Charing Cross had toilets so she hurriedly alighted. She pushed past the chanting parade, diesel exhaust and noise into the calm.

After just making it to the ladies' room, Ophelia found herself drawn towards the be-witching aroma of ground coffee beans and relaxed melody emanating from the cafe. She sat at the window and watched the morning slip by while her coffee cooled. She had an interview for a job she was actually interested in at end of the day but felt compelled to attend every interview since she was no longer employed.

She looked out among the crowds and noticed Mark coming out of Denmark Street and raised the mug to her face in case he looked up. It was unmistakeably him and uncanny how a city so big could still have you spotting friends or running into ghosts from the past at any moment. It shrank the world down to a blink of recognition and an uncertain smile or hasty turn of the head. Her heart skipped a beat feeling sympathy. She was also worried Laura was watching and judging her determination in avoiding her husband's grief.

-

Elise sat amongst her colleagues vaguely aware that deep down this was exactly where she had always wanted to be. An excited buzz swept through the pub as people wearing paper crowns and tinsel laughed and even sang carols. It was a week before Christmas and already everyone seemed lost in the season. All work in the capital seemed to cease or noticeably slacken after the second week of December though Elise usually noted the change vicariously. She normally would be in retail or doing volunteer work so it always seemed frenzied and busy. It was funny to feel so relaxed. She had a few shifts at Shelter and at a hospice in Forest Gate but otherwise planned on being busy with work. Elise finished her mulled wine, bemused at joining the crowd that relaxed in December. She was making a tidy sum using her creative talents and was appreciated for it. She felt happy but cautious. At any moment she could be rumbled and exposed as an interloper or fake. The fear was baseless but pulling at a loose thread in her subconscious.

They plastered calling cards in phones boxes throughout Camden, Kings Cross and the West End hitting pubs along the way. The cards showed a young girl about 18 in a cardigan and threadbare gym slip. The description read out that she was a Russian doll and a bit shy. It then urged the reader to get to know her by visiting her web page or calling the phone number. The web site introduces the same model in a photo of her in a bedsit in the same gymslip and tells you her name, her age and how she was tricked into coming to London and held as a slave in the UK sex trade. The further you went into the site the more you read about her family, and then all the other women like the Russian Doll. The press coverage would start a week later and then roll out into a big campaign about the illegal sex trade. Elise was secretly proud of her idea despite dismissing any praise from the agency. Seeing her idea brought to fruition at such speed and reaching such a vast audience was almost too good to be true.

Her mum had called twice over the last week leaving messages of who was attending lunch on Boxing Day and pestering for a wish list. Elise wondered if the calls were more to convince her to change her mind since she never rang that often in the previous years. An echo of desperation or anxiety grew with each message. A small part of Elise delighted in tormenting her mother though hopelessness and frustration seemed more prevalent. She knew it upset her ageing mother who really seemed unable to relate or understand her only daughter. She walked an eternal tightrope between pleasing her loving parents to asserting her own life against her pushy overbearing parents. She wished more than anything that she could want the same things as they did but she never quite could.

As she waited among the crowd of drinkers, workers, friends and Londoners she was suddenly acutely aware of how lonely she was. That feeling shrunk her to the point she began to worry the bartenders would never spot her. She wondered if this loneliness was a global phenomenon or exclusive to London or even just her.

She watched the girl pulling a pint for a loud chap in a pinstripe suit and a Father Christmas hat. He gazed wolfishly at her cleavage. The girl caught his eye and turned her head in disgust, meeting Elise's sympathetic nod. She smiled and walked over to take Elise's order.

-

Ophelia got to the office at three in the afternoon after promising to help out before she left on Monday. Steve was in a meeting with a client so she put the kettle on, checked and sorted through the emails while she peeled off her sweaty coat. She was always amazed at how close the Tubes and buses were when it was so cold outside. The rain made it worse; no wonder Londoners were such a miserable lot. With light snow falling there would be more smiles instead of sneers and snowball fights instead of stabbings. She smiled at her fleeting sense of optimism knowing the snow wouldn't make much of a difference and instead fuel hacks to write headlines about "snow chaos". Tossers, she thought.

She was relieved to have a few moments alone in the office to assess her feelings for the recent jolts of electricity between her and Steve in the office. She wasn't sure if she was just lonely and enjoyed the feeling of attraction and anticipation or if there was genuinely something there. Steve was such a cryptic chap and she found it hard to read him. Often he told her some twee joke that she heard in grade school but was surprised to find them both laughing. On Monday morning after a particularly bad interview he was strangely comforting and offered really solid advice. Whatever it was she felt she certainly didn't feel in control.

She hastily put together a tray of tea, coffee and some semi-stale biscuits. According to Steve's diary it was a client visit and it looked like he blocked off the entire after-noon. She crept in quietly, trying not to disturb their discussion. She found she could-n't meet his gaze, however she could see a broad smile from the corner of her eye as he waited for her to set the tray down.

272

"Ophelia, you remember Mr. Jakas, don't you?"

She looked over and smiled at the paunchy chap with a receding hairline who looked like a lot of Steve's shifty clients. Mr. Jakas smiled and looked poised to speak before apparently thinking better of it.

"Of course, hello. How is the missus?"

"Separated, I'm afraid." He didn't seem afraid in the least; he just continued to smile.

"I'm sorry to hear that. Shall I hold your calls, Steve?"

"Thanks." He nodded and she backed out of the stuffy room.

She slouched into the desk chair and began to go through his myriad of distraught and threatening messages. She tried to make a game of it, guessing whether it would be a sad or angry call by the tone of the caller's initial greeting. She tried to decide if hysterical would be counted as sad or angry when her mobile rang. She hadn't recognised the number and was hoping it was about one of the many CVs she sent off the week before.

"Is this Ophelia Graf? It's me, Cordelia. I got your parcel."

"Hi!" All the air rushed out of her lungs with the greeting.

"Did I catch you at a bad time? I can ring back later?"

"No, no, not at all. I have all afternoon, really. Wow. I wasn't sure if I'd hear from you at all."

"The parcel arrived today at work. I was really surprised to hear from you. I pretty much gave up a few years back after dad died."

"Dad died?"

"Three years ago. Heart attack in his sleep. Came back from the bar, passed out in front of the TV and never woke up."

"I had no idea."

"It was in the local papers. I even went around and told some of your old friends from school hoping they could pass on the message."

"Never heard from anyone."

"You seemed to disappear."

"Listen, Cordelia. I'm so sorry. I had to make a clean break. I never meant to leave it so long. I've thought of calling or writing so many times but things got in the way, or I got scared and the longer I left it the harder it got until it seemed out of the question."

"Mom came back."

"Mom?"

"She showed up for the wake and to the funeral service. She looked bad. Like she was worse off without him if you can believe it. Smack. Half her teeth gone, sunken face. Skin and bones."

"Oh,"

"Yeah. She stayed at the house and I helped her get cleaned up. It's been about fifteen months now. She's got an apartment and a job at Dunkin' Donuts"

"You see her a lot now?"

"I try to get out and see her at least twice a month, sometimes more if she's having a tough time. Lately she's been seeing this guy so she's with him a lot. It's fine with me since work has been crazy lately. I haven't told her I'd heard from you yet."

"Cheers. It's all a bit much to take in at the minute."

"Yeah, I know. I saw you're coming over for Christmas. I know you'll probably want to stay in Portland with your friends but if you're free I'd love to see you."

"Sure! I haven't made any certain plans as such. I land and fly out from Boston so tell me what suits you."

Ophelia organised a date and wrote it in her diary. She hung up and exhaled. A nervous excitement pulsed through her as she tried in vain to return focus to work. She made a cup of tea, dumping the cold filmy tea from earlier down the tiny office basin. She was still trying process all the news Cordelia had given. It shouldn't have surprised her too much that her father died. He wasn't the healthiest of dads and over 60. It then struck her that she wasn't sure how she felt about his death. With Laura they were close friends and she missed her friend and was involved in her life. It also hit her quite hard that they were so close in age. With her father he seemed more like a distant relative or someone from another lifetime. She also wasn't entirely sure if it was fear or anger she felt for him after all those years and whether she was sad or numb about his passing. She didn't know if there was anything more to say to him if he were alive. In many ways she buried her father when she came to London.

It was more surprising that her mother reappeared. It was easy to create myths and stories to explain her disappearance. She never called or wrote so she must be dead. How else could a mother simply vanish? It was easy to cast her father as the villain. He was there, angry and drunk. Ophelia sat, stirring milk into her tea and realised she never once considered his position.

It was so easy to hate him for losing his temper, spending their grocery money on booze and even not looking for her. He was a man of few words and he drank too much but he had to love them to stick it out and look after them after their mother left. She wasn't sure why he never bothered shipping them to relatives or even into care. He always seemed to resent them being there. She tried to shrug the thoughts off hoping they'd slink back into her past.

Steve smiled as he walked Mr. Jakas out. When he returned he stood before Ophelia's desk expectantly. Ophelia looked up.

"Right, we're having an office Christmas dinner to see you off to the States."

"We are?"

"Yes." He suddenly grew sheepish in his pause. "Unless you need to pack?"

"Are you kidding? I packed this morning."

"Great. I'll get our coats."

-

Taxis arrived for Elise and her colleagues to the office do at the Drunken Monkey. Elise shared a cab with Nas, the project manager, Louise the marketing exec and Funmi the comms manager. Funmi wore dizzyingly high heels and was already merry from the pub crawl. Nas was still laughing at how she fell into the taxi.

"You'll be right as rain once we get some food down you."

"Shut up, Nas. I'm perfectly all right."

Funmi mock glowered at him and continued to carefully apply some lip gloss. Louise was fairly new as well so she and Elise tried to follow snippets of gossip between Funmi and Nas.

"She always makes a complete tit of herself at these things. Hopefully she'll have the good sense not to go dancing afterward this year but I somehow doubt it."

Funmi sighed at Nas, returned her compact to her bag and smiled at Louise.

"This your first office do with us, isn't it? And you, too, Elise. Well, what better way to form an opinion of your co-workers?" She looked in her wallet and then over to Nas. "Have you any cash for the fare?"

Nas waved her off. "Don't worry, I've got it. Thought I gave my missus all my money but I still have some bills."

"I just wish they took cards."

Funmi opened the door and gingerly stepped out. The street glittered with frost causing Funmi to lean on Elise as they weaved their way into the restaurant. Nas held the opened door and scanned the room.

"Fook me, they did book the entire venue."

"Too bloody right after the year we've had."

Funmi noticed the look of incomprehension flicker past briefly on Louise and rolled her eyes up trying to find the words. "It was record year in terms of profits and awards. We all put in a lot of hours so it's the least they could do."

Elise looked around for familiar faces that she had names for hoping she didn't seem lost or clingy. She was famished but felt a little out of place being so new. Watching everyone laughing and chatting Elise wanted both to join in and to curl up in a dark corner and hide.

Her stomach rumbled so she made her way to the tables. Finding several that seemed empty she settled into one and grabbed a pint from a passing tray. Her thoughts drifted to Laura. She got a gift for everyone that year but her. It had been a few months and the grief buried itself into her heart. The spot was still soft and she still caught herself missing Laura or wanting to ring her.

"Don't let the food pass you by!"

She started as Nas grinned.

"Sorry, was daydreaming."

He grabbed a few bamboo steamers and set them on the table. A few more people joined the table as the food piled up. Tim sat beside Elise and chatted to Nas. She busied herself with the wine and stewed aubergine overhearing snippets of conversations. Normally she would have happily chatted along with everyone but had lately found it hard making idle chat or even appearing interested in talking to anyone. She was grateful for the work since it gave her deadlines and kept her busy but otherwise just wanted to float around in an emotional cocoon until she was ready to feel happy or human again. Tim tapped her on the shoulder as she chewed some noodles.

"Hey, was it you that got me the giant chocolate t-rex?"

Elise nodded and attempted to smile without revealing a gob full of chewed noodles.

"Cheers for that. So how are you liking it at Opti-level?"

"Nice. How long have you been here?"

"God, since I left uni. So about four years now. You were the artist, right?"

"Yeah, I guess."

Elise noticed the silence seemed a little awkward and worried she was coming across as rude or obtuse.

"Sorry, it has been a long day. So what are your plans for the holiday?"

"Don't be silly. I heard the whole team went on a pub crawl posting the cards. I'm going to Kent to stay with my folks then skiing in Austria after Boxing Day with a few mates. How about you?"

"Oh, avoiding the family and just staying home. Might pull a few shifts at Shelter."

"So, what did you get?"

"Huh?"

"Secret Santa."

"Oh. Ummm a mug."

Elise wanted to seem interested and engaging but couldn't muster the energy. Aside from a more generous spread and trendier location it was like every other office party she attended. A lot of people got off their face, sicked up in the loos, snogged in corners or got spastic on the dance floor. People were the same all over, she concluded, and no matter what the occupation she would always feel that little bit out of place. It never mattered in the other jobs she had though she had thought she would finally be in an office where she felt she belonged. She was originally worried that she would disappoint and was now the one disappointed.

She wasn't even sure if her expectations were realistic. Laura always seemed happy in her work and was surrounded by co-workers she seemed to get on with and when Elise met them they all seemed interesting, fascinating even. She wished Laura was still around to talk to about it.

"Hey, you all right?"

"Huh? Yeah. Sorry."

"No worries. You just seem a bit preoccupied that's all."

"Yeah, I guess."

"Can I help?"

"No, cheers. Sorry to be such a drag."

"Not at all. Think a lot of people are distracted this time of year. Family commitments, shopping, borrowing, bills, looking at the state their lives are in. No wonder we spend most of the month pissed out of our skulls."

Elise smiled. "I guess you're right."

"Course I am. I majored in Human Behaviour at uni and now spend my days telling people why their lives are incomplete and why my clients' products or services will fill the void. Not the most noble career but pays well enough and keeps me entertained."

"Is this what you wanted to do?"

"I never really had my heart set on anything to be honest. I'm good at what I do so that's good enough for me."

He poured her some more wine as the chatter around the table filled the spaces between them. Eaton mess was brought round with coffee. Laughter grew in volumes as motor skills dissolved into sloppy gropes.

"And so it begins," he sighed.

"What?"

"It gets a little sloppy at the Christmas do every year. It's amusing if anything and provides fodder for gossips but like everything else in life, eventually forgotten about and inevitably repeated."

"Very philosophical."

"Thank you. My mother would be thrilled you thought so."

"Is she a fan of philosophy?"

"No. She's dead now."

"I'm sorry."

"Don't be. She had cancer which was no way to live. It was years ago."

"So where do you go at Christmas?"

"My partner's family does something and my dad goes with us. The first one was the worst but we managed."

"A friend of mine passed away a few months ago. I'm still a bit shocked."

"I'll bet. Grieving is a lot different than how it's portrayed in film and television. Some people turn into zombies, others grow hostile and angry, some get really neurotic or phobic about stuff that seems or is completely unrelated. My dad was angry at the doctors for not finding the cancer earlier or not saving her or sometimes he'd recall an instance where the doctors didn't respond quickly or a nurse forgot to bring tea and he would rage on about it for days. He was like that for the first six months."

"Then what happened?"

"My aunt on my mum's side had a go at him. She was proper East London like and just told him that what was done was done. Everyone suffered and he was making it even harder on everyone by carrying on the way he was and she told him to stop being such a selfish git. He looked at her after she finished and cried like a baby for days then one morning woke up and got dressed and just tried to return to normal. Didn't happen right away but gradually things got easier. He's even got a lady friend he sees for dinner or takes to the football every week."

"I'm just tired. No matter how much I sleep I can't be arsed. The work's helped loads. After my gallery show finished I was a bit worried I'd go stir crazy."

"Sure. I get that way. I was really depressed for a while after my mum passed away."

"What did you do?"

"I left! Ran away to Argentina and travelled through South America for six months on some savings and the money she left me. I did volunteer work, learned to surf, got legless then met my missus. It was good to get away and clear my head. I quit my job, left my flat and put my stuff in storage. I packed a big rucksack and left. It was brilliant."

"What did your dad do?"

"What could he do? I couldn't stand to be around him; he was doing my head in. I wrote to him and called the whole time and sometimes he actually wrote back. We're quite close now and I think it's because of that. He needed the space to grieve and so did I. If I stayed I doubt we'd be talking now."

On the dance floor a conga line had formed and managed to pull Tim off his seat and into the throng. Elise excused herself and escaped in to the ladies. She then made her way to the bus stop and headed home.

-

Steve sat across her transparent with excitement. Ophelia felt slightly overdressed in her cheap suit after seeing a few Hollywood actors and actresses donning their incognito uniforms of jeans and t-shirts with baseball caps or sunglasses. Steve raised a glass and suggested a toast.

"To small office Christmas parties."

Ophelia laughed and raised a glass in return.

"Thanks again, Steve, but really you shouldn't have."

"Nonsense. I take all my PAs to Claridges for Christmas. It's to make up for the shoddy pay and sexual harassment."

He smiled indulgently as his eyes scanned the menu. She tried to keep from looking around to see who else was dining. Steve slid a cracker across the table to and she passed hers to him.

"You do realise I am not wearing a paper crown?"

"Don't be such a Scrooge. I think it'll look lovely on you. You could be the queen of Claridges."

"Thanks but no."

Despite seeing him a handful of times he had the familiar nervous tics of a first date. She playfully scolded him about two persistent clients he consistently neglected and they shared a few bad jokes involving horses and parrots.

The elusive spark from the other day flickered on and off throughout the meal. A fear kept her senses rooted but her heart fluttered restlessly in her chest, eager to soar. She didn't want to be hurt and feel stupid like she did when she caught Grant with a co-worker. And she never wanted to experience the anguish Mark did after losing Laura. It was easier and less messy to keep emotions in check on tight reigns.

She reasoned the giddy feelings could easily be that she was caught up in the supposed magic of the season or most likely just tired of being alone. She tried not to overanalyse it and simply enjoy a nice evening out when her original plans consisted of beans on toast.

"So what are you up to over the holidays? Lots of panto?"

"We don't do panto in the States. I want to go sledding since they got snow and ice skating. I miss both of those. How about you? Any big plans? I think Julian Clary may be in Cinderella someplace this year…"

"Ooh, I may just! I will go to my brother's in Bournemouth. His wife just had a baby so my parents will stay there and I can see them all at once rather than drag it out. Then I'll catch up on work and call those pesky clients you keep nagging me about."

"How old is the baby?"

"Only a few months, I think."

"They aren't much fun at that age. All they do is sleep."

"Sleeping is better than screaming."

"Mm. Still, the whole baby business is a bit risky."

"Risky? How so?"

"Well, it's a bit of a lucky dip, really. You've no idea what you'll pull out and then you're stuck with it for 18 years or more."

Steve levelled his gaze at her before throwing his head back and erupting into a volcano of laughter. Diners looked over and they completely forgot where they were and shrugged at them.

"Ophelia, you cynical minx! That is such a brutal, yet very comical way of putting it."

"But you don't. That baby is its own person and however much the mother or father wants to share their passions or interests or experience that baby, child, whatever may not give a monkey's. Then when they get older and stop being cute it all gets a bit disappointing."

"I take it you've not come over all broody then?"

"Me? I'm broody right now."

She grinned coyly at him while the puddings were laid out.

"I have to really start looking for work in the new year."

"You can work for me as long as you like..."

"Thanks but it isn't that. I think I just want to get back into marketing. Not that I don't love speaking to your hysterical clients over the phone while I nurse a hangover. ."

After several bars and champagne cocktails they found themselves in a hotel bar with gin and tonics. Steve grinned as he scanned the surroundings.

"What a nice place. It seems like it's just us and a few hardcore alcoholics."

"You're so romantic."

"I am. Dance with me."

"To Wings? Are you fucking serious?"

"Yes."

His hand rested tentatively on the small of her back as they swayed. He gingerly clasped her hand and leant his head toward her. She was struck by the graceful movement of his feet reminding her how clumsy she was. In a way it was touching though more in the way that a hideous hand-knitted jumper made by your gran after a stroke is.

The evening sky was clear and the wind refreshing as they headed to Marble Arch. She was surprised at how tired she was. She loved how quiet and empty everything seemed in contrast to the pulsing throngs of people that dominated the pavement by day.

"If London were always this quiet, I would love it." She mused, absent-mindedly taking Steve's hand.

"If London were always this quiet you'd be bored. Besides if it were this quiet it just wouldn't be London." He gave her hand a squeeze.

"Think of all the things there are to do here; great gigs, pubs, green spaces. All the people are what make it such a fascinating place."

"Delusional optimist."

"Just living life to the fullest. I couldn't imagine living anywhere else. No place is perfect and just like relationships you take it warts and all."

Ophelia stumbled towards a bus shelter and Steve pulled her back.

"What are you doing?"

"Catching the night bus."

"Ophelia, crash at mine. The night bus is frightening enough to a group of sober blokes. I promise you I won't try anything funny."

"Okay…" She collapsed in his arms and he hailed a cab.

18 DECEMBER

She woke with a start. She lay still and opened her eyes and realised it wasn't her bed. She quickly recalled having gone for dinner and drinks with Steve the night before and grew rigid. She took a sidelong peek beside her and there lay Steve still as a corpse on his back with his hands crossed over his chest. She begin to giggle uncontrollably.

Steve's eyes opened and he grinned quizzically. "Good morning. What's gotten you so giggly?"

"You look like Count Dracula!"

"-or a perfect gentleman. You will note that I kept my hands to myself entirely. And let me assure you that nothing untoward happened."

"Thank you ever so kindly, good sir."

He sat up and folded his hands in his lap, waiting for the giggles to stop. Each time she was about to settle down she looked at him and started all over again.

"How about I make us some tea? Otherwise you're going to lapse into fits."

She nodded and watched him leave. Ophelia looked down and realised she was wearing a pair of his pyjamas and all of her clothes were folded neatly by the bed. Details leaked back as she recalled leaning on him and tried pulling his tie off and falling up the stairs to his flat. And then him helping her button the night shirt and into bed. She smiled and flushed warm at his conscientiousness. Steve was easily the nicest chap she ever met which then dawned on her why he was still single. She thought of every complete bastard she ever wasted time or energy on and the way her heart would always have to be glued back together with empty promises that next time would be different. She never bothered to use her head in matters of the heart and there was a great guy who she feels something for even if she wasn't sure what it was.

Steve returned, balancing a tray of tea and toast.

"Feeling better?"

"Sorry, you looked so funny and stiff sleeping that way!"

He set the tray down.

"You take milk and no sugar, right?"

"Cheers."

"What time's your flight?"

"Shit! Three and I have to be at Heathrow for 12."

"It's eight thirty now. I'll get you a cab home and then to Heathrow."

He passed her a mug and then went to order the taxi. He came back in looking triumphant.

"They'll be here at nine."

She set down the mug on the night stand and grasped his wrist. He looked down at her smile surprised. She pulled him towards her and kissed him. He kissed back eagerly and she embraced him, feeling like she finally took control of her life and released any doubt or misgivings.

-

Kat sat nervously in the lawyer's office next to Beth. Andrew toddled between them muttering thoughts in a language only Beth seemed to understand. She hated waiting and was convinced everyone knew she was pregnant and getting a divorce.

"I still can't believe that's the first thing he said to you."

"He's never wanted kids and has this stupid play in Canada he's focused on. Well, that and Final Fantasy."

"Will you go back to England?'

"Not sure. There's the job there and nothing here."

"Mother-in-law there!"

"Oh God, true. It didn't even dawn on me but she'd never leave me alone if I had a baby. His baby!"

"You don't know that. Ask the lawyer. Besides if Ian doesn't want kids and wants nothing to do with it you may get lucky."

"Lucky to be a single mother? Great."

"You totally certain about keeping it? You probably have at least a month to decide."

"I'm in two minds. Part of me wonders if I ought to not keep it since I'm alone, broke and don't want to be tied to him forever. Then when I think of how he just assumed I'd have an abortion makes me want to keep it."

"You can't have a spite baby."

"I can do whatever I want now. I don't have to answer to anyone."

"Let's see what the lawyer says about your options, okay?"

"Listen, thanks for doing this all for me. Driving me round and the whole crisis stuff."

"Come on. That's what friends do."

-

James sat in front of his laptop and stared hard at the blank screen. He still hadn't thought of what to write and had a lunch with his agent later in the week. He was relieved to hear Elise coming down the stairs.

"Hey Cinderella. How was the ball?"

"Nice enough. How's the book?"

"What book?"

"Still nothing?"

"No and I really don't want to be penning hardcore sex stories for the rest of my life. I'm getting old and I hate that I've nothing to show my mother."

"You could always get something part-time. Some of the trouble might be that you're cooped up on your own most of the time. You don't have anything to write about since you're not up to much."

"I'll have you know this house doesn't clean itself. And I have lunches out."

"But the day-to-day stuff we take for granted like jobs or projects with other people form the groundwork for nearly every great story I can think of. The richness of the different characters, the necessary evil that draws them together regularly- it's all life. The stuff we do in the meantime is overlooked but it's what happens between the exciting bits."

"So I get a McJob and then spit out Wuthering Heights? Hmmm, I'm just not seeing it."

"No. I'm being serious. It forces interaction and will inspire you. Just get something a couple days a week at a cafe or shop."

"If my writing keeps on like this I just might."

"Are there a lot of people due round for the tree trimming Saturday?"

"I think quite a few. Maybe fifteen."

"It'll be kind of strange since Laura, Kat and Ophelia won't be there."

"But you'll have me?"

"I always have you."

"Are you bringing anyone from the office?"

"Ooh still early days for that."

"I'm thinking of making some devilled quail eggs and mini goats' cheese tarts for it."

"Sounds good, Delia."

"Are you going in today?"

"Am tempted just to see the state of everyone but think I might not bother. I've a new project I want to get started on."

"You've only just finished everything for the exhibit."

"This was something I've been meaning to do for a couple years now. I collected all those email addresses and mobile numbers and am sending out a survey."

"A survey about which toothpaste they use or how they vote? A one woman census bureau."

"I'm not saying another word. If you're nice I'll send you a survey."

"I'll get you a clipboard for Christmas."

-

Ophelia felt blessed that she managed to get to her flat in record time and grab her bags. She felt more cursed when she returned to the waiting taxi to find the M11 was a gridlocked snarl. The driver assured her he could get to the airport through London in good time. She tried not to panic at every set of lights or when a bus managed to get in front of them. They paused at one set of lights and a blur of red caught her eye.

She was amazed to see an army of Father Christmases making their way across Hyde Park. They were in all shapes, colour and quality from a cheap beard and cap to some very convincing suits and bellies. They shouted, they laughed, sang and shook sleigh bells as they stopped all traffic for a good five minutes. Ophelia was tempted burst from the black cab and join them. The sheer thrill of merging with this mass of festive cheer tickled her until she couldn't help but smile. Pedestrians and drivers alike turned and stared at the surreal moment unfolding before them.

The cab driver looked over and simply muttered, "Fucking nutters"

-

The flight over was filled with anticipation and worry. She was worried the plans she arranged with Caroline and Cordelia might go pear shaped involving tears, accusations, screaming or an awkward talk show combination of all three. She thought of how Kat was taking driving lessons and how she was facing her own demons since Laura died. It had been two months and though their lives all still continued undaunted, they were paying their respects in their own way.

After the meal trays were collected Ophelia thought about Steve and the kiss they shared. She didn't want it to be awkward when she came back, leaving them at square one, but was grateful for the time apart to get her feelings straight. Laura had always been her favourite sounding board. She also wondered how Kat was doing. She kept meaning to email or call but knowing she would meet her at Logan airport made her a little lazy.

-

Kat managed to keep from crying that afternoon and assured Beth she would be fine to drive to the airport to meet Ophelia. She loudly played the radio whilst going over the meeting with the lawyer in her head. Everything changed so quickly. Suddenly she had to make several big decisions very quickly. Nothing felt real from the cells multiplying within her to the daunting tasks that awaited her across the ocean. She knew she had to return at some point for the divorce but she wasn't convinced she would stay there once the ink dried on the decree. She could put money down on a condo in Saugus or in the UK once the dust settled. It was a novelty thinking of what she wanted after spending years trying to fit her life around Ian's. She turned down jobs that might require her to move and was pretty stuck where Ian wanted to stay to accommodate his largely unpaid theatre work. It was exciting seeing a world full of possibilities before her.

She caught sight of Ophelia and waved her down. Ophelia dragged her suitcase over and smiled. It was odd seeing Kat outside London. Kat hugged her tight. Ophelia hugged her back when she realised Kat was sobbing.

"Hey, what's wrong? Are you missing Ian?"

"I'm divorcing him and I think I need to have an abortion!"

Kat sobbed harder as the words uttered aloud shattered any possibility of denial.

"Whoa, slow down. I only just got here. Start from the beginning."

As they made their way to the hotel Kat told Ophelia everything. Ophelia paid the front desk staff and she wheeled up her bags.

"Wow. That totally dwarfs my news about snogging the lawyer. Have you called Planned Parenthood yet? Even if you're not completely sure what you want to do they have counsellors so you have all the options."

"I haven't done anything yet. This all seemed to happen at once."

"And I'm sure Elise can help with a solicitor. It'll all be fine. I know it's all overwhelming but you'll get through this."

"Are you hungry? It's dinner time unless they fed you on the plane?"

"Airplane food? Are you serious? What's good around here? You can stay on the spare bed if you like and we can ring round tomorrow to see what your options are. Who knows, maybe it's not so busy at Christmas time."

"When are you seeing that girl you bullied?"

"Caroline? Tomorrow. But if you need me I can reschedule."

"I'll be fine, honest. I'm just glad you're here."

Ophelia drove to Cambridge from memory and was amazed she didn't get lost at all. She parked the car and got a bus to Copley. The restaurant had really thick menus and Ophelia was a bit relieved she arrived early to read through it and get more coffee to keep her alert.

She sat nervously in the booth and waited. She started to worry Caroline would start off friendly and then snap and scream at her or Caroline presented her with all the receipts from years of therapy that stemmed from Ophelia's ruthless childhood cruelty. What else would she possibly say to her besides sorry? And then what would they talk about after sorry? Anxiety filled her as she dumped several packets of sugar into the milky coffee. She fretted that there would be awkward stilted conversation for an hour.

She glanced furtively each time the wait staff lead a few people to the other booths. Ophelia scanned them, looking for familiar features waiting for recognition on their part. As she waited she tried to think of all the things they could talk about. She took her diary out and tried to coordinate the rest of her trip. She noticed Laura's birthday would have been in a few days. She couldn't help but wonder if she were the one to die who would have noticed or remembered her? Her friends would miss her at first but then they'd step back into the bustling stream of their own lives. No one would really carry the intimacies or memories like a sibling or a lover. That thought left her feeling surprisingly tender with sadness.

Caroline stood in the aisle and looked around. Ophelia got to her feet and smiled warmly as she made her way over. All of the things she planned to say promptly left her.

"Ophelia, hi! Wow!."

"Cheers. You look great! Thanks for coming."

"I wouldn't have missed it. I have to go to the bathroom, I'll be right back."

Ophelia watched Caroline and noticed she still had the same walk that made her stand out some as a kid. Her hip would rotate on the right like a crane lifting her leg and swinging it forward. It was a lot less pronounced now unless you were looking for it or mercilessly teased her about it. Her cheeks flushed red with shame for noticing it. She smiled warmly and openly as she approached the table and Ophelia relaxed a little, hoping she wasn't planning to glass her face with the water bottle.

"Thanks for coming out. It is great to see you."

"Not at all. I was able to combine it with work."

"Where do you work?"

"For myself. I design and make wedding gowns."

"How cool."

"Not really. The designs that sell best are hideous. Why a woman would want to re-semble a lace covered multi-tiered cake on her special day is beyond me. I'd rather design other things but the wedding gowns are so lucrative. How about you? What are you doing these days?"

"Nothing. I've been made redundant. That's English for laid-off."

"Oh dear, that's awful."

"Not really. In the UK you tend to get three months' pay and it was a welcome break. I was working at a marketing department and I hated it. I'm doing some temp work for a friend of a friend while I find another job."

"Same kind of work?"

"I'm still not sure to be honest. Listen, thanks again for coming. I really felt awful for years about the way I treated you. I think it's really admirable that you came to see me after I wrote to you."

"We were just kids. Besides, you weren't half as nasty as the boys. They were so vicious. Plus you had so much going on at home."

"How did you know?"

"Everyone knew, Ophelia."

"Wow. I had no idea."

"It was still nice to hear someone apologise. I used to go home in tears every day. By the time I got to high school my weight ballooned briefly from the stress."

"I am so sorry."

"Don't be. I started to do costumes for the drama department and found out I was really good at it. I made friends, lost weight, got happy. We can draw a line under it and move on. Life is far too short."

"True. Well, thank you. So how long have you been making wedding gowns?"

"Oh, ages. In college I started throwing pieces together for myself, then for friends and family. And when my best friend got married I did the dress for her and the bridesmaids and then people started to ask until I had to quit my day job and did it full -time. I suppose it's a dream job but still frustrating when a client won't take your advice and ends up with some knock off design inspired by some 80's music video that I've had to put my name to. I almost want to send them to Filene's or Marshalls but I've got a mortgage to pay. You married?"

Ophelia held her hands up and smiled. "Not yet anyway. Still busy making my way through the endless pile of Mr. Wrongs. You?"

"Divorced. Caught him screwing a co-worker. At least I'll get to design another dress for myself. I took great comfort in taking nearly everything. Still, always good to get some practice in. Marie's supposed to get married in September, though we all think he's a bit of himbo. Nice guy and good to her but a bit blank. Make a great dad, I guess. How about you're sister?"

"I'm seeing her Christmas eve for the first time in years."

They spent the afternoon talking. It hadn't even occurred to Ophelia that they'd have anything in common. She was relieved to finally be able to face her seamy, darker self and atone for past cruelties. She still felt terrible about making her so miserable as a child but the past was past and she could only be a better person now, which in London was a struggle on a good day.

James and Mahesh fought for space on the worktops as they chopped and mixed, waiting to add to their concoctions on the hob. Joe tidied the house half-heartedly in the knowledge it was going to get trashed by guests. Elise kept resetting her alarm to wake up and help but sleep kept pulling her back under the duvet. Her dreams were too interesting to leave and she found that when she wasn't busy finishing pieces for the gallery opening or meeting deadlines for Opti-Level her shoulders slumped forward and she felt drained of energy. Her thoughts wandered back to Laura and inevitably she thought about how much she missed her. Sometimes she didn't have the energy for thoughts of any kind and Laura's death would haunt her the moment her thoughts were idle. It forced her to wonder what her purpose was which seemed to then prompt the question of whether there was a point to anything. Investing time or effort into anything seemed like such a risk if you could snuff it at any minute.

"Elise?"

Joe called up the stairs hoping she was home.

"Yes?"

"Are you still heading to the shops?"

"Yeah. Why?"

"It's nearly half three."

"Must've fallen asleep again. Sorry! Be right down."

She kicked the duvet off and dabbed at her cheeks with her sleeve. She rifled through her drawers and found some tights. She threw on some layers and shuffled down the stairs. Joe was about to carry some laundry up to the airing cupboard when he paused to examine his housemate.

"Have you been crying?"

"Huh?"

"Your nose and eyes are a bit red and shiny."

"Dust. My allergies are playing up. I have to tidy my room. It's a tip."

Elise tried her most convincing smile and edged by to get the shopping list in the hall. She felt a bit silly crying about Laura. It had been three months and everyone else seemed to move on. She couldn't understand why her death left her feeling so depressed. The grief was hard to articulate and she wasn't even sure it was only about Laura. She knew with the new job and exhibition she really had lots to be happy about which made the sadness all the more embarrassing. It was impossible to put the sadness into words and tried to hide it from James and Joe mainly because she didn't want to have to explain how she felt or why. She quietly grabbed the list and left.

Dusk was looming and the air was balmy. Shops had decorative tinsel in the windows with Christmas greetings. The local pound shop boasted stockings, gift wrap and decorations. Trees were leaned up against a fence with families scrutinising the size and prices. An almost tangible energy surged through the high street. Elise could see the yearning on children's faces as they passed shop fronts. People seemed either harried or generous as they made their way around the streets. Elise slipped into the

305

international food store armed with her list. The clerks chatted in Armenian as she filled her basket with last minute ingredients and emergency wines. She regularly stopped here on late nights since the night bus would stop outside, allowing her to roam the aisles and pick up sweets or nuts on her way home. Once or twice she was escorted to her house by the night clerk when she was too drunk so she always made an effort to do most of her shopping there when she was sober. She brought an over-stuffed basket to the till and the older woman smiled.

"Hello. You have quite a lot today?"

"Yes, we're having friends round."

"For Christmas?"

"Yeah."

"Are you worried?"

"About the guests? No. Why?"

"You look sad."

"I guess maybe a little."

She smiled sweetly and added a box of Gurabia to the bag after she rang up Elise's purchases. Touched by her generosity, Elise smiled and tried not to cry as she thanked her.

-

Ophelia drove up the highway to Portsmouth fiddling with the radio dial. She settled on an oldies station which seemed to change their format or decade since she was last over. Instead of doo wop classics from the 50's and 60's there was disco or Simon & Garfunkel. She tried to stay focused on the road since there was slush from an earlier snowfall. Most of the other drivers seemed oblivious to the change in the road conditions which only made Ophelia more nervous about driving. She wasn't due to meet Cordelia for another two hours but was worried about getting lost and Cordelia would assume she lost her nerve.

They agreed to meet at the Portsmouth Brewery. Portsmouth looked different from the last time she was there ten years ago. There was little chance of her running into familiar faces or recognising any if she did. It was teaming with holiday shoppers outside but the brewery was fairly quiet by comparison. It felt comforting to sit behind the glass watching chaos while nursing a beer. Holiday music from the Pogues and the Pretenders weaved through the gentle hum of conversations that took place around her.

Despite seeing photos she couldn't help but worry if she would recognise her. Cordelia was a stroppy teenager when Ophelia last saw her. Shoppers bustled past the window. The skies were blue and the snow seemed to take a break. Children clutched candy canes as they were lead by mothers clutching bags of shopping. She must have been lost in the mobs for a good few minutes before noticing a figure beside her, appraising her.

"Cordelia! Hi!"

She rose to her feet and embraced her warmly. Ophelia was struck by the realisation at how much she missed her after all the years they were apart. She realised that she felt completely alien as a grown woman. She looked more like their mother than ever but had the same dark hair as Ophelia and their dad. The small scar above her brow was still a visible reminder of the cruelty of her older sibling.

"You look great! And so grown up from when I last saw you."

"Maybe because I was 12 when you last saw me?"

Ophelia flinched, wounded by the jibe.

Noticing this, she quickly added, "Sorry. I hope you weren't waiting too long?"

"No, it's been nice to stop and rest."

"Just look at you! No more Doc Martens or black eyeliner."

"Ha, ha."

"I hope you brought photos; I want to see what you've been doing for the last ten years."

"I didn't order you anything since I wasn't sure what you'd want."

"Are you eating? I'm starved. Have you eaten here before?"

"No I was never old enough to get served here when I was younger."

Cordelia caught the waiter's attention and he took their orders. They managed to fill the time waiting for the food with safe, small talk about weather differences, news headlines and holiday plans for the new year. It felt so strange to be chatting with her sister as if she were a work colleague or acquaintance. Ophelia wanted to apologise for leaving, being mean and tell her every detail of her life since she left but something held her back. She wasn't sure where she stood with her or if she was angry or hurt or happy to see Ophelia either. She desperately wanted to feel the same easy intimacy they had as children but they were missing over a decade.

Cordelia seemed like a confident and happy woman. Ophelia remembered how much of a mess she was at her age. She was out of Birbeck for a year and was sharing a flat with Laura in Tottenham. She had such a hard time holding down crap jobs waiting tables or answering phones in between going to gigs and interviewing for a proper job. She had no idea what she wanted then and was so frustrated feeling as if she would be in limbo forever. Cordelia had none of that anger or confusion. She was planning her career path and was saving to buy a nice house in the new year.

What baffled Ophelia most was that Cordelia was taking care of their mother and not in the least bit angry or resentful that she left. They were nearly finished with their mains and talk had returned to their current lives. Ophelia told her about the redundancy and Laura's death. They managed more than a bottle of wine so were speaking with less restraint and seemed more relaxed.

"Did you ever tell mum about dad's drinking or temper?"

"I think she knew. It was one of the things that drove her away."

"If she knew, then why did she leave us with him?"

"Because dad had a job and wasn't hooked on smack. Drinking's bad but he wasn't leaving dirty needles around or having other junkies over. I think in some ways she made a really difficult decision to leave but in her mind at the time it was the best thing for us as far as she was concerned. Dad may have hit us or had a temper but he always made sure we had food and went to school. He wasn't the best dad in but at the same time he did the best he could. Imagine being in his shoes with two daughters and your wife ups and leaves one day with no explanation and you're stuck coping with that and two kids as well. It wasn't easy and to his credit he did try."

"I suppose... but he was just so cruel."

"He was human. He was grieving. He loved mom and really had a hard time with her disappearing. When she left he had no idea if there was someone else or something he did or what."

"It would have been easier if she died."

"You say that but he may have been worse in a way."

"I guess. But when I think of our friends and their families..."

"It may have seemed better but I bet they all have their own skeletons clanging around in their closets. No family's perfect."

"True but there's a limit to what everyone is willing to tolerate and I would've rather been alone than cowering in my closet when he got home drunk after darts."

"You had more trouble with mom vanishing, I think. You had her around for longer and were so close to her. I can remember her nodding off or spacing out and hated it. Maybe a small part of me knew she wouldn't be staying, I don't know."

"Maybe you were just more resilient."

"We were so different as kids, I think. You wanted everything to be perfect."

"I didn't. I wanted everything to be stable. Their fights were terrifying."

"He really did love her. If you think about how he grew up I think it puts it into perspective."

" Remember when she tried overdosing on pills and we had to call 911 since he was making fun of her? You have to break the cycle somewhere."

"I suppose, but you can always start now. He reacted to things in his own way."

"I don't think I'll be having kids somehow."

"You don't know what the future holds."

They managed another bottle of wine before Cordelia got a cab home. Ophelia waved to her as she left and cried a little over the years they had missed and all the things left unsaid. She knew they'd never be as close they way they were as kids but she was glad for the feeble attempt at bridging the gap. Ophelia hoped Cordelia knew the depths of remorse she felt over all the mean things she said or did. As she sat alone waiting for the bill she had to accept that this was the best she could do and look forward from now on instead of tormenting herself over the past.

Later that evening she dreamt that it was Laura in the back of a black cab waving. The mist curled into ghostly figures that slowly sailed forth with the taxi into the distance. She woke in the lonely hotel room with tears trying to recall Laura's face.

People began to arrive after seven. Elise was still upstairs sitting on the edge of her bed trying to get ready, willing herself to be happy and sociable. She could hear greetings and pleasantries exchanged in the hall while scarves were unwound, shoes were removed and bottles were presented. It seemed strange knowing Laura wasn't coming. Last year she spontaneously led everyone in a sloppy rendition of The Twelve Days of Christmas. It took ages to recall what all twelve days were and by the end everyone had given up and started to randomly shout out a made up gift. It was the sort of thing that couldn't be replicated or planned but exactly the sort of thing Laura was known to do.

With Kat and Ophelia in the States it seemed to amplify her loneliness. She had friends arriving downstairs but her closest friends were all far away. She had to get out of London for Christmas. If today was hard Christmas would be much more diffi-cult. She considered seeing her parents but worried that would make her feel even worse. It was an effort keeping a brave or neutral face with friends. Having her mother pry or offering daft suggestions meant to help would only make it worse. She knew she had to finish getting dressed and go downstairs before someone came up looking for her.

Music, chatter and laughter met her on the landing. The house smelled of mince pies, samosas and mulled wine. The tree was up by the window. Quiet anticipation glowed amongst the candles casting glints of light on the box of decorations. Gifts were strewn beneath the tree already collecting needles from the branches. She put on a smile hoping her heart and spirit would follow suit.

Joe was in a cardigan and shirt but paired it with shiny red rubber hot pants.

"Hey, Joe."

"There you are! I didn't think we'd see you. Everything okay?"

"Yeah, just busy on that project."

"Ian's here. Have you heard from Kat?"

"No, why?"

"He just seems a bit distracted is all."

-

Kat finished breakfast and sat, waiting to see if she could manage not to be sick. Andrew dabbed his sticky fingers on the table picking up bits of cereal and offering them to Kat. Beth orbited around the table pouring coffee and wiping up stray crumbs.

"How are you? Feeling queasy?"

"So far so good. And still not sure what I'm going to do."

"The doctor seemed to think you're about a month and a half along. So you've got a bit of time yet."

"Hardly seems like enough to decide."

"No time frame will seem enough for those kinds of decisions. What are you up to today?"

"Seeing Ed for lunch and a movie."

A knowing grin spread across Beth's face.

"It isn't like that. We're just mates," Kat remarked.

"I didn't say anything."

"You didn't have to. Your Cheshire smile said it all."

"He just seems a bit taken with you."

"He was about five years ago. It's a bit different now especially with me being married and pregnant."

"Like that's ever put a man off before. Just be careful. Your hormones and trouble with Ian probably have your heart all over the place."

-

Everyone had an ornament or two. Some brought ornaments they made or found and the rest were from the box James had in the attic. The living room was crowded with friends and familiar faces but it only served to remind Elise of who wasn't there. Ian hung a star on the lower branch and caught sight of Elise.

"Hey. How's things?"

314

"Good. You? Congratulations on the play'"

"Cheers."

"When do you go?"

"Not til April. Got another few months. How was the exhibition?"

"Went really well. Thanks."

"Listen I'm sorry I didn't make it."

"No you're not. Just like you're not sorry about how you treat Kat. So long as you're happy or taken care of it doesn't matter what happens to her."

"Is that what she said?"

"It's obvious to everyone."

"When's she back?"

"For fuck's sake, she's *your* wife."

"I'm not so sure."

Elise was going to press him further but he was drunk and she was in a cantankerous mood. Instead she drank mulled wine and watched the tree transform into a blur of tinsel, lights and baubles before passing out on the sofa.

-

The large UPS truck parked outside of Beth's house. Ed smiled on the porch in his uniform when Kat opened the door.

"Hey. Thought I'd grab you before I drop the truck since my last delivery was nearby. Is that cool?"

"Sure. Nice uniform."

"Ha! If you're nice I'll let you try it on. Ready?"

"Sure."

They dropped the truck at the depot and got in Ed's car. The snow was already starting to collect black patches of car exhaust and brown flecks of grit. Kat stared out thoughtfully as they left the business park.

"Why can't it stay clean and new?"

"The snow? Then how would you ever appreciate the first snowfall? I reckon the snow is a perfect reflection of our attitude towards it. At first we're all like 'Ooh, pretty!' Then we gotta shovel the stuff and we're like 'Aw crap!' and finally we just get sick of seeing it and it goes."

"I missed it."

"You've been gone too long then."

He smiled and turned on the radio. Train in Vain from the Clash came on and Ed gleefully turned up the volume. He started singing loudly and urged Kat to join in. They rolled the windows down and sang out. The icy wind hit her cheeks as she sang the words. She felt far from London, her troubled marriage, angry boss, Laura's death and everything else that made her miserable over the past five years. Moments like this made her want to stay stateside and pick up where she left off. She knew she was on borrowed time and had to make a decision about the pregnancy and then figure out where and how she would start over. The song faded out and a commercial came on.

"You hungry?"

Kat smiled, "always."

Ed parked the car and they headed to Chinatown on foot. Kat thought Downtown Crossing looked a lot more crowded than she ever remembered.

"Is Stairway to Heaven still open?"

"Oh man, you remember that place?"

She smiled. "What can I say? I'm old school."

Ed took her hand and gave it a squeeze. Her pulse quickened and he led her by the hand. "I haven't been there in ages. Want to check it out after we eat and see if it's still there?"

"Sure. You ever go to the tea room upstairs?"

"Nah. Heard about it though."

The restaurant was busy with tired shoppers and cranky kids. Kat could see the Naked Eye strip club clearly from the window. Ed poured them each some jasmine tea. He snuck a glance at her and smiled. Kat buried her head in the menu and tried to remember she was a responsible adult instead of a star crossed teenager.

"What are you doing for Christmas?"

"Just going to my folks. My sister's supposed to be there with her husband and daughter. They were at his parents' for Thanksgiving. What about you? Are you at Beth's?"

"Not sure yet. My friend Ophelia's over from London so we might hang out."

"Well you're both welcome at chez Woods. My mother would love to entertain two London lasses."

"Cheers."

After sharing a few dishes they returned to Winter St. The basement space that once housed Stairway to Heaven was derelict with crumpled newspapers and beer cans alluding to the rough sleepers that had taken up residence in the hall. A rat scurried past causing Kat to jump.

"Fancy seeing if the Tea Room's still here?"

Ed nodded and they waited for the lift. As the doors opened Kat was reminded why she would hold her breath on her way up to the Tea Room.

"This lift always stank of wee!"

Ed smiled at her trying not to breathe in. "Lift?"

"Sorry. Elevator."

"You're so British now."

"Hardly. I've been there five years so you practically pick up the slang by osmosis."

"British and educated."

"I didn't fit in there at all. I never realised how American I really was til I left."

"So now that you've gotten so patriotic are you gonna move back?"

The lift opened and the smell of sandalwood drew them to the entrance. The mystic themed paintings still graced the walls with crystals and stones dotted about. There was comfort in the fact that one Boston institution was stubbornly constant. Kat hoped it would always stay as she remembered it and that going forward she would always associate it with Ed and the way he made her feel that afternoon. She asked for two readings. The girl returned with two steaming Styrofoam cups and explained the wait shouldn't be more than 30 minutes. Kat and Ed relaxed and sank into a sofa with their tea.

"You still haven't answered me."

"That's because I still have no idea what I'm doing."

He nodded and gently blew into his tea.

"The only thing I've decided is that I'm getting a divorce." She looked into her tea. "I should've left a while ago."

Ed placed his hand on her shoulder and rubbed it. "Everything has a way of working out. You'll make the right decisions for you whatever they are. Even when we make the wrong decisions we live with them and make them right."

Kat nodded and tried to keep the tears in. "Some of the decisions affect other people."

"Screw other people. You have to do what's right for you. Ain't nobody else gonna look out for your best interests or your dreams since everyone's busy looking out for themselves."

She sipped her tea. "I'm still trying to figure out what my dreams are. How about you? What are yours?"

"Right now I'm just hoping to save enough for a house."

"Don't bother, it's overrated."

"What?"

"I'm a homeowner and it sucks. I'm responsible for all the repairs, maintenance, upkeep, blah, blah, blah. It's not worth it."

"Yeah but you have security."

"Security for what? To be tied down? I'd rather be able to up and move, go on a long holiday and not have to worry. The less you have, the less you have to lose."

Just then a man in a suit with white hair and moustache called Ed's name.

-

Ophelia checked into a nearby hotel in Portsmouth, New Hampshire. It was cheaper than the one in Massachusetts and had free internet access. She wanted to check her emails since she got to Boston to see if Steve sent any messages since their farewell snog. She experienced a swift flutter in her stomach whenever she thought of him or the passionate clinch in his bedroom. She admitted to herself that she did feel something more for him but the feelings were proving hard to identify in the haze of mistrust and self doubt. Getting involved with Steve exclusively and intimately seemed straightforward but there was a small, yet insistent, inner voice worried about self preservation and a shadow of doubt cast over her desires to be worthy of such affections.

She recalled two weeks spent on Laura's futon after one ugly break-up. Laura was adamant that his infidelities had nothing to do with her and how all of his nasty accusations had more to do with his own issues and hang ups. Ophelia wanted to believe her back then but was secretly convinced otherwise. After two days of facing her demons she realised that she no longer had to tolerate monstrous relationships herself. She had as much right as Cordelia or Caroline to be happy. She had always been afraid that if she wasn't dating a monster she would have to take the role herself as she had with Cordelia. She wondered if a small part of her felt she deserved it.

She thought of how polite and good natured Steve was and worried she might not be capable of loving him or anyone.

Laura would be outraged Ophelia was reticent now with her heart. The acute awareness of her absence stung. She needed Laura for her advice and encouragement at that moment. In her heart she knew just what Laura would say and would have to find the strength within to listen to her heart. She realised as she sat in the lobby facing the cool blue light of the monitor that it was those small acts of courage that would keep an element of Laura alive for her.

As the browser opened she realised she missed London and the life she made for herself there. The realisation threw her as the page loaded onto the screen. She spotted an email from Elise asking after Kat.

>Hey Feelie
>Hope you got there okay. How was the flight?
>Saw Ian at our party and he seemed even stranger that I thought he'd be. Has >Kat heard from him?

Ophelia explained all she knew and felt like a gossip as soon as she sent it. Steve sent a friendly email asking if she arrived safe and included a joke about a parrot in a freezer. It was nice to hear from him but it wasn't the message she hoped for. She wasn't sure what she wanted from him but she was fairly sure it wasn't a parrot joke.

23 DECEMBER

Elise sat on the top deck of the bus and let her thoughts flit between the email Ophelia sent her to the meeting she was due to have with Marcus in an hour. She wondered how Kat was dealing with everything especially in such a hormonal state. Then she started to worry about meeting with Marcus. He sent her a meeting invite last week and she couldn't help but think it was about her contract. She really enjoyed the work and her colleagues so for the first time she found herself wanting to stay. The fear of losing her job sat uncomfortably with her. She wasn't accustomed to caring about her day jobs. It wasn't so much that she was afraid of getting the sack as she dreaded being told she wasn't any good at something she enjoyed doing. She craved encouragement from her folks. She wanted them to understand how important her work was to her. She didn't want to be defined by a husband and never understood why in that day and age it was so important to her parents. Wasn't her happiness enough?

Her ringtone sliced through the worry and she answered without even checking who it was.

"Elise it's your father."

"Hello daddy."

"Now I'm sure you know why I'm ringing. Your mother's awfully worried about you. She said you're not planning in coming for Christmas."

"...no, I hadn't planned on it."

"Darling your mother and I would really like to see you. I'm not sure what's gotten you so upset but I think it's worth discussing if it's going to keep you away. Now what is it?"

"Nothing, daddy. I've just made other plans."

"Rubbish. What other plans?"

"I'm volunteering at Shelter on Christmas morning."

"Well then you can come in the afternoon. What's the fuss?"

"Going is the fuss. I'll be tired after that, daddy."

"Elise your mother and I aren't going to be here forever. All we want is to see you and have the family together for Christmas and Boxing Day. Now I hardly think that's asking a lot. If something's bothering you I should think we could discuss it when you're here."

Elise wanted to find the words to explain how hurt and rejected she felt but instead grunted a defeated assent. She hated herself for giving in and hurried off the phone as she neared the office.

Marcus was happy to see her and ushered her into his office promising some kind of tea hand picked by monkeys. Elise was intrigued so she hurried inside and sat down. Marcus followed and handed her a teacup.

"It's a green tea but the monkeys apparently have this great intuition abut what leaves are best."

"Cheers."

"As much as I love that the tea is from monkeys it's not why I had you come in today."

"I figured as much."

"The client rang on Friday and really loved the response the campaign's had so far. And the other ideas you've had have really impressed the account manager as well as myself."

"Thanks. Glad they liked my ideas."

"So much so that we want to get you working on a few other accounts. So I figured I'd get you in before we break up for the holidays and give you some food for thought."

Elise was relieved and flattered. She tried not to worry that all of her good ideas were spent and instead focused on the teacup.

"We were hoping in the new year you may want to go perm? You'd have some flex time to continue with your art."

Elise was stunned. She wanted to accept it then and there but a tiny nagging doubt held her tongue. Sensing her hesitation Marcus continued.

"You don't have to answer today. That's precisely why I suggested you think about it over the Christmas break. Any big plans?"

She sighed hating the cliché as it left her lips. "Going to my parent's."

The snow lay heavy outside absorbing any noise. Front windows were lit to showcase smiling children throwing ribbons while parents hovered nearby with steaming mugs and camcorders. Kat returned her gaze from the window to Andrew's delighted shrieks. Beth and Joe exchanged gifts and smiles over Andrew's pure ecstasy. A small part of her felt a fleeting pang of regret before she remembered her marriage bore no resemblance to theirs. She focused a steely will on her nausea and handed gifts to everyone.

"Happy Christmas!" Kat shouted.

"Merry Christmas yourself. How are you feeling?"

"Okay. What time are you going to set off?"

"Round noon maybe? When's Ophelia coming?"

"I'm going to pick her up, actually."

Joe sat on the floor playing with Andrew and one of his new trucks. Kat had to look away to stop from crying. She couldn't tell if she was honestly touched or if it was her hormones wreaking havoc with her emotions again. The night before she descended into tears after "I Saw Mommy Kissing Santa Claus" was on as Joe and Beth tried not to laugh. Beth and Kat went to the kitchen for coffee refills and bin liners.

"Say hi to Ed's mother for me. She used to work at the insurance firm I was at before I had Andrew."

"Sure. And please stop giving me that look. I know you're worried. I'll be fine."

"It's not just you I'm worried about. Ed seems to be a bit smitten and you're not only going through a divorce but not even living in the same country."

"It's not like I haven't been honest with him. Besides nothing's happened since that night I got shitfaced and snogged him. I'd feel too weird doing anything in my condition anyhow."

"Your condition! You sound like an old lady!"

"Seriously. I feel more like I have some weird STI with the nausea and symptoms and all. Or like I'm possessed."

"When are you going?"

"Friday the 27th at ten."

"Are you sure you don't want me to come with you?"

"Definitely. I'd feel awful if you had to get a sitter to accompany me to my abortion."

"We could always bring him and I'd just tell the protesters we already have one."

Kat smiled at Beth before they erupted into peals of laughter.

-

Elise jogged up Tottenham Court Rd to Store St. She asked the driver to meet her there rather than pick her up at the Shelter. The vegetarian sausages felt thick and heavy in her belly as she made her way to the car. Nancy had turned up again looking worse than she had the year before. She saw too many familiar faces and wished more could be done than spending a few days passing out teas and having chats knowing that their situation won't be much different and she can return to her comfortable life.

She was relieved to see Chester was driving an unassuming sedan and waved as the car came into view. He waved back and started the car.

"I haven't kept you ages, have I?"

"Nah, just texting the missus."

"Shit, I'm so sorry you had to come all the way out here and get me."

"Nah, she's fine. Her mum's over and they're making dinner. Gets me out of the house and pays double."

"Fair enough. The roads should be fairly empty so shouldn't take you too long. Thanks, by the way. And happy Christmas."

"Happy Christmas to you! How've you been keeping? Been a while since we seen you."

"Busy. How bout you?"

"Can't complain."

The ride was smooth and Elise insisted on tipping Chester for his time despite his protestations. As the car snaked down the drive two of Elise's cousins ran up to the car. Ellie was nine and her brother Harry was six. Ellie had a look of thunder on her face as Elise stepped out of the car.

"What's happened?" Elise asked.

"You're late!"

"Sorry?"

"We've had to wait to open our presents because of you."

"Ellie, I'm so sorry. I was helping some friends."

"And you smell funny. Now we'll have to wait for you to get cleaned up."

Elise rolled her eyes already regretting her promise to her father. "I'll be quick as can be. Why not try and sort the gifts by name and arrange the notepads to jot down who they're from?"

Ellie slowly walked back to the house unconvinced as Elise raced up the stairs with her overnight bag straight into her room. Elise stood in the shower in her room's en suite and tried to get into a cheerful and festive mood. She felt out of place at her family home and missed her place in Hackney. She dressed and brought down her gifts for everyone. Her mother was seated by the tree in the family room sipping champagne as Ellie ordered Harry around the tree and shouted at him when he piled the gifts wrong. Her aunt Jean was reading the Radio Times curled up on the sofa beside her mother.

"Where's daddy?"

"Choosing the wine with your uncle. They'll be here in a moment. Glad you finally managed to arrive."

She tried to ignore the comment and sat in the chair across from them. The canapés were out on the coffee table beside a Wedgewood teapot. She poured herself some tea and tried to relax despite the uneasy silence. Jean abruptly closed the magazine and placed it near her feet.

"Your mother told me about your new job. You must be so pleased."

"How do you mean?"

"Well to finally have a good job in a creative field."

"Oh. Yeah I guess so. How are you and Uncle Phillip?"

"Very good. Thank you."

Ellie continued to direct Harry's stacking before pausing. "Mummy can I open the first gift?"

"Yea, of course dear. As soon as we're all together."

At previous Christmas gatherings Elise prepared questions and topics that would guarantee a relatively peaceful visit. This year she hadn't really planned on going nor could she find the energy to bother preparing. She sat quietly trying to focus on her

330

breathing so that she wouldn't fall asleep. Her father and uncle could be heard down the hall to her relief. Time seemed to slow since she entered the family room. He came in carrying a decanter full of red wine followed by Uncle Phillip with the tray of glasses. Unwrapping the gifts took ages as it always did. There were rules that were strictly followed such as one person was to open a gift at a time, they had to show it to everyone and then write down what it was and who it was from. The whole tedious process took an average two hours more if there were a lot of people or a lot of gifts. Elise usually received frumpy clothing her mother thought she should wear or books her father thought she should read or tickets for holidays with her family that she tried to beg off. She gave up asking for things since her requests often went unheard or ignored.

An hour into it she was desperate to leave or fall asleep or start screaming. Volunteering at Shelter seemed to only further emphasise how the other half lives and that Elise's family was that other half. It wouldn't bother her as much if she felt close to them but she didn't. There had always been a formal distance since she was small that was aggravated by years in boarding schools.

Three hours later the last gift was opened. Paper was strewn about the living room, the wine decanter empty. Elise carried a sleepy Harry to the dining room.

"I think we should invade Iraq. Hussein is as bad as Hitler. He's a global threat."

Elise rolled her eyes at her mother's memorised statements from the Telegraph. "He's not a direct threat to the UK. If anything we stand to lose a lot of money that could be spent on helping the British people since it'll go to the military, we'll lose the lives of countless men and women on a hunch as well as the possible risk of straining relations with UK Muslims. The invasion is a terrible idea. They still haven't found any weapons."

Elise's father looked up from his roast and smiled. "Dear, they wouldn't put all this money and effort into invading if they didn't have proof."

"If they have sufficient evidence then why aren't they sharing it with the British public? If they're going to send all of these troops over they owe it to their families to justify the risk."

Elise went quiet thinking of how awful it was to lose Laura and couldn't understand how any human life could be so cheap to anyone. Sensing the imminent argument, Elizabeth changed the subject.

"Did you hear June's son Oliver came out?"

Elise snorted at her mother's shock. "Mother it was pretty obvious."

"What a waste."

Elise stopped and cocked her head at her mother who was now a bit tipsy. "How do you mean, mother?"

"He's an educated, handsome and well mannered man."

"His being gay doesn't change any of those qualities."

"It does for young women hoping to find a good husband."

"But not everyone wants that."

"Yes, you've made that painfully obvious, dear."

"It's only painful to you, which in my opinion's pretty selfish."

"Why must you be so aggressive with me?"

"Maybe my aggression is a response to your conditional love."

"And here we go. Why do you always have to cause scenes at family gatherings?"

"Why do you insist I come if you're going to criticise me the entire time?"

Her father set his cutlery down. "Elise, please. You're upsetting your mother."

"What about me? I seem to get upset every time I visit. Why do you keep asking me round if you can't accept me for the person I've become?"

Elizabeth got to her feet and shuffled her children out of the room as the voices escalated into accusatory shouts. Elise followed suit and skulked up to her room ten minutes later. She took out her laptop and emailed Ophelia to say she'd be joining her in Boston tomorrow. She tried to regulate her breathing but couldn't stave off the tears. She collapsed onto her bed and surrendered to frustrated sobs until she drifted off to an uneasy sleep.

When she woke the sky was welcoming hues of pink and violet in anticipation of dawn. Her eyes felt tender from the tears. She felt foolish and vulnerable standing in the bathroom recalling last night's harsh words. Her visits home always seemed to end this way. She exhausted every possible strategy though admitted to herself that this time she made no effort. She was tired from the volunteer work, annoyed about their absence from her gallery show and weary from years of the same arguments. She filled the sink with cold water and soaked her face.

She gingerly crept downstairs to the kitchen and turned the light switch on. She got the mash and sprouts from the fridge. She heated them in the microwave and added a dollop of margarine. She poured a glass of tap water then shuffled to the breakfast room.

The Sunday Telegraph was still scattered across half the table. The crossword was nearly complete with a few pens near some scribbles. As she ate the leftovers she eyed the room for a pad of paper or a notebook, finding a corner peaking out from under the sports pages. She tried to start the letter three times before finding the right tone. As she stirred the mash and sprouts together she tried to calmly catalogue all the perceived slights she was dealt over the years whether deliberate or not. She tried to explain how hurt and alone she often felt because of them and that while she didn't have any suggestions or answers to fix things she did want their relationship to improve. She explained she was leaving for Boston early on Boxing Day and promised to ring with an address once she arrived.

-

Kat sat on the chair in the hotel room while Ophelia finished dressing.

"Is there like a special place where hotels all get their furniture?" Kat asked.

"I know, right? Do you have the directions?"

"Yes. Hey can we stop for Chinese on the way? I'm suddenly really craving egg foo yung!"

"Sure. Whatever the parasite needs to keep you from sicking up on me."

"Do you think this means I'm not maternal?"

"No. I think it means you're divorcing a man who doesn't deserve your love and the last thing you need is the financial, emotional and physical drain of a wailing mini-Ian who will keep you fettered to his awful family for the rest of your life."

"Wow. Nicely put."

"I try."

They managed to find a Chinese restaurant and were relieved to find it open. The staff seemed thrilled to have more customers to break up the monotony. They sat down and were surprised to see three other tables filled with people. Ophelia looked over and shrugged.

"Jehovah's Witnesses?" Kat offered.

"Shhhhhh, they might hear you! Then you'll never be one of the few who get in to the VIP heaven!"

"We should try and just get a few small things. I bet Ed's mother will have puddings."

"You can say desserts here, remember? So how do you know Ed again?"

"From years ago, way before I met Ian. We ran into each other and have been spending time together."

Kat began to get nervous, worried Ophelia would be able to sense some attraction between them. She was starting to fret that his family might, too. She hadn't done more than hold hands with him since their kiss that night but she couldn't stop thinking about him. She would have dreams of him kissing the back of her neck, caressing her how she always longed to be touched, wanted by someone and then wake in a sweat frightened of her desires and yet disappointed that they were only dreams. She was convinced everyone could see directly into her heart where she harboured these secrets. She wondered if her feelings had become transparent like her pregnancy symptoms and everyone was judging her accordingly.

Ophelia was lost in preoccupations of her own; her meeting with Cordelia nagged at her. She wanted to see Cordelia again but worried it would sour the good feeling from their first meeting, bringing all their old resentments to the surface. Once the bitterness emerged they would resume their old roles of bully and victim. She wondered if everyone was doomed to play the roles they first created for themselves with some people mired in some compulsive satire or tragedy. As the Chinese tea was poured by the waitress she thought about Cordelia and wondered if she was with their mother. She buried her mother when she left home and if given the choice to raise one person from the dead she thought Laura deserved it more than her mother.

"You okay? I thought I was supposed to have the hormone surges."

Ophelia looked up and realised she was crying.

"Sorry. I was miles away."

"I can tell. You all right?"

"Yeah. Just thinking of Laura and my sister."

-

Ed was crawling around on all fours while his niece fed him pieces of a chocolate Santa. He barked and sat up panting with his tongue lolling out. The little girl was wearing a red velvet dress that bore evidence of chocolate fingers. Her strawberry blonde hair was starting poke out of a tight bun resting on her crown. She waved as Kat and Ophelia poked their heads in from the front hall.

"I have a chocolate face!" She sang waving sticky fingers. "And this is my dog Mr Fluffy."

Ed barked a greeting and sniffed behind her ears prompting fits of giggles. He picked her up and held her upside down.

"Nelly these are my friends from England, where the queen lives."

Her giggles ceased and her face grew serious with awe.

Kat and Ophelia waved. Ophelia rooted around her purse and managed to find a Cadbury Flake, Tube map and two pound coin to present his niece. The improvised exotic offerings were a bigger hit than the Barbie doll Kat grabbed at the 24 hour Walgreens on Route One. Ed's mother Carol fussed over them and insisted they drink some eggnog.

"Wow. I can't believe I nearly forgot about eggnog!"

337

Ophelia's spirits brightened as she tried to remember the last time she drank it. Ed leaned in and whispered loudly.

"It's loaded with whisky and rum. You've been warned."

He winked and sank back into his chair. Nelly kept asking Kat and Ophelia to read out all the Tube stops on her Tube map. Ed's sister was dozing on the sofa snoring softly as her husband flicked through the channels. Carol brought out a huge glass pitcher along with gingerbread men.

"It's too bad you girls missed lunch. The turkey was perfect. I can always make you turkey sandwiches. Just ask."

"Thanks, Mrs Woods."

"Kat, please call me Carol."

Kat smiled sheepishly and nodded. The smell of the eggnog made her ill so she had ginger ale and watched Ophelia get tipsy after a glass. Ed laughed at her losing track of her words.

"Didn't I tell you? The turkey helps. That and the fact I've had all of December to build up a tolerance."

Kat and Ophelia felt comfortable and completely at home. It was the first Christmas in years that either enjoyed. As the evening progressed they all ended up in the sitting room on the other sofa watching cartoons with Nelly. Ophelia found everything in them hilarious and Kat would tear up at any twee scenes because of her hormones.

Ed put his arm around her and handed her tissues. Carol sat across them in a recliner.

"Did Ed tell you I got divorced?"

Kat looked over in surprise. She didn't think Ed told his mother much at all but was relieved Ed hadn't told her she was pregnant. Carol continued casually.

"It all seems overwhelming at first. And then you get to stages of grief, guilt, anger; just like you do with a death. The one word of advice I wish I was given was that you haven't failed or wasted years when you were married. You learn so much in marriage; negotiation, sacrifice, patience...tons they never mention at the wedding. Even though the marriage dies the relationship doesn't. It simply changes. It's ugly at first though most changes are. But sometimes you're still left with a great friend if you're lucky."

Kat thanked Ed's mother through tears. She hoped Carol would be too drunk to remember this tomorrow. Nelly was slumped against Kat who was picking flecks of sticky candy cane out of her matted hair. Kat smiled at the temporary patchwork family she managed to stitch herself into for the day. She recalled how Laura always insisted that friends were merely family you had the luxury of choosing. Kat always believed her but the truth of her words resonated deeply at that moment.

26 DECEMBER

Elise sat under the harsh lights of the Heathrow terminal. She couldn't understand how the world's busiest airport could be so shabby. She managed to buy a ticket and was sat eyeing the departure boards for her gate number. She blew on her tea wondering if her mother found the letter or bothered to read it. She took out her notebook and reviewed the survey she prepared and went over to the internet terminals. She got out her list of email addresses and typed out the following:

Hello

You may not remember bumping into me but my name is Elise Blythe-Hughes. I'm a London-based artist and my recent project is compiling responses to the following questions. You can reply with your answers via email or write them out and post them to the address included at the bottom of this email. You do not need to answer all the questions or even include your identity. Your time and help with this is appreciated.

Does everything happen for a reason?
What was the easiest time in your life so far?
What was the hardest time in your life so far?
Who has influenced you most?
What has made you the person you are?
Have you settled for mediocrity?
What is your greatest regret?
How do you define happiness?
If you had a week to live, how would you spend that time?
Where do we go when we die?
What do you need to change about yourself?
What did you want to do as a child when you grew up?
What are you doing now as an adult?
What's missing in your life?
Why not you?

Elise found an online translation site and translated the missive into ten other languages and BCC'd everyone in the contacts list. She figured even if a small number of people responded she would have enough to work with.

-

Ophelia woke with a throbbing headache. Kat was retching in the hotel loo. She fumbled around in her purse for aspirin before realising there was nothing to drink. She reluctantly rolled out of bed and knocked on the bathroom door.

"You all right in there?"

"…yeah…think I'm done. Sorry about that. Did I wake you?"

"Nah, was half awake anyway. Did you want to come downstairs with me for some breakfast?"

Kat opened the door and forced a smile. "Sure. I bet you they don't have fry-up."

"They don't even have Boxing Day. Come on."

After eating, Ophelia checked her email and saw Elise was arriving that afternoon. "I'll have to get her at Logan. Guess her family visit bombed. You coming with me?"

Kat looked at her slippers. "I was gonna hang out with Ed again…"

"Seriously?"

"He asked me to dinner and it's a nice distraction since I have the procedure tomorrow."

"Fair enough. I'll go on my own. Are you staying here tonight or at Beth's? Or are you at Ed's?"

"Ophelia! Stop! Do you mind if I stay here at the hotel with you?"

"Only if you don't mind sharing a bed with Elise. Unless she booked something else though she's not exactly one to plan ahead."

-

On the flight Elise was sat next to a Buddhist nun in grey and burgundy robes. She tried to seem nonchalant and returned her warm smile after she stowed her bags in the overhead compartment. After the plane took off the meal trolley made its way down the aisle. They exchanged smiles again seeing they both picked the vegetarian option. After finishing the meal, Elise poured her small bottle of wine.

"What brings you to Boston?"

"The Munsusa temple in Wakefield."
"Would you be interested in answering some questions for a survey I'm doing?"

The nun politely agreed and Elise dug her notebook out of her bag. She turned to a fresh sheet of paper and wrote out the questions and answers as she asked them.

"How do you define happiness?"

"We all have the power to be happy. It's a matter of conscious choice."

Elise finished the survey and thanked her neighbour. She slipped on the airline issue headset and found herself struck by her response about happiness. She found it hard to believe that happiness was that easy but after her second glass of wine she considered there was certainly some truth in that belief. Before Laura died , never stopped to question what she was doing or what direction her life took; she simply accepted it and made the best of it. The few months following Laura's death, Elise fed her grief until it smothered her, allowing herself to sink deeper into depression. The nun's response forced her to wonder if it was that easy to fix.

-

Kat sat across Ed and smiled. She wondered why every Bickford's in the US seemed to not only have the same décor but also the same views from the window. They ordered coffee and sundaes.

"Sorry, it's the only thing I'm in the mood for."

"It's fine, seriously. I'm down with having dessert first. Just don't tell my mom!"
"I won't, I promise." She smiled and gave the scouts honour hand gesture. "Your mum was lovely. Thanks again for having us. We had a great time."

"Was your friend okay? She was totally wasted when you two left."

"She's feeling it today."

"Mom ought to bottle and sell that stuff."

"Ed, I want you know I have had so much fun hanging out with you."

"....but... Is there a 'but' coming?"

"Sort of. I can't know what state I'll be in after tomorrow and I've decided that I have to return to London even if it's just to sort my divorce out. Have I totally wrecked our night?"

"You worry too much. I know you got a lot going on and I'm just glad to spend time with you while you're here. If you come back I'll still be here, probably in the same job, same apartment, but I may get more tattoos."

"Thanks."

-

Elise jogged over to Ophelia as if they'd been apart for decades. Ophelia couldn't help but laugh, hopeful that Elise's recent bleak cloud had lifted, allowing rays of her old sunny disposition to filter through.

"You're chipper. Are you still drunk from the free booze on the plane?"

"Feelie! I'm glad to see you. Where's Kat?"

"Off with an old flame. Feel like coming with us to get her abortion tomorrow?"

"Uh, sure. Is she okay?"

"I think she's trying to just make the right decisions and not get too emotional. Looks like she'll have a lot ahead of her."

"I asked my dad and he gave me the names of two divorce lawyers he knows. We could ring them this week."

"Which brings me to the obvious question: what the fuck happened?"

"Same thing that always happens. I was tired from the volunteer shift, my bratty cousins were driving me mad and my mother started on about how being gay was a waste and I took the bait. I lost my rag and stormed out. It's like I'm forever trapped at 17 whenever I see them."

"I'm sorry."

"I left a note this time."

"You wrote your parents a Dear John letter?"

"What? No. I just told them how I felt and that I wanted a relationship with them but something had to change and I was happy to work with them on changing things."

"Did you need to crash at my hotel?"

"Actually that would be great. Cheers."

27 DECEMBER

Ophelia drove down Interstate 95. Kat sat beside her, trying not to doze off. Kat looked over.

Ophelia looked over quickly before returning her gaze to the road. "What time did you get in?"

"Four." She whispered feebly.

Elise poked her head between them. "Did you bring balloons to your party?"

"There was no party. I am having the procedure today so that was the last thing on my mind. We just snogged a little and I fell asleep on him. All totally innocent. I told him I'm flying back on the 30th."

"What airline are you two flying back on?"

"Virgin." Ophelia answered as Kat's head snapped back to wake up. "Kat, just take a nap. We'll wake you when we get there."

"Sorry. I think it's more nerves than anything. I tend to shut down and sleep when I get stressed."

Elise patted her shoulder and Ophelia watched for the exits. She turned the radio on to fill the silence. They managed to arrive only ten minutes late. Ophelia drove them to the front of Planned Parenthood.

"We're already a little late. Elise can you take Kat in and I'll find parking?"

Elise nodded and helped Kat out of the passenger seat. She ushered her past the small group of protesters and muttered. "Fuck them, Kat. They don't know you. This is one of thousands of decisions you make in your life. It won't define you and this will eventually fade into your past. They don't know you and have no right to judge you. Keep your head high."

Kat squeezed her hand and whispered her thanks. She refused to show any tears to the group of shouts, pleas and accusations. There was so much happening to her at the time that none of it felt real. She knew eventually it would all catch up to her but she needed to be numb to get anything done. Ed and Beth had commended her strength and she laughed at them; it wasn't strength but self preservation. She had to get through the next few months. She filled in the forms and the two of them sat in the waiting room.

Elise patted her hand. "Want me to go in with you?"

"I'm fine. I don't think they'd let you anyway. I just want to get it over with and focus on getting the rest of my shitty, I mean shiny new life together."

Elise sat back. "When you get back, you can stay at mine until you meet with the lawyer and figure you out if you can stay at the flat. Ian's folks are nearby so he could probably stay with them and you could stay in the flat. I guess it depends on how much of a dick he decides to be."

The nurse called Kat. She stood, took her bag and followed the nurse down the corridor. Ophelia managed to find a space and dumped all her change into the meter which only gave her an hour. She walked towards the clinic and was surprised to be met by the protesters since she wasn't having anything done.

An older woman shouted. "Please don't kill your baby!"

Ophelia stopped dead in her tracks. "Excuse me? Are you going to carry it for nine months, go through the agony of labour, pay to raise it, educate and feed it? Love it? I bet you're the same kind of person who's voting to get people off welfare or to kick out immigrants. What even makes you think I'm getting an abortion? These guys do birth control, HIV tests and pregnancy tests. That's why it's called Planned Parenthood and not Abortion Superstore! If you're so big on God, why don't you leave it to him to judge and go home to your own children?"

She stormed in irritated and looked for Kat and Elise. Elise waved her down. Ophelia complained about the exchange she had with the protester and Elise laughed about her outburst.

"That is class! I can't believe you told her off."

Ophelia took her coat off and laid it over her lap. "I wasn't going for an abortion. Where did she get off?"

"We didn't say anything to them. I just gave Kat a pep talk as we walked by the mob. Did you get my questionnaire?"

"Huh? Oh, yeah. I'll fill it in when I get back to London. Did you check for responses yet?"

"No, though I managed to get a nun on the flight to fill it in."

"Bonus. Reckon she'll be okay?"

"Kat's strong. I think it's a tough decision but she had to. What else could she do? She can go back, get the divorce and start over with a clean slate."

31 DECEMBER

Ophelia watched the cartoon plane cross the digital Atlantic leaving a dotted line in its wake. The cabin lights were dim and several travellers donned masks sleeping slack-jawed. Kat came from the loos brandishing two small bottles of wine.

"They let you get two?"

"I told em one was for a mate. You get the next round though."

"Fair enough. How long will you be waiting at Heathrow for?"

"Only an hour or two. Her plane lands at half nine. I'll grab a coffee and switch on my mobile. I'll probably have an hour or two of texts to catch up on."

"And delete all the 'Happy Christmas' ones."

"Oh god, yeah. I forgot about those. You getting a cab or is Steve picking you up?"

"Ha! I don't think he gets back until the third. I'll take the tube. If I'm feeling really extravagant I'll take the Heathrow Express. Any more thought on whether you're staying in London? Ed looked like he was gonna cry when you left him at the gate."

"He is really sweet, isn't he? I'm actually thinking of going to uni in September and finally get a degree."

"In what?"

"Not sure; either accounting or languages. Something stable I can use in the UK or US or even further abroad. The divorce stuff should be sorted by then, right?"

"Sounds about right."

"I'm hoping it might get sorted by June and if I get a decent settlement I might put some aside for a flat then take the rest and finally travel to Polynesia. I've always wanted to go but would never be able to afford to go when I was with Ian especially since I would've had to pay for both of us."

"Are you going to study in London?"

"Possibly. I'll have to see what's more affordable."

"What about Ed?"

"You sound like Beth! He's talking about coming out for a week in the spring. UPS has UK branches so if things go well when he visits he'll see if they might let him transfer. Even if he only worked here for a bit we could see if things would work. And the time apart will let me deal with the divorce and abortion."

"Plus it'll help you figure out if he was a bit of fun or something more."

"Yeah. I know it's all a huge mess but can't help but feel optimistic."

-

Elise saw the throng of people craning their necks for a view of the bags as they slowly paraded past on the conveyor belt. She stepped back and turned on her mobile while she waited for the crowd to thin out. She texted Kat promising to be no more than twenty minutes. Her messages trickled through; she had a text from Opti-Level wishing her a happy New Year and hoping she'll be joining them permanently in January. She smiled, touched by the sentiment. She was flattered that her work would be worthy of attention and even pursuit. She noticed a voice message.

"Elise, it's daddy. Your mother's still really upset. She doesn't know how to talk to you without upsetting you and it's breaking her heart. How about we come down to you after you return from Boston so we can talk this out? We both really love you and I fear there has been some miscommunications on both sides over the years. We would hate it not having you in our life. It just seems like whenever we try to do something nice or talk to you we just seem to make you angry. We never know what's to do or say. You're our only daughter and we love you so much."

Her father began to get tearful and tried to hurry off with a reserved good-bye. Elise felt her heart sink and worried she had been unfair. As soon as she got home she would have to ring her father and arrange for them to come over. It would be hard to drop her defences and insecurities but she didn't want to live with regrets of unsaid apologies or questions like she had with Laura. When she looked up she could see her bag left on the carousel slowly orbiting in the lonely crowded airport. She smiled and skipped forward to collect her bag and seize the impending New Year.

-

Ophelia lugged her case to her front door. She thought of Cordelia and how she was probably doing something with their mother. Her heart still felt as if the thaw was a ways away but the possibility existed which in itself was quite novel. She never considered redemption a possibility until after Laura died. She also realised that perhaps there wasn't a specific checklist or path to follow in life. The hard part was trying to find any direction besides just getting by. She thought of some of her friends who seemed to be exactly where they wanted to be or were meant to be. Then there were others that were just as deep in it as she was.

She said as much to Steve after their kiss and he explained that sometimes overanalysing was the worst thing to do. He had the philosophy of not getting bogged down in questions or theories and instead just went with it. Ophelia told him he was full of horseshit but as she dropped her bags and coat in the hall that morning it seemed to make sense.

London seemed less claustrophobic once she realised it was where she wanted to be. There was plenty of opportunity and promise where she was; she just had to stop being so afraid to try or take the chances when they showed themselves. Ophelia knew she had to stop worrying about being comfortable and to simply start doing what felt right. All the vague limitations and excess of worries seemed to have been stripped away over the past few months while she cocooned herself in grief. Laura's death made her realise she wasted far too much time waiting for the world to change when it was just her perspective.

The flat was dark except for the blinking beacon on the answering machine. She followed the red light and went over to the phone.

"Ophelia, it's Cordelia. I'm sorry if I seemed defensive the other day. I'm really glad you got back in touch. I missed having a sister. Maybe in the summer or fall you can come up and stay with me? Happy New Year. I love you."

"Hello, Miss Graff this is your favourite solicitor ringing to wish you a merry Christmas and Happy New Year. I'm back in the big smoke on the 4th and would love to take you to the theatre for some panto if you're free. Call me on my mobile."

The flat seemed less empty with the voices echoing from the machine. She smiled as she slipped her bunny slippers on feeling that she was exactly where she needed to be.

The official *All Change Please glossary*

If you aren't from the UK or spent a decent of amount of time in this area of the world, many of the words used within this novel might not make any sense to you whatsoever. Since the characters of *All Change Please* care deeply about you, they have supplied a glossary for your convenience so you can better understand the language barrier.

999 - UK equivalent of 911

Ace – Cool!

Aggro - Trouble or fights after football matches, short for aggravation.

All right? - Mainly used in London and the south and always phrased as a question it means "Hello, how are you"? You would say it to a complete stranger or someone you knew and is often pronounced "Aw right?". The response is "All right"? in return. Used
by blue collar workers or younger people.

Anorak – A person weirdly interested in something/ obsessive nerd or geek

Arse - Ass though can also be used as a verb "I can't be arsed today"

Auntie - Pet name for the BBC

Bang - Nothing to do with your hair - this is a rather unattractive way of describing having sex. Always gets a smile from Brits in American hair dressers when they are asked about their bangs.

Bangers – Sausage

Barmy - Crazy

Beastly - Used by the upper classes to describe someone unpleasant.

Bees Knees - This is the polite version of the dog's bollocks. So if you are in polite company and want to say that something was fabulous, this phrase might come in handy.

Bell End – Penis

Bender - Pub crawl or heavy drinking session

berk - Cunt rhyming Slang, short for 'Berkshire Hunt'

Bespoke – Custom Made

bint - Derogatory term for woman

bird - girl or girlfriend

Biro - Pen

Bits 'n Bobs – Various things

Bladdered - Drunk

Blag - Get for free

Bleeding - An alternative to the word bloody. You'll hear people say "bleeding hell" or "not bleeding likely" for example.

Blighty – Britain

Blimey - Exclamation of surprise. "Gor Blimey" or even "Cor Blimey" is all a corruption of the oath God Blind Me.

Bloke - Guy

Bloody - Curse word used for emphasis, "Bloody Hell" "Don't be so bleeding stupid"

Blooming - Polite version of "bloody"

Blow off - To fart

Bob's Your Uncle – There you go! Or Tah dah!

Bog Roll – Toilet Paper

Bollocks - Testicle but ut used to say something is rubbish you can say it's bollocks or if something is really great it's the dog's bollocks.

Bonk - Have sex

Boot - Trunk of a car

Bottle - This means courage. If you have a lotta bottle you have no fear. From probably the Dutch courage people get after too many pints of lager.

Box your ears - Generally meant a slap around the head for misbehaving.

Brassed off - Pissed off with something or someone, you are fed up.

Brill or Brilliant - Great!

Bugger - Similar to shit or fuck is an exclamation you wouldn't utter in front f your gran.

Bugger all - If something costs bugger all, it means that it costs nothing. If you have bugger all, it means you have nothing.

C of E - The Church of England.

Chat Up – Flirt

Chav – White trash

Cheeky - Flippant or naughty

Cheers - Thanks

Chin Wag - Chat

Chips – French Fries

Christmas do - Christmas party

Chuffed – Proud or really pleased

Cock-up – Screw up

Cor - Another one of those expressions of surprise. "Cor blimey" or "cor love a duck", heard a lot in East London or Essex.

Cow – Idiot

Cracking - Great!

Crap - The same word in both countries but used more frequently here often as in "that's total crap".

Crikey - Another exclamation of surprise.

Crisps - Potato chips packet of crisps is the UK equivalent of bag of chips

Daft - stupid

Dear - Expensive.

Dim - A dim person is stupid or thick or a dimwit. Dimwit - Someone a bit on the dim side.

Do – Party

Doddle - Something that is a doddle is a cinch, it's easy. Unlike ordering water in Texas with an English accent, which is definitely not a doddle!

Dodgy – Suspicious or crooked

Dog's Bollocks – Awesome but not said in front of your gran.

Dog's dinner - A real mess.

Don't Get Your Knickers in a Twist – Calm down

Donkey's years - Cockney rhyming slang for "years". If someone hasn't seen you for a while they may say they've not seen you for donkeys.

Duffer - Useless, feckless or idiot.

Easy Peasy – Easy

Engaged - When you call someone on the phone & the line is busy, in the UK it's in engaged.

Faff - Procrastinate, lollygag or dither.

Fag - Cigarette

Fag end - Cigarette butts

Fancy – Like

Fanny – **Vagina.** The Brits think the term "fanny pack" is hilarious.

Fit – Hot

Fiver – £5

Flog - To Flog something is to sell it. It also means to beat something with a whip, but when your wife tells you she flogged the old TV it is more likely she has sold it than beaten it (hopefully!).

Fluke - If something great happened to you by chance that would be a fluke. When I was a kid my Mum lost her engagement ring on the beach and only realised half way home. We went back to the spot and she found it in the sand. That was a fluke. Fortnight - Two weeks; an abbreviation of "fourteen nights".

Fringe - The UK equivalent to bangs

Full of beans - Full of energy.

Getting off - Making out or snogging them.

Git - Jerk

Give us a bell - Call me. You often hear people use the word "us" to mean "me".

Give You A Bell – Call you

Glasgow kiss - To head butt some one

Gob or Gobby - Mouth or mouthy as in someone has a bigmouth or is a rude loud-mouth

Gobsmacked – Amazed

Gormless - Slack jawed yokel

Guff - Fart

Gutted – Devastated

Haggle - To haggle is to argue or negotiate over a price. Most people that wangle stuff are usually quite good at haggling. I just learnt that in the USA you dicker over a price, particularly for used cars!

Hash - # or pound sign on a phone

Her Majesty's Pleasure – To be in prison

Hiya - Short for hi there, this is a friendly way of saying hello.

Hoover – Vaccum

Nick - To steal

Nicked - Something that has been stolen has been nicked. Also, when a copper catches a burglar red handed he might say "you've been nicked"!

Nosh – Food

Nut - To nut someone is to head butt them.

Nutter – Crazy Person

Off your trolley - If someone tells you that you're off your trolley, it means you have gone raving bonkers, crazy, mad!

On about - What are you on about? That's something you may well hear when visiting the UK. It means what are you talking about?

On the job - Hard at work, or having sex.

On the piss - Out to get drunk.

On the Pull – Out to pick up a one night stand.

On your bike - Get lost.

One Off – One time only

Pants – Underpants, also can mean something is crap or rubbish.

Pear shaped - When something goes completely wrong.

Piss up - Drinking session or visit to the pub with mates.

Pissed – Drunk

Plonker – Idiot

PMT- Premenstrual Tension, UK equivalent of PMS

Ponce – Poser

Porkies - Cockney rhyming slang short for "porky pies", meaning lies.

Posh - High class

Potty - Crazy

Pound - UK currency £

Prat - Idiot or jackass

PTO - Abbreviation for "please turn over". Another used is "Please see overleaf"

Pukka - Super

Punter – Customer/Prostitute's Client

Quid – £ pound, the US equivelant of calling the dollar a buck.

Quite - Exclamation of agreement.

Read - If someone asks you what you read at university, they're asking what you majored in.

Reckon - To suppose

Redundancy - Laid off.

Reverse the charges - Collect call

Right - Very or quite as in he was being a right ball ache

Ring - Call or phone

Roger - Have sex or a seeing to. As in He rogered her senseless or She gave him a right old rogering.

Round - Your round would mean it's your turn to buy the drinks for your mates in the pub.

Row - Sounds like "cow" and it means having an argument, can be used a verb if two people are arguing they are rowing.

Rubbish – Garbage or slang as in 'That's crap!"

Sack/sacked -To be fired from your job.

Sad - Lame

Scouser – Someone from Liverpool

Scrummy - Delicious, used to describe treats or comfort food.

See a Man About a Dog – Do a deal or to go for a poo

Send-up - Make fun or someone or roast them.

Serviette - Napkin

Shag – Have sex

Shagged - Past tense of shag, also used to describe feeling tired.

Shambles – A mess

Shambolic - Messy or chaotic

Shirty - Cheeky or surly

Shite - More polite way to say shit.

Sick - Vomit or to vomit as in puddle of sick or sick up one's lunch

Skint - broke

Skive – Lazy or avoid doing something, skipping school or work is skiving

Slag - Slut or tramp, also to slag someone off, is to bad mouth them in a nasty way.

Slapper - Slut or tramp

Slash - Having a pee

Sloshed - Drunk

Smarmy - Sycophantic

Smart - Well dressed

Smashing - Wonderful

Snog - Passionately kiss

Sod - As a noun it usually means git or as a verb "Sod off" is equivelant to "Piss off"

Sod all - Nothing

Sod's law - Murphy's law - whatever can go wrong, will go wrong.

Sorted - Fixed

Spend a penny - Go to the toilet. It comes from the fact that in ladies loos you used to operate the door by inserting an old penny.

Squiffy - Buzzed or a little bit drunk

Stag Night – Bachelor Party

Starkers - Naked

Stiffy - Erection

Stonking - Huge

Strop - Sulk

Stuff - UK equivelent to screw; verb as in "Get stuffed" or "Stuff this"

Suss - Figure out as in they've sussed him out

Swotting - Study hard, a Swot is grade A student

Ta - Thanks

Tad – A bit

Taking the biscuit - UK equivalant of Takes the cake.

Taking the mickey - See taking the piss. Variations include "taking the mick" and "taking the Michael".

Taking the piss - Making fun of someone, putting them on.

Tenner – £10

the filth - the police

The Telly – Television

Throw a Spanner in the Works – Screw up

Tickety-boo - Running smoothly

Todger - Penis

Toff – Upper Class Person, from toffee nose

Tool - Idiot

Tosser – Idiot also see wanker. Tosser as in tossing one off or masturbate.

Totty - Nice piece of ass.

TTFN - Abbreviation of "ta ta for now". Catchphrase of a Radio Two DJ in particular.

Twat - Another word used to insult someone who has upset you. Also means the same as fanny but is less acceptable in front of your grandmother, as this refers to parts of the female anatomy. Another use for the same word is to twat something, which would be to hit it hard. Get it right or I'll twat you over the head!
Twee - Dainty or cute overkill

Two finger salute - AKA the V sign is the UK equivalent of flipping the bird or giving the middle finger.

Uni – College/University

Up for it – Willing to have sex

Up the Duff – Pregnant

Wacky backy - Marijuana!

Waffle - talk on and on without getting to the point.

Wangle - Getting freebies

Wank - Masturbate

Wanker – Idiot or more accurately jerk-off

Wazz - Have a pee

Well - Very

Welly - Wellington boots or rubber rain boots

Whinge – Whine

Wicked – Cool!

Willy - Penis

Wind up - If something you do is a "wind up" it means you are making fun of someone and if you do it often you are a wind up merchant.

Wobbly - To "throw a wobbly" is to have a tantrum

Wonky - Odd, wrong or unstable.

Zed - The last letter of the alphabet.

For Boopie & Bucky

I often see these long thank you lists at the back of books and when I am stuck on a train and neglected to bring a second book I read through every page to keep busy and I always wonder if anyone else besides the intended recipients of gratitude read them. This book took 7 long years to complete and in those years a lot of people helped me through the completion of this book.

My biggest thanks goes to Mike Sloan for taking time to read the book and agree to publish it and for all the hard work that goes into getting it ready for print. Thanks to Bluebell Martin who helped shape the primordial soup of a story into a readable novel. Polly Courtney and Philippa Brewster were instrumental in encouraging me and advising me to keep going until I succeeded. Also thanks to Lucine Shahbazian, Kathy Gifford and Liz Akers for actually taking time to read the book in its early forms and give honest feedback. I also must give a warm thanks to my daughter, Marielle and partner Mohsin for their support and encouragement.

About Danielle West

Danielle West is one of the brightest new authors today and has an amazing success story. Originally from Boston before moving to Toronto and then London, she has lived in forts in the woods, cardboard boxes and in fancy high rise flats. Danielle has been a go-go dancer for Boston punk bands, helped start the UK's first roller derby league, had her own soap making company and eventually embarked on a professional mixed martial arts career. Over time she began penning what would become *All Change Please*, her first published novel.

All Change Please was written over the course of seven years on Danielle's Blackberry smart phone while she travelled back and forth to work on the Tube in London, UK. The book has been influenced by her own and friends' experiences, all of which has helped craft a moving story and shape Danielle into the fierce competitor she is today and has strengthened her resolve in adding more literary works to her belt. She has been published in such magazines as *Fighters Only* and *Train Hard, Fight Easy*. This is her first novel.

Danielle is in the early stages of creating her second masterpiece of fiction while she trains for her next series of MMA bouts and prepares to move to Singapore.

Please contact Danielle West at *batgirl13uk@facebook.com*